At Marietta's gen
sexual exciteme
turned his back

"Sing some more, Marietta," he said, knowing that her singing would quickly dampen his desire. "I do so like to hear you sing."

"Really?" she asked, eyes shining.

"You have no idea," he said as he picked up his chambray shirt.

Marietta was thrilled. Her singing had had the desired effect. She would use it as her chief tool to tempt him. And once she had seduced him, had given herself to him, he would surely fall in love with her. So much in love he would not force her to go to Galveston to her grandfather. He would take her wherever she wanted to go. And she wanted to go back to Central City and the opera!

Marietta inwardly shuddered at the prospect of allowing Cole to actually make love to her. She didn't really know what to expect. Wasn't sure she would know what she was supposed to do when the time came.

She was worried. But she had no other choice. If she was ever to be free of him, then she would have to let Cole make love to her. It would, she knew, be quite a sacrifice on her part.

But it would be worth it.

NAUGHTY MARIETTA

NAN RYAN

MIRA

ISBN 1-55166-676-6

NAUGHTY MARIETTA

Copyright © 2003 by Nan Ryan.

All rights reserved. Except for use in any review, the reproduction or
utilization of this work in whole or in part in any form by any electronic,
mechanical or other means, now known or hereafter invented, including
xerography, photocopying and recording, or in any information storage or
retrieval system, is forbidden without the written permission of the publisher,
MIRA Books, 225 Duncan Mill Road, Don Mills, Ontario, Canada M3B 3K9.

All characters in this book have no existence outside the imagination of the
author and have no relation whatsoever to anyone bearing the same name
or names. They are not even distantly inspired by any individual known or
unknown to the author, and all incidents are pure invention.

MIRA and the Star Colophon are trademarks used under license and registered
in Australia, New Zealand, Philippines, United States Patent and Trademark
Office and in other countries.

Visit us at www.mirabooks.com

Printed in U.S.A.

For seven of my favorite writers
who are also valued friends

Marsha Canham
Lori Copeland
Heather Graham
Virginia Henley
Kat Martin
Meryl Sawyer
Christina Skye

One

June 1872

Midnight in Galveston, Texas, a Southern coastal city still under the occupation of federal reconstruction troops seven long years after the end of the War Between the States.

A man who had given the ultimate for the Confederacy's cause—his only son's life—sat alone in the paneled library of his spacious seaside mansion. He was grimacing in agony, his teeth were clenched, his eyes closed.

Seventy-eight-year-old, wheelchair-bound, Maxwell Lacey—crippled in a fall from a horse years ago—was suffering. The increased dosage of laudanum failed to kill the pain. The disease that was slowly ravaging his frail body was incurable; he would not recover. Nor, he realized, would his passing be an easy, peaceful one.

The pain refused to go away. It was unbearable. He could stand it no longer. He *would* stand it no longer.

Maxwell Lacey opened his eyes, gripped the arms

of his chair and anxiously wheeled himself across the room and around behind his massive mahogany desk. Grimacing in misery, he opened the bottom desk drawer and took out the old Colt revolver he had carried as a young man. Perspiration dotting his pale, drawn face, he calmly loaded the weapon, raised it and placed the cold steel barrel directly against his right temple.

His finger on the trigger, he glanced across the room. His watery eyes fell on the poster advertising Marietta's starring role in her most recent opera. Maxwell Lacey swallowed hard and blinked to clear his vision. Focusing on the diva, he gritted his teeth against the worsening pain and slowly lowered the revolver.

Shaking his gray head, he laid the weapon atop his desk. He folded his age-spotted hands together, placed them beneath his quivering chin and sat quietly for a long moment, staring fixedly at the poster. Lost in the mists of memory, he was tormented with anguish and regret.

He thought back over the years to when he was young and the mansion was filled with children's sweet voices and his wife's throaty laughter. Now the big house was silent and lonely, had been for a long, long time. All were dead: his son, Jacob, his daughter, Charlotte, his devoted wife, Annabelle.

Maxwell stared at the poster as tears rolled down his wrinkled cheeks. And he came to a decision. He would attempt to right some of the terrible wrong he had done.

Suddenly, for the first time in days, the pain eased.

Maxwell Lacey sat in the shadowy library of his opulent home all night, patiently waiting for the summer dawn. Come morning, he sent a servant to summon his attorney to the mansion.

Upon his arrival, Marcus Weathers was immediately shown into the library. Puzzled, the attorney stepped inside and greeted his client.

Turning his wheelchair around and without so much as a "good morning," Maxwell instructed Weathers, "Draw up my last will and testament!"

The lawyer frowned, his eyebrows knitting. "You already have a will, Maxwell. Don't you recall, you made it several years ago."

"I'm changing it, so get out your pen and start writing," Maxwell bellowed.

"Why the urgency?" asked Weathers as he took a seat facing Maxwell's desk. "Has something happened? Are you…?"

"Yes," Maxwell Lacey interrupted. "Doc LeDette was here last evening. The prognosis is not good. I haven't long to live and I want to…I have decided that I am going to…. Damnation! What is that infernal hammering?"

The steady, rhythmic hammering just outside the steel-barred window elicited no curiosity from the darkly bearded prisoner whose cold blue eyes stared unblinkingly at the ceiling.

In the shadowy cell at the rear of the Galveston city jail, Confederate war veteran and condemned prisoner Cole Heflin lay on his bunk with his hands folded beneath his dark head and his long legs stretched out and crossed at the ankles.

Cole Heflin knew what the hammering meant. A gallows was being constructed. A hanging was to take place at noon. And he, Cole Heflin, was the man who would be hanged. He had been charged with burning Hadleyville—a Northern munitions-supply station—during the war. The Northern press had dubbed him "the man who burned Hadleyville." Secretary of War Stanton had declared the act a crime against the Union. A crime for which he would hang.

Cole did not fear death. He had faced it many times in the bloody four-year struggle in which most of his friends had perished.

Reflecting on his thirty-four years on earth as he calmly awaited the fast-approaching hour of his death, Cole realized with little regret that he would be leaving no one behind to mourn his passing. His mother and father had long since gone to their final reward and the pretty young woman who had promised to be his faithful sweetheart and wait for him until he came home from the war hadn't. She had waited only a few short months before running away with a wealthy New Orleans cotton broker.

There would be no tears shed over his passing, including his own. But he did have regrets and remorse that he had not kept his pledge to Keller Longley.

Cole's eyes clouded as his thoughts turned back to that hot summer day in 1864 when his best friend, Keller Longley, died in his arms on the battlefield atop Lookout Mountain.

When the war began, Cole and Keller—friends since their Texas childhood—made a solemn vow. Should one survive and the other die, the survivor would take care of his deceased comrade's family.

Cole swallowed hard as he recalled that terrible moment just before Keller died. "You'll look after Ma and little Leslie, won't you, Cole?" Keller had managed to say weakly, clutching Cole's shirtfront as his lifeblood flowed out of him.

"You know I will," Cole assured him as he cradled Keller in his arms and cried like a baby.

Now Cole ground his teeth in frustration. He hadn't kept his promise to Keller. He had failed his friend, hadn't been able to look after Keller's widowed mother and baby sister. Cole closed his eyes and grimaced, a muscle clenching in his lean jaw.

Before the war Cole had been a young, struggling attorney. But he couldn't practice law when the war ended. A fugitive with a price on his head, he'd had to lie low. Had to constantly keep on the move in an effort to elude the occupation troops and avoid being caught and hanged for burning Hadleyville.

Finally, in desperation, he had attempted a bank robbery to get money to help Keller's mother and sister. He had been caught. An alert captain on the provost marshall's staff had matched the captured felon's face to the old federal death warrant.

What would have been five years in Huntsville State Prison for the failed bank robbery became a federal death sentence. He would hang for the burning of Hadleyville and the destitute Longley women would be left to struggle on alone.

The hammer of the ancient clock in the town square struck the hour. The jailer's booming voice drew the reclining prisoner from his painful reverie.

"It's time, Heflin," the jailer said as the heavy cell door swung open and he held out a pair of silver handcuffs.

Cole slowly turned his head, nodded and agilely rolled up and off his bunk. Rising to his full, imposing height of six foot two inches, he extended his wrists and said, "Crowd forming?"

"A big one," said the burly jailer with a broad smile.

"Well, let's go give them what they came here for," said Cole calmly.

Flanked by two armed federal marshals, Cole Heflin walked out of the Galveston City Jail and into the sun-splashed square where the newly built gallows dominated the cloudless blue skyline.

"Here he comes!" The excited declaration swiftly swept through the gathering as the throng parted to let the prisoner through.

"The bastard's getting what he deserves!" exclaimed a well-dressed, transplanted Easterner who spat contemptuously at him as Cole passed.

The expression on Cole's face never changed.

"I don't care what he's done, he's too handsome to die!" shouted a brazen young woman and, elbowing her way through the crowd, she stepped right up to Cole and threw her arms around his neck, kissing him soundly.

A mixture of whistles and boos rose from the shocked spectators. Other less forward young ladies threw bouquets at the tall, dark Southerner, while a majority of the men, Confederate veterans who considered Cole a hero, shouted admiringly, "Hurrah for the brave Johnny Reb! The man who burned Hadleyville!"

Cole climbed the gallows' steps to the wooden platform where a new rope hung down in an ominous loop from the sturdy overhead beam. There stood an old robed padre and the hangman, dressed all in black.

The jailer cautiously uncuffed Cole. Cole gave him no trouble. Instead, he stepped into place directly below the looped lariat and atop the trapdoor.

The rope was lowered, the loop slipped down around Cole's neck. The hangman produced a black hood. Cole declined.

The hangman asked, "Any last words, Heflin?"

"No," said Cole as the priest stepped closer and began to read passages of scripture.

The hangman was tightening the noose around

Cole's neck when an out-of-breath gentleman, soon identified as Marcus Weathers, forced his way through the crowd, shouting, "Stop! Don't do it! I have signed orders from Colonel Patten of the Federal Occupation Forces for you to cease and desist!"

The shout drew everyone's attention to the well-known attorney. In his raised hand was a blue legal document. Marcus Weathers rushed up onto the platform and handed the papers to the executioner. The document was read and then, frowning, the executioner announced, "Take the rope from the prisoner's neck. The hanging's off!"

Two

A low moan went through the crowd.

Amid rising jeers and cheers, Cole stood stunned and totally still as the jailer roughly removed the noose from around his neck.

"You're free to go, Heflin," the big lawman said, clearly disappointed.

Marcus Weathers stepped forward, smiled at Cole and said, "Come with me, Mr. Heflin. The carriage is waiting."

"Where are we going?" Cole asked.

"You'll see," replied Weathers as he took Cole's arm and slowly guided him down the gallows steps, through the buzzing mob and toward the black carriage.

Cole was driven a short distance to the city's waterfront. The carriage soon turned into a long palm-bordered avenue that led to an opulent seaside mansion. The white two-story building was located at the center of a great expanse of well-manicured acreage. It gleamed in the late-morning sun and Cole quickly realized its inhabitants were afforded an unobstructed view of the Gulf of Mexico.

Cole was ushered into the imposing mansion and immediately directed to a large, darkly paneled library where an old man sat in a wheelchair.

Maxwell Lacey smiled when Cole entered the room and said, "Welcome to my humble abode, Mr. Heflin. Won't you have a seat."

Cole continued to stand. "I'm afraid you have the advantage, sir."

"I usually do. Or, at least, I try to," Maxwell Lacey said with a chuckle.

Cole didn't share his amusement. "Who are you? What's this all about?"

"You'll know soon enough what it's about, Mr. Heflin. But allow me to introduce myself. I'm Maxwell Lacey. You may have heard of me."

"No, I haven't."

"No matter. Would you like a drink?"

Cole accepted. An unobtrusive servant immediately handed him a bourbon. Cole turned the heavy shot glass up to his lips and drank thirstily.

Maxwell Lacey dismissed the servant with a wave of his hand and said, "Please, sit down, Mr. Heflin. Let's have a little talk."

Cole drained the glass, set it aside and folded his long body down onto a comfortable sofa. Lacey wheeled his chair out from behind his desk and moved closer. He continued to smile as he sized up the lean, darkly bearded man.

The man he had chosen to do his bidding.

Maxwell laced his fingers together in his robe-covered lap, leaned forward and said, "I know all about you, Heflin. You're the man who single-handedly burned Hadleyville during the war and—"

"Ancient history," Cole interrupted with a dismissive shake of his head.

"Not ancient history to the occupying federal forces," Maxwell Lacey reminded him. His eyes flashed when he added, "You were tried and convicted *in absentia* years ago and sentenced to hang! Took them seven years to catch you."

Cole shrugged his wide shoulders. "What's that got to do with you?"

"Everything, Heflin. I saved your life. Had the federal commander order you taken down from the gallows. I am a very powerful man in Galveston. And a rich one. I greased the necessary palms, pulled the necessary strings to have your life spared."

Cole raised one well-arched eyebrow, looked Maxwell Lacey in the eye and said, "My sincere thanks. But again, why?"

With an ominous laugh, the old man ignored Cole's question and stated, "I expect to be repaid for your deliverance. You will do exactly as I ask, Mr. Heflin."

"And why would I ever do that?"

A sharp pain pressed Maxwell's spine. He paled, but continued as though Cole had not spoken. "There is a special young woman, a Miss Marietta Stone, an opera singer in Central City, Colorado." He pointed across the room to the poster featuring Marietta. "She is my granddaughter and my only living relative.'' He paused.

''Go on,'' Cole said.

''I am dying—I have only a matter of months, perhaps weeks, to live. My granddaughter *must* be brought to Galveston before I pass away.''

''And you've chosen me to go get her, bring her here.''

''Exactly.''

Cole looked thoughtful, as if he was considering the proposition. But when finally he spoke, he said, ''No, I don't think so. Find somebody else.''

Maxwell's wrinkled face instantly turned scarlet with anger. He thundered, ''Damnation! If just anyone could bring her back from Central City, you'd be swinging from the gallows this very minute! I saved your life. You owe me, young man!''

''True,'' Cole admitted, pausing briefly. ''I'll go,'' he finally answered. ''But here are my terms. Before I leave for Colorado, you'll pay me ten thousand dollars cash.''

''Ten thousand dollars! Why, this grand house didn't cost much more than that. You're out of your mind if you think I'll give you that kind of money.''

Cole sat calmly, said nothing.

''That's highway robbery! You're in no position to demand anything,'' barked Maxwell Lacey. ''Let me remind you again, I saved your life. You *will* go after my granddaughter or you'll go right back to the gallows and be hanged.''

Still, Cole didn't budge. "Ten thousand or your precious granddaughter stays in Central City."

Maxwell Lacey was not a man used to being bested. His first inclination was to order this arrogant upstart out of his house. Send him back to the gallows. Let the ungrateful bastard swing. But time was short. Running out. His days were numbered.

"Very well," he said grudgingly, "I'll pay you the ten thousand."

Cole smiled for the first time since entering the mansion. He said in a low, level voice, "You will have your attorney deposit the money in the Gulf Shores State Bank this afternoon. I'll leave for Colorado in the morning."

"Agreed," said Maxwell and he, too, was smiling. His attorney had, by telegraph, queried both Union officers and fellow Confederate officers and all had agreed that Cole Heflin's word was as good as his bond. "Weathers is waiting in the parlor. He will accompany you to the bank."

Cole nodded, rose, shook the old man's hand and then turned to leave the library.

But he stopped abruptly when Maxwell Lacey said, "Ah, one last little thing I didn't mention, Heflin."

Cole turned. "Which is?"

Maxwell looked sheepish when he admitted, "Marietta may not want to come with you."

Cole frowned. "Jesus, are you telling me I'm supposed to bring this woman back against her will?"

Maxwell nodded his head. "Absolutely! I'm certain she'll refuse to come. It's a long, complicated tale and of no concern to you. Your orders are to bring my granddaughter safely back here to me.''

Cole made a face. "Just how am I supposed to persuade this woman to—''

Lacey interrupted, "If you can't convince her to come peacefully—which I fully doubt will happen—snatch her right off the stage! Kidnap her! Use force if necessary. Do whatever you have to do, but bring her back. You understand me?''

"I don't like this," Cole said.

"Why, Heflin, what's kidnapping to an arsonist, a bank robber?" Cole gave no reply. Lacey continued, "You don't have to like it, just do it. I'll give you the ten thousand you've demanded and fully finance your trip." He lifted a hand and indicated the soiled jail garb Cole wore. "Buy yourself some decent clothes, travel in style and stay at the best hotels." He paused then, looked hopefully at Cole.

Cole said, "How do you know I won't take your money and disappear?''

Lacey replied, "I don't. But I'm a pretty good judge of character and I'd bet everything against it."

"I'll bring your wandering granddaughter home to you, Mr. Lacey. Count on it."

Central City, Colorado

"No, no, you must start over!"

"Not again!"

"You heard me," said Madam Sophia.

Marietta made a face, sighed heavily, but cleared her throat and began anew.

It was early afternoon. Marietta Stone, a twenty-five-year-old, red-haired opera singer, was practicing her roulades and glissandos under the tutelage of her two-hundred-and-fifty-pound voice coach, Madam Sophia.

Teacher and pupil were ensconced in Marietta's private quarters, a luxurious five-room suite above the Tivoli Opera House. In a few short days, Marietta would debut at the grand opera house in a production of Verdi's *La Traviata*.

She was the star.

The young singer took her voice lessons seriously. She was determined to become a famous soprano in the glamorous and exciting world of opera. She never doubted that she would achieve the fame she sought.

Marietta was a woman as obstinate as she was beautiful. She believed that she could change, if not the world, her world. As indeed, she had. Endowed with intelligence, determination and great beauty, she had been successful in the dogged pursuit of her goals.

"No! No! No!" scolded the frustrated Italian voice coach as Marietta reached for a high note and went a trifle flat. Marietta immediately fell silent. Madam Sophia, shaking her head, said, "Try again and remember to breathe properly as I have shown you. You must learn to enunciate and strengthen your vocal cords.''

Marietta was not stung by the reprimand. She trusted her voice coach completely. The acclaimed— and well-paid—Madam Sophia was an expert in the physiology of voice production and control. Marietta felt fortunate to have such a talented teacher. And, she was pleased that she was Madam Sophia's only pupil.

''You will begin once more,'' instructed Madam Sophia, ''and practice breathing properly so that you can reach those high notes without going flat!'' Madam Sophia paused. ''You must be better before dress rehearsal.''

Marietta nodded, took a deep, slow breath. She began the musical scales, but was momentarily interrupted by a knock on the suite's door. Marietta stopped her exercises. The rotund voice coach frowned.

''That will be Maltese,'' said Marietta.

Madam Sophia exhaled with annoyance. ''Must he come here while we are practicing?''

''He won't stay long,'' assured Marietta.

Madam Sophia held her tongue, said no more. She couldn't object too fiercely. Taylor Maltese paid her handsomely to tutor Marietta.

Marietta hurried to the mirror to examine herself. She pinched her cheeks, bit her lips, drew the feathered lapels of her pink satin dressing gown together.

Then turning, she said, "Sophia, let my visitor in, please."

Muttering to herself in Italian, Madam Sophia opened the door and then hurried out once the dapper, immaculately dressed suitor had entered. A slender man of medium height with silver-gray hair, hazel eyes and a ruddy complexion, Taylor Maltese was an extremely wealthy, middle-aged bachelor. He owned and operated a number of Colorado's most prosperous gold and silver mines as well as Central City's newspaper, the Gilpin Hotel and many of the stores and saloons of the thriving mountain hamlet.

He also owned the Tivoli Opera House, which was more of an indulgence for him than a commercial venture. He loved music, opera…and his beautiful leading ladies. Especially his current leading lady, the opera's star, Marietta.

Maltese had a spacious three-story home high on a bluff above Central City, as well as a huge stone mansion down in Denver, which was his primary residence. His great wealth and position in society made him the target of many hopeful women longing to become Mrs. Maltese. They were wasting their time.

Since the moment he had first seen her, Maltese had been totally smitten with the young, lovely Marietta. His first glimpse of the flame-haired beauty had been a year ago on the stage of his own Tivoli Opera House. He had come to see a production of *La Bohème*. He hardly noticed the celebrated soprano who was the star. Marietta, in a bit role as a café customer in the chorus immediately caught his eye. He was entranced. And had been ever since.

He so adored Marietta, he was afraid to press her for fear he might lose her. He longed to take her in his arms, but he didn't dare. He had seen flashes of her fiery temper and didn't want that anger directed at him. So he contented himself with nothing more intimate than kisses on the cheek and the pleasure of her company.

Now Marietta turned her most dazzling smile on her aging suitor and played the coquette, to his delight.

"What did you bring me, you naughty boy?" she purred, swaying seductively toward him, eyeing the bag in his hand. She moved in close, draped one arm around his neck and playfully tickled him under the chin with her long, painted fingernails.

Maltese beamed with joy. He held the bag behind his back and said, "You have to guess, sugar."

Marietta toyed with the lapels of his custom cutaway, tilted her head to one side and said, "Mmm, let me think. A hat? Jewelry? A red ball gown?" She put out the tip of her pink tongue, licked her top lip and said in a soft, sultry tone, "No, no, I know what it is. It's shoes!"

It was a game the two of them frequently played. Marietta knew exactly what he had brought her. Didn't have to guess. Her bewitched suitor had given her dozens of pairs of shoes. Shoes of every kind and color. Soft leather pumps imported from Italy. Saucy satin slippers from Paris. Even a pair of hand-tooled cowboy boots.

Now as he laughed merrily, Marietta continued to play her part. She reached around behind him, took the bag, drew it up and peeked inside.

"Would you...put the shoes on for me, sugar?" asked the hopeful Maltese.

"Why, of course, Maltese," said Marietta. She took a seat on an armless velvet chair and made a big production of trying on the dainty new dancing slippers.

Her enchanted admirer sank onto a sofa nearby and watched as if she were totally disrobing. Marietta, cleverly allowing her long dressing gown to part just enough to give him a fleeting glimpse of a shapely, stockinged knee, winked at the heavily breathing Maltese.

She stretched her long right leg out straight and turned her foot one way then the other, as if she was carefully inspecting the new slipper. From beneath veiled lashes she stole a quick glance at her admirer. Beside himself with sexual excitement, Maltese tugged at his choking cravat. The pulse in his throat beat rapidly.

He'd had enough, Marietta quickly decided. Didn't want him having a heart attack.

She modestly pulled her robe together, rose to her feet and said sweetly, "It's such a warm day, isn't it. Shall we have a glass of icy lemonade? Cool off a bit?"

"Yes," Maltese managed to say weakly. He drew a clean white linen handkerchief from his breast pocket and nervously blotted his shiny forehead. "Oh, yes, sugar, that would be nice."

Three

Cole Heflin arrived in Denver, Colorado, on a warm, still evening near the end of June. Tired and stiff, he stepped down off the train and took a moment to stretch and unwind. He raised his arms skyward, groaned and lowered them. Ignoring curious stares, he bent forward and touched his toes several times. He straightened, leaned back from the waist and twisted one way then the other.

Once he'd worked the kinks out of his legs and back, he made his way through the crowded train depot and out onto the busy street. Cole walked the short distance to the corner of Larimer and Eighteenth, and the Windsor Hotel. A well-heeled fellow traveler had assured him that the British-built hotel was the very best accommodations Denver had to offer.

Cole stepped into the Windsor's vast lobby and looked around. His fellow traveler had been right. The Windsor was an oasis on the frontier. Elegant parqueted floors, sixty-foot mahogany bar and full-length diamond-dust mirrors.

The uniformed clerk raised a disdainful eyebrow

when the bearded, shabbily dressed Cole stepped up to the marble desk. Cole was unbothered by the man's high-handed attitude.

"Have a corner suite available?" he asked the scornful clerk.

"Sir, our suites are quite expensive and I—"

"Answer the question," said Cole with a smile. "Any suites available?"

"Well, yes, but—"

"Good. Top floor. Front corner suite will do." He reached for the register, turned it around and signed it as the snooty young man went to get the key.

"Suite 518," said the desk clerk and reluctantly handed the key to Cole.

Key in hand, Cole said, "I noticed a haberdasher across the street."

"Why, yes," said the clerk, "Miller and Son is one of the oldest—"

"Fine," said Cole as he took a bill out of his pants pocket and laid it on the marble ledge. "Have someone from Miller and Son bring several suits—size forty-two long—to my suite so I can choose one. Also a white shirt, underwear and pair of black leather shoes, size eleven. And, have a barber sent up. I need a haircut. Think you can manage that?"

The clerk looked anxiously around, then eased the bill off the marble desk and nodded. "Half an hour. Will that be acceptable?"

"Perfect," said Cole who turned away just as a

small group of expensively dressed ladies swept through the lobby on their way to the dining room.

One, an attractive brunette who could have been anywhere from thirty to forty, glanced at Cole, nodded and smiled. Cole winked at her. She blushed and hurried to catch up with her friends.

Cole stood and watched her walk away, liking what he saw, wishing he could get to know her better. She went out of sight and he dismissed her. Eagerly he headed for his suite, taking everything in, admiring the fine furnishings of the stately hotel. The Windsor, with its grand staircases, was built to resemble Windsor Castle.

It looked like a castle to Cole.

Once in his luxurious suite, he admired the elegant furniture, oversize bed and gold-plated bathtub. Cole promptly made himself at home. He stripped off his soiled clothes, flipped the tub's gold faucets and marveled as running water flowed swiftly into the tub.

After a shave and haircut, a hot bath, a couple of shots of bourbon and a fine cigar, Cole dressed in the new suit of clothes he'd purchased from Miller and Son.

The transformation was dramatic. He hardly recognized himself. His tanned face was smoothly shaven and his shaggy black hair neatly trimmed. The new apparel, a well-fitting suit of lightweight navy flannel, pristine white shirt and maroon cravat, made him look like a gentleman.

Cole laughed at the idea. He was no gentleman.

And he'd like to meet a woman who wasn't a lady. Perhaps later in the evening he'd stroll down to Holladay Street and visit the famous Mattie Silks.

But first he'd have dinner. He was starving.

Cole went down to the dining room and was shown to a table on the wall. Once seated, he casually looked around. His attention was immediately drawn to a round table where the laughing ladies he'd seen in the lobby were enjoying a leisurely meal.

The attractive dark-haired woman that he had winked at began glancing boldly at him. She smiled seductively then lowered her lashes. Cole leaned back in his chair and returned her gaze. The flirtation continued as he ordered dinner.

When the ladies finished their meal and rose to leave, the shapely brunette hung back and pointedly looked his way.

Without sound, Cole mouthed the words, "Suite 518."

She flushed, turned and hurried away with her friends.

Cole chuckled.

Dinner arrived—a thick juicy steak, fried potatoes, hot bread and butter—and he forgot the brazen brunette. When he'd finished his meal and left the dining room, he debated the visit to Mattie's. He decided against it. He was too tired. A night's sleep was what he needed most.

A half hour later, back in his suite, Cole was naked and ready to crawl wearily into bed. But just as he pulled the top sheet down and put a knee on the mattress, there was a knock on the door. Cole frowned. He wrapped a towel around his waist, tied a loose knot atop his hip and crossed the room to open the door.

Before him stood the bold brunette.

"I...I am not in the habit of doing this sort of thing," she promptly assured him.

Cole grinned lazily. "Why, no, of course not," he said as he reached out and gently took her arm. He drew the woman inside and closed the door behind her.

For a moment they stood there face-to-face, neither speaking. Cole towered over the woman. She pressed her back against the solid door and gazed at his wide, sculpted shoulders, his broad chest, the white towel covering him. Her breath was now coming in shallow, anxious little gulps. Her heart was beating rapidly, the swell of her full, pale bosom rising and falling above the low-cut bodice of her snugly fitted suit jacket.

Cole raised a hand, cupped the side of her throat. "I'm glad you made an exception for me."

"Yes, well, I...I can't stay long," she said. "My...my husband is expecting me home by ten."

"I see," mused Cole, letting his hand slip down to the buttons of her bodice. "Then we'd better waste no more time."

He dropped his towel to the carpeted floor and swiftly unbuttoned her jacket. He pushed the opened jacket apart, slipped his long fingers inside her lace-trimmed camisole, and eased the slick satin garment down to release a full, creamy breast. She drew a quick breath as if surprised, but made no move to cover herself. And she exhaled heavily when Cole licked his forefinger and circled her stiffening nipple with his wet fingertip.

The brunette's soft hands fluttered along his slim hips before seeking his already straining masculinity. Cole took his cue from her. Without so much as a kiss, he shoved her full skirts up and, with her help, deftly relieved her of her underwear. Looking into her flashing eyes, he swept a warm hand across her flat stomach, then slipped his fingers between her legs. She swooned and tilted her pelvis upward, eagerly pressing against his exploring hand. Cole was amazed. She was as hot, wet and ready as if he had spent an hour arousing her. He took his hand away, pushed her skirts higher up, around her waist.

"Want to tell me your name, darlin'," he asked and cupped the twin cheeks of her bottom, pressing his body against hers, letting her feel his firm erection throb against her bare belly.

"No," she quickly responded. "And I don't want to know yours. Just put it in. Hurry."

Cole didn't hesitate. The brunette winced, then sighed with pleasure when he lifted her a little and guided his hard flesh up inside her. She clung tightly to his neck, lifted her stockinged legs and wrapped them around him.

They stayed right where they were, making hot,

impersonal love. Cole pumped and thrust and slammed her rhythmically against the heavy door. The brunette bucked and lunged and egged him on, digging her sharp nails into his shoulders. Two total strangers, out of control, mating like lusty animals. Kissing and licking and biting. Grunting and panting and growling.

But only for a few short moments.

Soon the brunette began experiencing a deep, wrenching climax. Cole joined her in the release.

She cried out in her ecstasy and viciously bit Cole's bare shoulder.

But the second her climax had passed, she lowered her weak legs, took her arms from around his neck and pushed Cole back. She anxiously reached for her pantalets, turning away to put her underwear on before dropping and smoothing her skirts. She whirled around to face Cole as she pushed her exposed breast back inside her camisole and buttoned her bodice.

"I must go," she said.

"Thanks for visiting," he replied.

"My pleasure," she said with an impish smile, clearly giving his statement a double meaning. He laughed and so did she. She lifted slender shoulders in a shrug and said, "Now I really must go."

But before she left, she reached out and cupped his now-flaccid flesh. She licked her lips, sighed and said, "I wish I could take this with me and have it whenever I want it."

Grinning easily, he teased, "Don't you have one like it at home?"

"Hardly!" The smile left her face and a clouded expression came into her dark eyes. "Not like this. Nothing like this."

She reluctantly released him, turned, opened the door and rushed away without saying goodbye.

For a moment Cole stood naked in the open doorway, shaking his head. Then he shrugged, closed the door and yawned. It wasn't the first such encounter he'd had with a stranger and it probably wouldn't be his last.

He'd lose no sleep over her or any of the others. Women, so long as they were easy on the eye, were all pretty much the same to Cole Heflin. They all behaved alike. Hard to tell one from another.

He smiled.

God, it was good to be alive.

Cole crossed the silent room, blew out the lamp and fell sleepily into bed.

Late the next afternoon the narrow-gauge train chugged its way higher and higher through the winding and steep-sided Clear Creek Canyon. The newly built railway ended at the mining and smelting town of Blackhawk, more than eight thousand feet up in the mountains.

Cole stepped off the train at Blackhawk and, swinging his suitcases, walked the mile up the steep hill to Central City. The high altitude and thin mountain air made him feel short of breath and slightly light-headed. He stopped outside the Gilpin Hotel and considered checking in. He leaned against the building, took a minute to catch his breath, then moved on.

As he strolled unhurriedly up Eureka Street, he noticed the posters advertising Verdi's opera, *La Traviata,* and it's young star, Marietta Stone.

Cole paused before one of the posters, studied the likeness of Marietta. He exhaled heavily. Here she was, the toast of Central City, a content, fulfilled young woman. And he had come to take her away from it all. He hated to do it, but he had no choice. He'd promised Maxwell Lacey he would bring the woman to Galveston and he would, whether she wanted to go or not.

The summer sun had completely slipped below the Front Range. In the gathering twilight, Cole walked up the street to the newly opened Teller House Hotel. The four-story hotel's wide entrance opened onto a floor of solid-silver bars. He checked into a top-floor room with furnishings of exquisite walnut and damask and a fine Brussels carpet.

Cole looked around, shrugged out of his suit jacket and stretched out on the soft bed. He folded his hands beneath his head and gazed up at the crystal chandelier at the room's center.

How should he go about getting the pretty opera star out of Central City and back to Galveston? He had the sinking feeling that it was not going to be easy.

He wouldn't worry about it. He'd take it one step at a time.

First on the agenda was tonight's performance of *La Traviata* at the Tivoli Opera House.

Four

Full darkness had fallen and there was a definite chill in the mountain air when Cole, dressed in dark evening attire, left the Teller House Hotel that evening.

Eureka Street was crowded. Laughing people spilled out of restaurants and saloons. Others milled about leisurely, stopping before glass-fronted shops. Many, like him, were headed to the Tivoli Opera House for the debut performance of *La Traviata*.

In minutes Cole reached the imposing opera house, which was built out of stone, brick and iron. The main entrance was wide; swinging doors afforded passage into a spacious corridor.

On the ground floor, at the back of the roomy foyer, was a large gambling club. Cole instinctively moved closer, pausing just outside the crowded, smoked-filled casino. He was sorely tempted. It had been ages since he'd sat in on a good poker game.

He thought about the ten thousand dollars in the Gulf Shores State Bank. Ten thousand that belonged to him. His to do with as he pleased. His expense money—a thick roll of bills—was suddenly burning a hole in his pocket. With effort, he resisted the strong lure.

He turned away and moved with the growing crowd up a flight of stairs to the theater. The grand stairway divided two spacious sections of the theater. The ornate and elaborate audience room was large, and the dress circle, where Cole was to sit, was reached by a second set of stairs. The circle extended, horseshoe shaped, around the room.

Opera chairs with adjustable seats were of ornate cast and upholstered in scarlet plush. Cole found his and sat down in the comfortable chair. White-and-gold hand-turned balusters formed balustrades around the horseshoe circle. The railing was covered with scarlet plush.

Cole looked around with interest. On the right side of the stage, high up on the wall, was a large private box, mirrored and upholstered in scarlet like the dress circle. Lambrequins and lace curtains gave the private box a degree of privacy. The box was presently empty.

Cole's attention returned to the main floor of the grand theater. The wide aisles were beautifully carpeted in red, the walls were painted in brilliant colors, the ceilings handsomely frescoed. Everything was red, gold and white, and revealed by brightly burning gas jets.

Just below the scarlet-curtained stage, a fifteen-piece orchestra was seated in a circular box. They played an overture as the auditorium began to fill with patrons.

Cole had patronized few opera houses, but he felt certain this one was as grand a theater as could be found anywhere in America. Cole lifted and studied his program.

La Traviata
by Giuseppe Verdi
Characters

Violetta Valéry, a courtesan..................Soprano
Dr. Grenvil, Violetta's physician...............Bass
Alfredo Germont, lover of Violetta............Tenor

Cole glanced through the rest of the cast, then read the brief summary of the opera's story at the bottom of the page.

A tale of the tragic romance of Violetta Valéry, a beautiful courtesan of Paris, and Alfredo Germont, a sincere and poetic young man of a respectable provincial family.

Cole finished reading and lowered the program.

The theater had quickly filled to capacity. Every seat in the house was taken. While there was a scattering of handsomely dressed couples, the majority of the first-nighters were men. Men who were not handsomely dressed. A rough-hewn, sunburned lot in work clothes looking sorely out of place in this palatial amphitheater.

Cole wondered briefly if it was the opera's celebrated star, Marietta, who had attracted such an unlikely mix.

Impatient for the curtain to go up, Cole again glanced at the private box high up on the wall near the stage.

It was no longer empty. A silver-haired, impeccably dressed gentleman sat in the plush box, a look of eager anticipation on his face. Something moved behind the gentleman. Cole's attention was drawn to the back of the box.

Beneath a sway of lace curtains, half hidden in shadow, stood a tall, spare man with shifty eyes and a nasty-looking scar on his cheek.

The conductor rapped his baton.

The noisy crowd quieted.

Cole quickly turned his attention to the stage. The scarlet curtain rose. The opera began. Act 1 opened on the richly furnished drawing room of Violetta Valéry in Paris. A party was under way. Several bit players sang their parts.

Cole quickly grew restless.

He had no interest in the supporting cast. He had come to see Marietta.

At last the star appeared onstage amidst deafening cheers from the appreciative patrons. Cole blinked, then stared, feeling as if he'd just been struck in the solar plexus.

Marietta was so incredibly beautiful he couldn't believe his eyes. Cole drew a quick intake of air and felt his heart lurch in his chest.

Flaming red-gold hair framed a perfect face with flawless apricot skin, large, dazzling eyes, a small upturned nose and a ripe, red mouth fashioned for kissing. Tall and slender with soft feminine curves, she wore a luxurious ball gown of shimmering turquoise silk adorned with thousands of tiny semiprecious stones.

Marietta's character, Violetta Valéry, was determined to ignore the precarious state of her health in a ceaseless round of enjoyment. Marietta looked anything but sick. She was young and healthy. Fantastically vital, alive and vivacious. And she was so breathtakingly lovely, so ethereally beautiful, she might well have been an angel come down to earth. Cole gazed at the vision in turquoise, totally mesmerized.

The flame-haired beauty took a step forward, smiled and bowed to her admirers, giving the adoring throng a fleeting glimpse of her soft, pale bosom. Amidst whistles, catcalls and cheers, she straightened, pressed her lips to her fingertips and tossed a kiss to the audience.

At once she had them all—including Cole—in the palm of her hand.

But then she began to sing.

Cole's jaw dropped.

He frowned.

He stared in stunned disbelief at the gorgeous Marietta, wondering if the discordant sounds he was hearing were actually coming from her.

They were.

Marietta's mouth was open wide and she was singing at the top of her lungs. She did not have a beautiful voice. Far from it. It was a slightly shrill singing voice that went displeasingly flat when she reached for the high notes.

Bless her heart, she had everything else. She was young, beautiful, a good actress, had great stage presence and wore the elegant costume as no one else could. She was captivating to watch. Graceful. Commanding. Sure of herself.

Still, Cole shook his head with incredulity, wondering how on earth such an untalented singer was allowed to grace the stage of this or any other opera house. The woman simply could not sing.

Puzzled, Cole glanced around. He caught the expressions on some of the weathered faces of the men in the audience. They were smiling, yet looked as if they were in a small degree of pain. Apparently he was not the only one who found Marietta's singing voice somewhat jarring.

But if that were so, why had they come to hear her? Why the full house? Why would anyone come to hear a singer with a decidedly displeasing voice?

How could this untalented woman, lovely though she was, be an opera star?

Cole's gaze returned to the well-dressed, silver-haired gentleman seated alone in the box. The man was beaming down at Marietta as if he had never heard a sweeter voice.

"Oh, holy Christ," Cole muttered under his breath, knowing instinctively that the gentleman was no doubt the starry-eyed suitor of the tone-deaf singer.

Cole sat there and endured the cacophony for several long minutes, then finally could stand it no longer. Opera was tough enough to take when the performers had beautiful voices.

"Excuse me," he whispered, rose, and made his way out to the wide, carpeted aisle, bumping knees as he went.

Resisting the temptation to put his hands over his ears, he eagerly exited the theater. But he didn't leave the building. He went down the grand staircase to the first floor and into the gaming room. Tables of green baize rested beneath crystal chandeliers. The shuffle of cards, the click of the dice, the spin of the roulette wheel were seductive. Cole, his heartbeat quickening, loosened his black silk cravat. But he did not succumb to his strong desire to gamble.

A long polished bar stretched the length of the back wall. He headed directly for that bar and for a stiff drink.

A bald, rotund man stood behind the bar, wiping

glasses on a clean white cloth. He looked up, smiled and asked, "What'll it be, sir?"

"Bourbon," said Cole. "And hopefully a bit of information."

The fat man smiled and said, "Try me. I know just about everything that goes on in Central City."

"Then you're my man," Cole said with a smile before he downed his bourbon in one long swallow and shoved his glass across the polished bar. The barkeep poured him another. Cole said, "And your name?"

"Harry," he said with a grin, rubbed his gleaming bald pate and added, "Not that kind of hairy."

Cole smiled, reached a hand across the bar. "Cole Heflin, Harry. I was just upstairs at the opera."

"I figured," said Harry, firmly shaking Cole's hand.

"The star of the opera can't sing, Harry."

The barkeep laughed heartily, jowls and belly shaking. "You noticed, did you?"

"I noticed. I also noticed a prosperous, silver-haired gentleman seated in a private box who appeared to be taken with the opera's lovely young star, Marietta."

Nodding, the barkeep looked around, then leaned across the bar. "He's absolutely mad about that red-haired singer."

"I assumed as much. Who is he?"

"Taylor Maltese," said Harry as if Cole should recognize the name.

"I'm a Texan," Cole explained.

"Then you don't know who he is?"

Cole shook his head.

Harry said, "He's Taylor Maltese, owner of the Maltese Mining empire. Rich as old Jay Gould. Owns silver mines all over these mountains as well as many other lucrative enterprises."

"And this Marietta, she's his…?"

"Yes, she sure is." The barkeep laughed and confided, "I've never seen a man as smitten with a woman as Taylor Maltese is with that gorgeous redhead. He's like a puppy dog, always following her around, nipping at her heels, begging her to toss him a bone."

"And does she?" Harry just grinned and gave no reply. Cole pressed on. "I noticed a rather evil-looking character standing at the back of Maltese's private box. Scar face and all. Bodyguard?"

"He's called Lightnin'," the barkeep said, nodding.

"Lightnin'," Cole repeated.

"That's how fast he is on the draw."

"I see," Cole said thoughtfully. "Lightnin' the only bodyguard?"

"No, there are a couple of big, burly brothers, the Burnett boys. They shadow Marietta."

That was bad news for Cole, but he didn't let on. He sipped his second bourbon and said, "You know, I can understand this wealthy man's infatuation with Marietta. She's sure a pretty thing, isn't she?"

"Looks like an angel," agreed the barkeep.

"But there's something I can't understand," said Cole. "She can't really sing very well, so how is it she's the star of an opera."

The barkeep roared with laughter. "How do you think? Maltese owns the Tivoli Opera House."

Cole laughed. "That explains it."

"Maltese is so in love with that luscious singer, he pays his miners hazard pay to fill the opera seats every evening to cheer and praise his darling!"

Five

Harry disclosed that the wealthy Taylor Maltese provided his adored Marietta with luxurious living quarters; a five-room rooftop suite above the Tivoli Opera House. Not only that, the multimillionaire had persuaded a renowned Italian voice coach to come to Central City to tutor Marietta. It was rumored that he paid the woman generously to teach and train Marietta. Exclusively. The voice coach was allowed to have no other students.

Cole listened as the talkative Harry supplied answers to questions that hadn't been asked. "The voice coach, Sophia somebody, I don't know her last name—you should see her, she's bigger than me." Harry laughed then and patted his big belly. "She lives in a nice little cottage near the opera house. Maltese pays the lease. Some folks wonder why she doesn't live with her only pupil. There's plenty of room in Marietta's private quarters. But I guess Maltese doesn't want anyone around when he visits his ladylove." Harry winked conspiratorially.

Cole smiled and said casually, "I'm surprised he allows Marietta to live alone. Isn't he worried she might entertain someone other than him in her quarters."

"Not a chance of that happening," said Harry. "He watches her like a hawk. Or, rather, his minions do. She goes nowhere without the Burnett boys tagging along. And, when she's at home, one or the other of the brothers stands guard below on the sidewalk. Night and day. Maltese is no fool. The way I see it, she's his, bought and paid for. And Maltese protects his property."

"Can't say that I blame him," Cole replied. Just then, people, laughing and talking, began streaming into the foyer beyond the gaming room. Cole turned his head, glanced in their direction and said, "Looks like the opera is over."

"Yes. I'll be pretty busy now," said Harry.

"Time for me to be getting back to the hotel," said Cole. "Nice talking to you, Harry."

"Same here," said the barkeep. "You come again." Harry screwed up his florid face then and added, "I'm losing my touch. We've talked for more than an hour and I know nothing about you other than the fact that you're from Texas."

"Not much to know," said Cole. "I'm just your typical music lover, in town for a few days."

When the final curtain came down, Maltese rose and exited his private box. His hands were red and stinging from applauding so vigorously. Marietta had taken several curtain calls and the audience, on its feet in a standing ovation, had whistled and called her name and tossed fresh-cut flowers onto the stage.

Now the great auditorium was swiftly emptying and Maltese, anticipating giving his beloved a congratulatory kiss, hurried backstage. The unsmiling, scar-faced Lightnin' was a couple of steps behind.

Inside the flower-filled dressing chamber, Madam Sophia, proud of her charge's performance, was embracing and complimenting the beaming Marietta. The two women had grown close in the months they had spent together. Marietta had few female friends, save the motherly Madam Sophia. She confided in Madam Sophia, told her things about herself that no one else knew. Once resentful and in complete disdain of Marietta, Madam Sophia had now become understanding and protective of the beautiful young woman.

Madam Sophia was aware of her pupil's limited singing abilities. But she knew how desperately Marietta wanted to be famous, so she was determined to mold her eager pupil into a star despite her less than perfect singing voice.

Marietta wasn't the first opera singer she'd coached whose voice was not exceptional. And, Marietta had everything else. With her youth and beauty and acting talents, she was surely destined for some degree of stardom.

"Did you count the curtain calls?" Marietta asked breathlessly, her face flushed with excitement, her eyes shining.

''Seven,'' replied Madam Sophia, giving the taller, younger woman one last affectionate pat on the back. ''Now turn around, dear, and I'll help get you out of the costume.''

Sighing happily, Marietta dutifully turned. Madam Sophia's plump fingers went to the tiny hooks going down the back of Marietta's gown. As she worked, Madam Sophia said, ''Such a grand opening night! Every seat filled and—'' An urgent knock on the dressing room stopped her in midsentence. Madam Sophia clucked her tongue against the roof of her mouth. ''Maltese, I presume. Shall I tell him you're not dressed?''

''No,'' said Marietta. ''You can let him in. I'll finish behind the dressing screen.''

Madam Sophia grabbed her charge's arm, whirled her back around. ''With him in the room?''

Marietta laughed off Madam Sophia's chagrin. ''That's what dressing screens are for, Sophia. Is my dress completely unhooked?''

''It is,'' said the coach, hands going to her wide hips.

Marietta nodded. ''Then open the door for Maltese.''

''If you undress behind the screen, he'll see the tops of your bosom,'' scolded the disapproving Madam Sophia.

''Nonsense,'' said Marietta. ''He'll see nothing. Now, please, answer his knock and then you may go.'' Madam Sophia made a face.

Marietta laughed at her friend's needless concern

and assured the older woman, "Nothing will happen, believe me. I see to it that Maltese is always a gentleman with me." She danced around behind the screen. "You know I'm telling you the truth."

Madam Sophia lifted a skeptical eyebrow, crossed to the door and admitted the eager admirer. To Maltese she said, "Marietta has early rehearsals tomorrow."

Eyes only for Marietta, Maltese said, "I won't keep her up too late."

Madam Sophia bustled out in such a hurry, she bumped into Lightnin', who stood just outside the door. They glared at each other.

Maltese closed the dressing-room door and leaned back against it. "You were a sensation tonight, my dear," he said.

"You're so sweet," she replied with a flirtatious smile. "Give me a minute to get out of my costume and I'll be ready to go to dinner. Will you blow out the lamp?" Marietta asked and ducked behind the dressing screen.

"Of course, sugar," Maltese said as he crossed to the mirrored dressing table, lifted the lamp's glass globe and blew out the flame.

The lamp extinguished, now only a single white candle burned in a holder near the open back window. The small room was bathed in the candle's mellow glow. Shadows danced on the walls. It was a seductive atmosphere.

Marietta was soon to make it even more seductive.

His voice cracking a little, Maltese turned about and said, "So...you haven't changed yet?"

"No, Sophia and I were so busy congratulating ourselves I didn't get around to it. But don't worry, I won't be a moment," she said and favored him with another dazzling smile.

Marietta was a tall woman. Her head and shoulders rose above the covering screen. She lowered the sleeve of her turquoise gown down one shoulder and asked, "You don't mind waiting, do you?"

Maltese swallowed hard. "No, sugar. You take as long as you need." His eyes flashing with expectation, he reached for a chair, turned it around so that it faced the screen and quickly sat down.

Marietta knew exactly what she was doing. She would, on this festive evening, provide her middle-aged benefactor with a few memorable thrills. And she would do so without actually showing him anything or compromising herself.

She knew how it would excite him to know that she was stripping behind the screen. So Marietta stepped out of the turquoise costume and draped it over the screen.

She paused, rested her arms atop the screen and said, "I'm just dewy with perspiration from my strenuous performance."

"Are you, sugar?" Maltese managed to say, his wide-eyed gaze resting on her pale shoulders. "Did you want to go up to your quarters and take a bath before dinner?"

Marietta pretended to be thinking it over. "No, tell you what, Sophia was so thoughtful, she placed a basin of water here behind the screen. I'll just strip off everything and take a little sponge bath. If that's all right with you?"

Maltese was now practically speechless with excitement. He nodded his silver head vigorously and gestured with trembling hands.

"Does that mean yes?" she asked in a honeyed voice.

"Y-yes," he finally croaked. "Yes, absolutely."

"Good. I declare, I'm just so hot and sticky."

Marietta sensuously wiggled free of her lacy petticoats and tossed them atop the discarded costume.

"These tiny little hooks on my camisole are hard to manage," she informed him, her face screwed up in concentration as she worked at undoing the minuscule fasteners. She laughed then, and added, "If I can't get these little devils open, I may have to enlist your help."

Maltese's breathing grew labored and shallow at the exciting prospect. He watched with growing anticipation.

"Ah, there!" she said after a moment. "Finally got the last one."

"That's nice," he said, a cloud of disappointment crossing his perspiring face. But the disappointment evaporated as the lace straps of the camisole slipped down her shoulders. The frothy undergarment was soon draped across the screen's top and Maltese felt his heart hammer in his chest. His beloved—standing not six feet from him—was now bare to the waist.

He began to pant when Marietta lifted her arms, swept her long red-gold hair atop her head and pinned it there. The movement caused her shoulders to lift, the swell of her full, bare breasts to rise dangerously close to the top border of the screen.

Maltese anxiously licked his dry lips. He gripped his trousered knees with dampened hands; hands that itched to touch the beautiful woman who so tempted him. He could almost feel the warm heaviness of her white breasts in his palms.

Marietta, knowing what was going through his mind, chattered gaily as if nothing unusual were taking place, continuing to thrill her suitor without really giving him anything. When she slithered out of her lace-trimmed pantalets and tossed them over the screen, she sighed as if with great relief.

Maltese, red-faced now, pulse pounding in his ears, squirmed on his chair as she noisily kicked off her shoes, then peeled her silk stockings down and tossed them over the screen.

"Ah, there," she sighed, "everything's off and I'm as bare as a newborn babe. It feels *sooo* good. Sometimes I wonder why we must wear such hot, heavy underclothing." She laughed musically then and added, "Sometimes I wonder why we must wear any clothes at all, don't you, Maltese?"

"Y-yes, oh, yes," he groaned as his heart tried to beat its way out of his chest.

Just then a strong night breeze stirred the sheer window curtains. The candle flame danced wildly. The quick surge of light outlined—for a fleeting instant—Marietta's bare silhouette against the dressing screen. Maltese quickly put a hand to his mouth to stifle his rising moan of joy. Such undraped perfection! Such purity! And it was his, all his.

Light-headed, dizzy, Maltese felt his brain pounding out the message, "My darling Marietta is *naked*. Totally, gloriously naked. She is bare. Not wearing a stitch. And there's only a silk screen between us."

Marietta began to hum as she dipped a sponge into the basin of water and pressed it to her throat, then let it slide slowly down her chest until it disappeared behind the screen. Maltese had never known such sweet agony. He watched, entranced, as his naughty Marietta sponged off her entire body. He could see nothing, but he imagined that he could. He wished that she would announce which part of her lovely body she was presently washing. But, of course, she wouldn't. She was too much of a lady.

Maltese held his breath, hoping against hope that the candle would flare again. His chest tightened as he pondered whether or not she had reached the nether region between her long slender legs. God, he wished that she would tell him.

Marietta revealed nothing, just continued to hum.

Still, being afforded the opportunity to share this intimate bathing exercise with her was incredibly pleasurable and highly arousing. He could, if asked, truthfully brag that he had watched Marietta take a bath. But that would be raffish behavior.

Nevertheless, Maltese had high hopes that one day Marietta would be naked in a candlelit room with him and there would be no screen between them. He would be the one helping press the dampened sponge to her heated body.

This pleasant fantasy continued as Marietta finished her bath and got dressed. When she stepped out from behind the screen, she was fully clothed and fully aware that she had given her aging caller all the excitement he could handle for one evening. Nothing more would be required of her. A sumptuous dinner at the Castle Top and then a good-night peck on the cheek.

Maltese would leave her a happy man.

Six

Cole joined the departing crowd.

He left the opera house, but he did not immediately go to the hotel. Crossing the street, he approached a false-fronted business, now darkened and closed for the night. He stepped into the shadows of the roof's low overhang, turned and leaned back against the building. Arms crossed, Cole stood looking up at the top floor of the opera house.

Marietta's private quarters.

Cole wondered if she was up there now, entertaining her aging Romeo. He recoiled at the thought and quickly looked away.

From where he stood, he could see down the alley directly beside the opera house. The tall, spare man he'd observed in Maltese's private box was posted there by a side door near the back of the building.

Cole watched him for a moment, then looked back to the front of the theater. The crowd had thinned dramatically. Only a few stragglers remained on the sidewalk, talking, getting into carriages. Two men stood out—both were big, burly fellows dressed in work shirts and buckskins. Undoubtedly, the Burnett brothers that Harry the barkeep had told him about. Cole studied the brothers for a while, sizing them up, wondering how he was ever going to slip Marietta past them.

His attention was drawn once more down the side alley, when the door opened and out into the mountain moonlight stepped Marietta and her middle-aged lover.

Cole sank farther back into the shadows. He watched as the couple came up the alley toward the street. They turned onto the sidewalk and into the glow of the gaslights lining the avenue.

Again Cole was struck by Marietta's incredible beauty and for a moment he sorely envied the silver-haired man with whom she shared her time and her charms.

Cole's jaw tightened.

He continued to watch as the couple, arm in arm, strolled up the street. The scar-faced bodyguard called Lightnin' followed a few paces behind. Marietta and Maltese soon entered the bustling Castle Top restaurant at the top of the hill. Lightnin' stayed outside. An armed, unmoving, black-clad sentinel.

Cole again glanced directly across the street. The Burnett brothers still loitered outside the opera house. They would, he surmised, be waiting when Marietta got home.

Cole pushed away from the building and headed for his hotel. Back at the Teller House he undressed without lighting the lamp, tossing his clothes over a chair. He mulled over what he had seen and heard. And he grimaced.

Old Maxwell Lacey's beautiful red-haired granddaughter was the mistress of a wealthy, powerful man who was old enough to be her father. And it would not be simple or easy to whisk the gold-digging beauty away from Central City. Not with the lovesick Maltese certain to interfere.

Naked, Cole crawled into bed. He yawned and thought back over the evening. Like a quick jolt of adrenaline came the unforgettable moment when he'd gotten his very first glimpse of the gorgeous Marietta. Cole felt himself stir at the vivid recollection. She was without doubt the most beautiful, the most innocent-looking, the most desirable woman he had ever seen.

He wanted her. Wanted her now. Wished that she was here, naked in his arms.

Cole exhaled with frustration and silently cursed himself. He flopped over onto his stomach and pressed his surging erection into the softness of the mattress. He gritted his teeth, cursed his weakness and waited for this quick burst of unwanted desire to pass. He was annoyed with himself. And he was surprised. It wasn't as though it had been weeks since he'd had a woman. He'd had one just last night in Denver. What the hell was wrong with him?

Cole waited impatiently for the stirring sexual hunger to subside. All at once he recalled the discordant sound of Marietta's singing voice. He could hear it ringing in his ears. That did the trick. Desire fled. Heat passed. Cole relaxed.

He heaved a sigh of relief, turned onto his back, folded his hands beneath his head and wondered idly if the beautiful opera singer was in love with the Maltese mining magnate.

No, she wasn't. He'd bet his ten thousand against it. Harry, the barkeep, had said Maltese purchased the newly built Tivoli Opera House solely so that Marietta could star in all the productions. Marietta was cleverly, cold-heartedly using the lovesick Maltese to further her fledgling singing career.

Cole lay awake pondering how best to get the heartless little gold digger back to Galveston. He decided he'd have to spend a few days in town before he tried anything. He'd watch her closely, check out where she went and when. And with whom. Try to catch her away from her big bodyguards. If he could get her alone for just a moment, he would introduce himself. Tell her he was a fan.

Cole briefly considered courting her, but decided against it. He wasn't that big a heel. He would simply level with her. Admit that he had come to Central City to escort her home to Galveston and her waiting grandfather.

After all, he wasn't sure she would refuse to go.

"New York. London. Rome. Amsterdam. Madrid!" exclaimed a glowing Marietta after the morning's rehearsals. "Andreas, tell me that one day I shall sing in all those cities' fine opera houses!"

The other players had left the opera house as soon as rehearsals had ended. Only Marietta, Sophia and the opera's artistic director, Andreas, remained on-stage.

Andreas, a slender, refined man with sandy hair, a pencil-thin mustache and a fondness for the red-haired Marietta, smiled indulgently but was noncommittal.

He said, "My dear child, before you can hope to appear in the opera houses of London and New York, you must spend years mastering your craft. Listening to Madam Sophia, doing as she instructs. Learning, practicing, improving."

This was not what Marietta had wanted to hear. She sighed heavily and sank onto a chair. "Andreas, you know very well how much I practice. That's all I do all day, every day. Tell him, Sophia."

The rotund Madam Sophia agreed. "She works very hard, Andreas. Perhaps too hard."

The discerning artistic director, like the voice coach Madam Sophia, was all too cognizant of the unfortunate fact that the long hours of practice were not going to make a great deal of difference. Marietta, bless her, beautiful though she was and possessed of a great stage presence, was never going to sing in Rome and Madrid. She simply did not have the voice. But Andreas did not have the heart to tell her.

"Marietta," Andreas said, rubbing his chin thoughtfully, "I believe Madam Sophia is right.

You've been practicing too much. Both you and Sophia need to take a rest. Why don't you get out of that costume, get dressed up in something attractive and go out for a walk or a carriage ride." He smiled and added, "The fresh mountain air will be good for you."

Marietta's weariness instantly fled. She jumped up out of the chair. "You mean it?" She looked from Andreas to Sophia. Both nodded. Her emerald eyes now sparkling, she mused aloud, "I could go shopping or out to lunch. Or just take a walk. I'd enjoy that so."

"And it would be good for you," Madam Sophia said.

"You go, my dear, and enjoy yourself," said Andreas.

"I will," Marietta replied. "Oh, yes, I will!"

Marietta felt a great surge of excitement wash over her as she planned her little adventure. She had the entire afternoon to herself. No practice. No rehearsal. Maltese was down in Denver and wouldn't be back until late evening. She was free to do as she pleased!

Marietta, as happy as a child, impulsively dashed over to Andreas and gave him a big bear hug. The normally reserved artistic director was disarmed by her. He laughed and gave her small waist an affectionate squeeze. She released him and turned to Sophia.

Her arms around the short, stocky voice coach, she said, "Will you be a darling and help me dress?"

* * *

A half hour later, a smiling Marietta, fashionably garbed in a bronze poplin traveling suit, stepped out into the warm Colorado sunshine.

Her bright smile weakened a little when she saw both Burnett brothers in the alley. In her way. She wished, just once, she could go somewhere without them following her.

Marietta took a spine-stiffening breath and raised and opened her bronze silk parasol. She stepped up to Conlin Burnett, the older of the two brothers, and told him, "I am going to take a walk. By myself. I do not want either one of you getting in my way. I do not want you dogging my every step. In fact, I want you to just stay right here where you are. Will you do that?"

Con Burnett, twisting his battered hat in his big, callused hands, frowned and said, "Now, Miss Marietta, you know we can't allow you to go off on your own. Lightnin' would have our hides. We're supposed to look after you."

Marietta gritted her teeth. She was wasting her breath and knew it. Maltese swore he had hired the Burnetts to watch after her. She knew better. He had hired them to watch her.

Marietta whirled away and headed up the alley. The brothers exchanged worried looks and hurried behind her. She reached the sidewalk, looked up the street, then down. The parasol shading her delicate skin, she turned and sauntered up Eureka Street with no particular destination in mind.

Passersby, mostly men, recognized the lovely opera star. They stopped to speak to her, to tell her they had seen her perform. Pleased, Marietta smiled politely, shook some hands and graciously accepted praise and compliments. Her presence caused quite a stir on this still, summer afternoon. Everyone she passed warmly acknowledged her, spoke to her, lauded her.

Except one man.

The block ahead was empty, save a lone man leaning a shoulder against the striped pole in front of Duncan's Barbershop. He did not look like a miner. He looked like a gentleman. He wore a pair of snug-fitting buff-hued trousers and a starched white shirt, open at the collar.

He was not looking in her direction, so Marietta had the opportunity to study him while he remained unaware. She stopped a few feet from him and stared. The man was tall and lean with broad shoulders, deep chest and slim hips. His hair, neatly brushed and shining in the sunlight, was as black as the darkest midnight. His smoothly shaven face was so deeply tanned it was almost swarthy.

But oh, what a handsome face it was.

High forehead, proud roman nose, full, sensual lips and strong, harshly cut chin. She couldn't tell what color his eyes were, but she could see the long, black lashes that shaded them.

Marietta, feeling strangely faint, was half-afraid to move closer to the tall, dark stranger. Why, she didn't know. She swallowed hard and moved cautiously forward. She was holding her breath by the time she reached him.

And she was confused. He had to know that she was approaching him, had to see her moving in his side vision. But he didn't turn his head to look at her.

Not until the very last second. When Marietta passed directly by him, the man finally looked up and met her gaze. And Marietta thought her heart would beat its way out of her chest. Startlingly sky-blue eyes staring up from under improbably long eyelashes touched her, assessed her, frightened her.

Then quickly dismissed her.

Marietta was nonplussed. She hurried away, flustered and insulted. This darkly handsome man had looked directly at her, but was apparently not the least bit interested. Those beautiful blue eyes did not light up at the sight of her. Those sensual lips did not lift in a flirtatious smile. That lean, masculine body had not shifted, muscular shoulder had not left the barber pole. She had had no visible effect on him.

None whatsoever.

She wandered aimlessly up the street, both disappointed and excited. She was extremely frustrated that the handsome stranger had paid her no attention. At the same time she was strongly intrigued by his utter nonchalance. His obvious lack of interest made Marietta all the more interested in him.

That and the fact that he was a sultry, sexually suggestive, highly threatening male and just the sight of him had made her tingle all over. She wanted the feeling to last. She wanted to be close to him again. She wanted him to make her tingle. And she especially wanted to make him tingle.

Marietta paused half a block past the barbershop and the tall, dark, indifferent stranger. She lifted her chin defiantly, turned about and almost bumped into the lumbering Con Burnett. Her anger flared and she loudly berated him.

"I told you to stay out of my way!" she hissed.

"Sorry, Miss Marietta."

Cole heard the exchange and grinned. He knew what she was going to do. She was coming back his way. She had noticed him. She wanted him to notice her.

So he wouldn't.

Not yet.

Her heart in her throat, Marietta nervously approached the tall man who still stood there leaning against the barber pole. Cole waited until she was a few steps from him. Then he pushed away from the pole, turned his back on her and stepped down off the sidewalk. He unhurriedly crossed the street.

Marietta couldn't believe her eyes. It was all she could do to keep from calling out to him and ordering him to come back. She was filled with anger and despair as she watched him casually walk away from her. She continued to stare, longing to know who he was and where he was going and wondering if she would ever see him again.

She blinked when he turned into the silver-floored

entrance of the Teller House Hotel and disappeared. She was tempted to follow him, took a tentative step forward, and caught herself. She couldn't go running after a stranger. Besides, even if she could, the Burnett brothers would tell Maltese.

Marietta sighed, her slender shoulders slumping.

The excitement of her afternoon adventure was gone. She had no particular interest in shopping or having a late lunch. She just wanted to go home. Parasol raised, she walked dejectedly back to the opera house, ignoring the passersby who smiled and called to her.

Back in her private quarters, Marietta undressed, drew on a satin robe and paced restlessly. She was agitated. Fidgety. Unable to relax. She had seen an incredibly attractive man who'd set her pulses to pounding and she wouldn't rest until she saw him again.

Marietta abruptly stopped pacing, snapped her fingers and said aloud, "I will see him again. I will go to the Teller House tomorrow and have lunch."

Marietta did just that.

But to her disappointment, there was no sign of the dark-haired stranger. She hurried through her meal and left the hotel. She walked up the street toward the barbershop, hoping to find him leaning against the colored barber pole.

But he was not there.

From the front window of his fourth-floor suite in the Teller House, Cole watched Marietta leave the hotel, walk up the street. Her head was bare and her glorious red-gold hair, dressed elegantly atop her head, blazed in the sunlight.

He watched as she approached the barbershop. And he smiled when she stopped, reached out and touched the barber pole.

She was looking for him.

Soon he would let her find him.

Seven

Cole knew it wasn't going to be easy to catch the lovely Marietta alone. When she was with Maltese, the scar-faced Lightnin' hovered nearby. If Marietta went out alone, she was closely shadowed by those two big bruisers, the Burnett brothers. Maltese saw to it that his ladylove was well guarded at all times.

Still, Cole was confident he could find a way around the bodyguards. Impatiently he bided his time, waited and watched. And he smiled when, three days in a row, he saw Marietta venture out. From his fourth-floor Teller House suite he watched her stroll up Eureka Street, pausing before shop windows.

But her interest was not really in the merchandise displayed. She didn't gaze longingly into the plate-glass windows of the stores. Instead, she covertly glanced around, as if looking for someone.

She was looking for him.

Each day Cole waited until Marietta returned to her private quarters. Then he went out. He explored every inch of the little mountain hamlet, walking up one street and down another. He spoke to no one, attracted as little attention as possible. He hunted for the ideal place for a private rendezvous with Marietta. He found it on his third day out. The Far Canyon Café. A cozy little out-of-the-way restaurant nestled in the sheltering slopes near the top of the hill. The food was good, the wine cellar exceptional, and the high-backed banquettes afforded total privacy.

It was, Cole decided, time to end the little game of cat and mouse. The very next afternoon he dressed in a freshly laundered blue cotton shirt and a pair of dark twill trousers. Cleanly shaven, his hair neatly brushed, he left the Teller House resolved to carry out his mission. His mission was Marietta. Cole stepped out into the scorching June sunshine and looked up the street.

And there she was.

Marietta and her shadows were only a couple of blocks ahead. Cole proceeded cautiously, ducking into doorways, mingling with the milling crowds. All the while advancing, determined to meet Marietta, to talk with her.

He knew his opportunity had come when he saw Marietta enter a little shop on the corner at the far end of the block. Cole picked up his pace, hurried toward the store where the sign above read Lilly's Ladies Apparel.

The Burnett brothers stood on the sidewalk a few feet from the shop's front door. But neither noticed when Cole went inside. Their attention was momentarily diverted. An altercation had broken out across the street in front of the Golden Nugget Saloon. A crowd quickly gathered and bets were being placed on the bloodied pugilists. Con and Jim Burnett whistled and applauded, liking nothing better than watching a good fistfight.

Inside Lilly's small shop, Marietta was alone. There were no other customers. And the shop's owner, the diminutive Lilly, was in the back storeroom. She'd gone there after telling Marietta about the new shipment of lacy underwear that had just arrived that morning.

"Stay right here, Marietta," Lilly had said. "I'll go unpack some of the prettiest things for you to choose from. Shall I?"

"Definitely," Marietta had replied. "You know how I love the feel of silk or satin against my skin."

Alone now, Marietta was lifting a delicate white shawl from a display table, when she felt a presence behind her. A chill skipped up and down her spine. She turned, looked up and saw Cole. The shawl slipped from her hand and her heartbeat quickened.

For one long instant they inventoried each other and there was a definite challenge in their glances. Snared by his arresting blue eyes, Marietta automatically smiled and almost imperceptibly nodded to this darkly handsome man for whom she'd been secretly looking for the past four days.

Cole smiled back and asked, "Did you nod to me?"

"Did I?"

"I'm certain that you did."

"Well, perhaps," she admitted with a radiant smile.

Cole cautiously approached her. "Allow me to introduce myself," he said in a low, pleasing baritone. "I'm Cole Heflin, one of your legion of admirers, Miss Marietta."

He offered his hand. Marietta accepted it and felt a quick jolt of excitement race through her as his tanned fingers closed warmly around hers. She knew she should withdraw her hand. She didn't. She allowed him to continue holding it securely in his own and derived a strange thrill from the innocent act. She was certain this mere touching of hands had affected him too, because a muscle in his firm jaw moved as if he was clenching his teeth. Neither spoke.

They just stood there holding hands, looking at each other. It was a moment of electric silence. But although Marietta delighted in the firm pressure of his hand, she finally made an effort to withdraw her own. Cole tightened his grip. She was secretly glad.

"Then you have been to the opera?" she said, her emerald eyes aglow.

"Every performance since opening night," he lied.

"Ah, so you enjoy my singing, Mr. Heflin?"

"Words cannot describe," Cole said with an engaging smile. He gave her hand one last gentle squeeze, released it and asked, "I know it's awfully forward of me, but would you consider having lunch with me, Marietta?"

She was tempted. He was so compelling, so masculine, so attractive. The good-looking deeply tanned face, the jet-black hair that curled away from his temples. Those hooded eyes, as blue as the Colorado skies. That provocative smile, a smile that lifted one corner of his full lips a little higher than the other. And his hands, such marvelous hands, so strong and warm. Lean, beautiful hands with long tapered fingers. She was tremendously attracted and longed to know him better.

Still, she hesitated. Maltese was down in Denver again today, but his two hired minions, the Burnett brothers, were just outside Lilly's. They watched every move she made. Lunch with this handsome stranger was out of the question.

"I'm very flattered, but I—"

Cole interrupted, "Leave now and I'll stay behind. Go to the Far Canyon Café and I'll meet you there." Marietta's brilliant green eyes flickered and Cole knew she was weakening. He continued, "I'll go around through the alley behind the buildings. When I reach the café, I'll use the back door, come through the kitchen. It's almost two o'clock. The café will be deserted at this hour. No one will see us together."

Marietta took only a second to think it over before she whispered, "I'll be in the back banquette, away from the street."

Cole grinned boyishly. "I'll meet you there in fifteen minutes."

"Fifteen minutes," she repeated, and taking a step

closer, glanced nervously out the front windows and told him, "Don't turn and look when I leave."

Cole shook his head and said, "The next time I look at you will be across the table at the Far Canyon Café."

True to his word, Cole kept his back to the street as Marietta quickly exited the apparel shop. She had just walked out the door, when Lilly, carrying several frothy undergarments over her arm, came out of the storeroom, saying, "Marietta, there's an ice-blue satin nightgown that you...you—" She stopped, frowned, looked about and said to Cole, "Where is the beautiful lady, the red-haired opera singer?"

Cole looked around, shrugged wide shoulders and said, "No one else is here."

"But that can't be! Marietta, my best customer, was waiting until I—"

"Ma'am, the shop was empty when I walked in. Now, if you'll just show me that blue satin nightgown you mentioned. My wife might like it."

"Oh, indeed she will," said Lilly, tossing the bundle onto a table and withdrawing the slinky nightgown with a bodice fashioned entirely of delicate lace that left nothing to the imagination.

Cole said, "I'll take it. Wrap it up and I'll be back for it later." He withdrew some bills from his pocket and paid the beaming proprietress.

"Your wife is going to be so pleased, Mr.... Mr....?"

But Cole was gone. He stepped outside. The sidewalk was now empty. He walked to the end of the block, turned and slipped down through the alley. He headed for the restaurant.

Marietta blinked blindly when she entered the dimly lit Far Canyon Café. When her eyes adjusted to the change in light, she saw that she was the only customer. For that she was extremely grateful. If she was very lucky, no one would see her here. No one would ever guess that she had lunched with a stranger, a man who could be a dangerous outlaw for all she knew. The fine hair at the nape of her neck rose and she wondered if she was in danger. If she had any sense, she would leave now before he arrived.

Too late.

No sooner was she seated in a high-backed banquette in a private alcove at the back of the café than Cole Heflin joined her. He slid onto the soft leather seat across from her, licked his thumb and forefinger and extinguished the lighted candle at the center of the table. Smoke from the dying flame wafted and hung in the still air.

Unsmiling, Cole leaned back and gazed at Marietta through the thinning smoke, fixing her with those incredible indigo eyes. He said nothing, just stared at her. His intense scrutiny both embarrassed and pleased her. She could feel the blood rushing to her face and all at once her clothes felt uncomfortably tight.

Cole noticed the pulse in her pale throat throbbing

rapidly, saw the high points of color now staining her cheeks.

"Are you too warm, Marietta?" he inquired, shifting on the seat, leaning up to the table. "You look a little flushed."

"No, I'm fine, really," she managed to say and silently ordered herself to calm down.

"I wish I could say the same," Cole said as he reached up and deftly flipped open a couple of buttons going down the center of his shirtfront. "You don't mind, do you? I'm perspiring."

"No, of course not," she said and couldn't keep from focusing on the expanse of dark, muscled chest that the open shirt revealed.

"There, that's better," said Cole, then lifted a hand in the air to signal the waiter.

Soon Marietta relaxed somewhat and began to enjoy herself. Wine flowed into tall goblets of Venetian glass with elegant twisted stems. Crisp salads on gold-banded china and a basket of hot yeast rolls with butter were placed on the table before them. Neither was very hungry. But both drank thirstily of the red wine.

Cole was clever. He put Marietta at her ease, teased her, laughed with her, drew her out. Found out all he could about her without pressing her. Marietta was more than happy to tell him of her triumphs, her plans, her dreams. She had, she told him, been in Central City for a little more than a year. Her residence in the remote mountain village was temporary, she had no intention of staying here long.

She would, she told him, likely be leaving soon to grace the stages of opera houses in much larger cities. Her career in opera was only beginning. She hoped to one day appear in London and Milan. Cole nodded and smiled and listened and acted as if everything she said was of great interest.

Marietta was thoroughly charmed. This clandestine luncheon was, for her, most enjoyable. She couldn't recall when she'd had such a good time. Sipping her wine and leaning up to the table to listen as he talked, she learned that Cole Heflin was not only the handsomest man she had ever met, he was charming and witty and great fun to be with. In a pleasant wine haze, Marietta was now totally relaxed and happy. Sighing contentedly, she wished that she could sit here in this deserted café with this magnetic man forever. Just the two of them. Drinking, laughing, flirting. It was so incredibly thrilling and downright naughty to be having this secret meeting with a mysterious stranger.

And the danger made the rendezvous all the more exciting.

Holding her stemmed glass out for more wine, Marietta slurred her words slightly when she said, "You know something, Cole, you have just a hint of a Southern accent. Are you from Georgia or Alabama?"

"Texas," he said, filling her glass.

"Ah," she replied. "What part of Texas?"

But his reply was a question, "Where were you born, Marietta?"

She didn't answer and he noted a slight cloud pass behind her eyes. She wrinkled her perfect nose. Then giggled and changed the subject.

"This is the best wine I've ever tasted," she said and licked her lips. Then she tilted her head to one side and asked, "Do you have any idea what time it is?"

Cole glanced across the café, saw a large Seth Thomas clock on the far wall. "Yes, it's five minutes of four."

Marietta's eyes widened. "You're teasing me!"

"I would never do that," Cole said.

"Good heavens, I had no idea it was getting so late," she said. "I must go."

Cole shook his head. "Why? The afternoon is young. Let's order another bottle of wine and some rich, decadent dessert."

"No. No I can't," she said, and started to slide across the leather seat.

"Wait." Cole stopped her. "Listen to me, Marietta, and let me finish before you speak. Will you do that?"

She smiled and said, "Why, of course, Cole."

Cole drew a breath, reached across the table and placed his hand gently atop hers. He said simply, "My dear, I've come to take you home to your grandfather in Galveston."

For a moment Marietta stared at him in stunned

disbelief. Then her face flushed with anger. She yanked her hand free of his, slid out of the banquette and shot to her feet.

She shouted loudly, not caring who heard her, "Wild horses couldn't drag me anywhere near that cruel old bastard down in Galveston!"

"Marietta, your grandfather is dying and he—"

"Let him die!" she screeched. "Everybody dies!"

"That's mighty cold talk coming from the old gentleman's only granddaughter," Cole accused. "Let me take you home before it's too late."

Her eyes flashing green fire, Marietta snarled, "You are taking me nowhere, Heflin, and you'd better stay away from me! If you don't, I'll sic my bodyguards on you and they'll rearrange that arrogant face of yours! Get out of Central City, you don't belong here, Texan!"

"I will," Cole said calmly, remaining seated, "but when I go, you're going with me."

Furious, Marietta put both hands on the table, leaned down so that her face was only inches from his and hotly declared, "Not a chance, Heflin. For your information, a very rich and powerful man is madly in love with me and—"

"Maltese," Cole cut in. "I know. The little silver-haired fellow I've seen you with."

"Yes! I'll tell Maltese about you!"

"No, you won't."

"Yes, I will! I'll go straight to him and—"

Interrupting, Cole said, "You will do no such

thing. You're not about to admit to your aging protector that you secretly met with another man behind his back.''

Marietta had no retort. He was right. She couldn't dare tell the overly possessive Maltese about this meeting. Fuming, bested, she snapped, ''You deceitful bastard, pretending to be a fan!''

Cole grinned. ''Sweetheart, I could take lessons in deceit from you.''

''Oh! You can go to blazes, Texan!''

''I probably will, but not before I get you safely home to your grandfather.''

Eight

"Madam Sophia, you of all people know very well that opera is all about the soprano!" stated a disdainful Andreas. "After an evening in the theater, a patron barely recalls the preening tenor, the mezzo or even the forceful baritone. When the curtain comes down, it is the effect of the soprano that lingers!"

"I know, Andreas," said Madam Sophia calmly. "I've done all I can with Marietta. She tries so hard. And she is a wonderful actress. She has a riveting, instinctive stage presence. You have to give her that much."

"It's not enough. Marietta cannot sing!" said the artistic director.

Sophia smiled indulgently and waved away his concern. "Well, do not despair. We are not in New York or Paris. This is Central City, Colorado, and in case you've failed to notice, the theater is filled every evening."

The two were having afternoon coffee in Sophia's comfortable little cottage. Andreas and Sophia had become good friends since arriving in Central City. Veterans of European opera houses, they had a lot in common. Both were alone, both loved the opera and both were very fond of the mercurial Marietta.

Andreas replied, "Yes, the seats are filled, but we know the reason. If Marietta were appearing anywhere but here in this remote alpine village, she'd be playing to an empty house. Marietta cannot meet the vocal demands of grand opera, she hasn't the God-given talent. She definitely does not possess the *voix d'or*—the golden voice."

The rotund Sophia carefully set her coffee cup aside. She sighed and said, "I'm well aware, even if Marietta is not, that she has no bright future in opera. But I am not too worried about her. She is young and full of life and very beautiful. Men are drawn to her like moths to the flame. My hope is that she soon meets and marries someone more suitable than Maltese."

"Oh, I don't know," commented Andreas. "Maltese is one of the richest men in America. She could do worse."

Sophia shook her head knowingly. "He could never make her happy. Marietta needs a man with fire and passion to match her own. Someone who will *not* put her on a pedestal and worship her. A devilishly handsome rascal who is consistently and stubbornly all male who will not allow her to dominate him."

"The way she dominates poor old Maltese?"

"Exactly."

Andreas mused aloud, "You're probably right."

He smiled when he added, "I only wish she'd meet such a man tomorrow and leave the opera."

Andreas chuckled then and so did Sophia.

Cole remained seated after Marietta had rushed angrily out of the Far Canyon Café. He poured himself another glass of wine and lit an expensive Cuban cigar. He calmly considered his next move.

He had no idea what Marietta had against her grandfather, but he knew that she was not going to go peacefully. The prospect of whisking her out of Central City and delivering her a thousand miles south to Galveston was not a pleasant one. Long days and longer nights with an irate woman whom he couldn't let out of his sight. No stroll in the park, to be sure.

Still, her grandfather had stayed the hangman's hand and paid him handsomely and he had promised the old gentleman that he'd bring his granddaughter home. Had given his word. He would do just that.

Cole finished his wine and cigar and left the empty café. His chore, for the next several days, was to stay away from Marietta. He intended to let her get lulled into a false sense of security.

The tall, spare man with the long, nasty-looking scar on his right cheek slowly withdrew the knife from its leather scabbard. The razor-sharp blade gleamed in the sunlight streaming in through the store's front windows.

He smiled satanically.

He gripped the knife's smooth handle, liking the feel of it in his palm. His beady, narrowed eyes gleaming, he slid his thumb and forefinger the length of the blade several times, caressing it as if deriving sexual pleasure from the act.

"You might like this one better," said Jake Stone, standing behind the counter of Stone's Weaponry Store. He placed a black-handled, short-bladed knife before his customer. "This one might be easier to handle."

The man stroking the long shiny blade never glanced at the other knife.

"I'll take this one," he said and slipped it back into the leather scabbard.

He was strapping the sheathed knife onto the back of his low-riding gun belt, when the proprietor said, "A good choice, Lightnin'. Perfect for skinning trout or what have you."

Lightnin' finally looked up, nodded, paid for the knife and left. He stepped out onto the wooden sidewalk just as Cole happened past Stone's Weaponry. Cole was lost in thought, head down. The two men collided.

"Why don't you watch where you're going?" snarled Lightnin'.

"Sorry," Cole apologized and hurriedly walked on, silently cursing his timing.

Maltese's scar-faced bodyguard was the last person on earth whose attention he wanted to attract.

Lightnin' stared after Cole. He knew everyone in town, so he recognized Cole as a stranger. He wondered what the man was doing in Central City. He meant to find out.

He trailed Cole back to the hotel. After Cole had gone up to his suite, Lightnin' went directly to the front desk. The clerk looked up and smiled nervously.

"May I help you?" he asked politely, recognizing Taylor Maltese's evil-looking bodyguard.

Unsmiling, Lightnin' said, "That tall, dark fellow who just went upstairs. Who is he?"

The desk clerk cleared his throat needlessly. "I'm sorry, sir, but the manager of the Teller House, Mr. Darren Ludlow, has made it a strict policy of this hotel that we not divulge the identity of our guests."

Lightnin' looked around. The high-ceilinged lobby was almost empty. Only an elderly couple sat on one of the many sofas. Both were reading. Lightnin' whipped out the shiny new knife he had just purchased at Stone's. The blade flashed as he held the sharp point an inch from the frightened desk clerk's chest.

"I'm making a new policy," he said. "You have exactly one minute to tell me who that stranger is."

"Yes, of course," said the jittery clerk who quickly turned the registration book around so that Lightnin' could look at it. "The guest to whom you're referring is Mr. Cole Heflin from Texas."

"Heflin, Heflin," Lightnin' repeated the name, resheathing his knife. "When did Heflin get into town?"

"A week...no, eight days ago, I believe."

"What's he doing here and how long is he staying?"

"That I couldn't tell you," said the clerk, then quickly amended, "I mean, I don't know. He didn't say."

Lightnin' turned away and walked out of the hotel. His curiosity aroused, he headed for the opera house. The Burnetts were standing guard in the alley. Maltese was upstairs with Marietta.

Lightnin' went into the downstairs gaming hall. He stepped up to the bar and questioned Harry, the barkeep. Harry told him a Texan had come in for a drink the night of the opera's debut, but didn't give his name or say why he was in Central City.

"He ask you anything about Marietta?"

Harry's mouth fell open. "Ah, he might have mentioned seeing her perform, I don't recall."

Lightnin' scratched the long scar going down his right cheek. "You tell him anything about her?"

"No. I mean, what's to tell?" The fat man shrugged and shook his head. "I know nothing about her, other than that she stars in the opera."

Lightnin' left without responding. He went around into the alley to talk to the Burnett brothers. "Did Marietta go out this afternoon?" he asked.

Con Burnett answered. "She did, but we were with her every step of the way, Lightnin'."

"Where did she go?"

Jim said, "She went into that ladies shop up on the corner of Eureka and Glory. You know that place where they have all them dainty things for women."

"Anywhere else?"

"The Far Canyon Café," stated Con.

Lightnin's eyes narrowed. "How long did she stay?"

"Quite a while," admitted Jim, never noticing his brother's silencing frown. "We just got back here not ten minutes before you and Maltese arrived."

"Did you go in the café with her?"

The big brothers looked guilty. Con told Lightnin', "Miss Marietta ordered us to stay outside. Said she wanted to enjoy her lunch in peace."

Lightnin' frowned. "Either one of you big, dumb bastards bother to have a look through the front windows to see who else was having lunch?"

The Burnetts exchanged worried looks. Con spoke up. "I'm telling you nobody else went in that café. We'd have seen 'em if they had. Marietta was alone the whole time."

Lightnin' looked from one to the other. "All right. But you boys better start keeping a closer eye on that red-haired singer. I don't trust her. She's far too young and high-spirited for Maltese." He paused, kicked at a clump of grass with the toe of his boot and reminded them, "Our only loyalty is to Maltese. If Marietta ever steps out of line, I'd better hear about it before he does. You understand me?"

"Yes sir," the brothers said in unison.

"I don't think Miss Marietta would do anything behind Maltese's back, Lightnin'," Jim offered.

"That's your trouble, Jim, you don't think." He reached out and thumped the side of Jim's head. "Start using your noggin or you'll be out of a job."

"We will," said Con. "You'll see."

"When I say, 'Don't let her out of your sight,' I mean it."

"You can count on us," promised Jim.

Cole wished that when he grabbed Marietta, they could hop on the Colorado Central at Blackhawk and ride the narrow-gauge train down to Denver. But he knew that was out of the question. She would undoubtedly scream and carry on and have him arrested for kidnapping.

So the day after their lunch at the Far Canyon, Cole visited Pollock's Livery Stable where he purchased a fine-looking black stallion, assuring the stable owner he'd be back for the black within a day or two. He considered buying a pack burro, but decided against it. Once he had Marietta, he would need to make a quick getaway. A mule or burro would slow him down.

From the stable, Cole went directly to Central City's largest general store. Parker's Emporium carried just about everything anyone could ever need. Cole picked out a comfortable saddle and a bridle with long leather reins. He shopped around, tossed a couple of blankets on the counter.

He lifted a pair of soft chamois trousers, held them up to his lean frame and saw that they were way too small. He figured they would fit Marietta just fine. He tossed the trousers on the counter and looked for the smallest shirt he could find. He chose a white cotton one with a long tail and sleeves. He snagged two pairs of leather moccasins, one pair for him, one for Marietta. He lifted the moccasins, examined them and placed them on the growing stack of supplies.

Pete Parker came up to Cole, smiled and asked, "Can I help you find anything, my friend?"

"I believe that'll do it," Cole replied. "If you'll add all this up I'll be back to get it in a day or two."

"Sure thing," said Pete, then asked, "You aiming to take yourself a little trip, are you?"

Cole smiled and gave no reply.

The sun was already beginning to wester by the time Cole finished shopping and stepped outside. He squinted in the dying sunlight, reached into his breast pocket and withdrew a cigar. He bit off the end, spit it out and placed the cigar in his mouth. He scratched his thumbnail against a Lucifer and lighted the smoke, cupping his hands against the slight mountain wind.

He was shaking out the lighted match, when he looked up and saw Marietta. That bright coppery hair instantly caught his attention. She was with Maltese and the pair were coming down the sidewalk toward him. Behind them was the man called Lightnin'.

Cole's first impulse was to turn and rush away. But that would make him appear to be guilty of something. He stayed where he was. Didn't budge. Nor did he look at them when they passed. And he hoped that Marietta was clever enough not to look his way.

She was not.

Marietta tried very hard but couldn't keep from glancing at Cole. He never knew it. Neither did Maltese.

But Lightnin' did.

The hired bodyguard caught Marietta subtly stealing a look at the dark stranger.

He immediately wondered, Was something going on or had something already gone on between this Texan and Marietta? Lightnin' sensed trouble ahead. His hand automatically touched the pearl butt of the revolver on his hip.

He would, as soon as he got back to the opera house, threaten the Burnetts with their very lives if they didn't keep a closer eye on Marietta.

Nine

Cole stayed right where he was until the trio had passed him. Then he snapped into action. He went back inside Parker's Emporium and told Pete Parker he had changed his mind, that he needed the supplies right away.

"Toss in some beef jerky, a tin of crackers and a couple of cans of beans," Cole said to Pete. "I'll take the saddle and bridle with me now and be back for the rest of the things in the next half hour."

Pete nodded, then asked, "You want some help carrying that saddle?"

"I can manage," Cole said as he hoisted it up onto a shoulder.

He stepped outside, looked both ways and walked directly down to Pollock's Livery Stable. At the stables he dropped the saddle and went into the stall where his newly purchased black was penned.

Cole carefully examined the stallion and the big black neighed a greeting and playfully bit at Cole's shoulder. Cole stroked the stallion's sleek neck and murmured soothingly into a pricked ear.

Turning to the stable boy, he said, "I'll be taking

the black tonight. Have him saddled and ready to go by nine o'clock. I'll be back to get him."

"He'll be ready, sir," said the lad with a toothy grin.

Cole ruffled the boy's hair, then peeled off a bill and handed it to him. He was heading back to Parker's Emporium, when he passed Lilly's Ladies Apparel. Cole stopped abruptly, snapped his fingers and turned back. He had, until this minute, forgotten about the lacy blue satin nightgown he had purchased yesterday afternoon.

Cole glanced about, then went inside.

Lilly looked up and smiled warmly at him. "You have come for the beautiful blue nightgown?"

"I have," Cole said decisively.

Lilly hurried into the back room and returned shortly with a neatly wrapped package. Cole left the shop carrying the package under his arm, feeling foolish, wondering what on earth had possessed him to buy the nightgown in the first place. And why he had bothered to go back and pick it up.

Cole returned to Parker's, gathered his supplies and headed back to the hotel. As twilight blanketed Central City, Cole began preparing for the difficult journey ahead. After a long relaxing bath, he had dinner in his room, then dressed in riding clothes—dark trousers, gray chambray shirt, gray and black bandanna. And finally he put on the soft moccasins that would afford him not only comfort but the quiet step of an Indian as well.

Everything was ready. The hotel bill had been paid. His belongings—the fine clothes he'd bought while in Colorado—were carefully packed. Beside them on the bed was a nice gratuity and note to the hotel manager, Darren Ludlow, asking that the clothes be held until he sent for them.

The supplies for the trip were neatly rolled up in a blanket. His saddlebags were loaded. The black stallion was waiting at the stable.

And, if he judged the time correctly, Marietta was about to take the stage halfway down the block.

Maltese was seated in his private box at the rapidly filling Tivoli Opera House auditorium. He took his gold-cased watch from his vest pocket, checked it and sighed with rising pleasure.

As he waited for the opera to begin, he was—as usual—filled with pleasant anticipation. The kind of excitement that escalated with every passing moment.

The exhilaration never diminished. Each evening it was as if it were his first night at the opera, the first time he had seen the lovely Marietta. Each time the heavy scarlet curtain rose, he experienced a quick fluttering of his heart. And when Marietta appeared onstage, the fluttering became sharp palpitations.

Nothing and no one could thrill him the way she did. He had had, in his fifty-two years, everything there was to have in this world. Money. Mansions. Mistresses. Thoroughbred horses. Yachts. Private rail cars. You name it, it had been his. And until recently he had supposed that there was little left that could charm or amuse him.

But he had been wrong.

From the moment he'd first laid eyes on Marietta, he had been totally enchanted, had instantly felt as if he were twenty years younger. He was, he mused as he waited for the curtain to rise, a very lucky man. Maltese sighed again and turned around.

"Lightnin', am I not the luckiest man you've ever known?" he asked the man standing at the back of the box.

"No doubt about it," Lightnin' replied without a change of expression.

"No doubt about it," Maltese happily repeated, then turned back around.

Lightnin' slowly, ruefully, turned his eyes heavenward and shook his head.

Backstage in her dressing room, Marietta was high-strung and unusually jittery. The astute Sophia was aware of Marietta's condition, but was puzzled. She had never seen her young pupil so anxious. She couldn't imagine why Marietta would suddenly be suffering from a case of stage fright.

"Something is bothering you," Sophia gently accused, her eyebrows lifting. As her plump fingers worked with the tiny hooks going down the back of Marietta's costume, she said, "You've never experienced the least twinge of stage fright, so it isn't that. Tell me what is upsetting you and I'll help if I can."

Marietta frowned at herself in the freestanding mirror and sighed heavily. She bit the inside of her lower lip and strongly considered confiding in Sophia. She had always been truthful with Sophia and she needed to tell somebody that she was in imminent danger.

She needed to confess that she had met a handsome Texan who had pretended to be an admiring fan. Admit that she had been flattered and had foolishly agreed to a secret luncheon with the stranger. That there she'd learned he was an impostor. A hired mercenary paid by her grandfather to deliver her to Galveston.

Marietta was confident that she could trust Sophia. Sophia knew her better than anyone and she never judged or censured.

"There," said Sophia, "your gown is completely fastened up the back. Now, tell me what's wrong."

Marietta turned to face her friend. "Oh, Sophia, you know me too well. There *is* something I need to tell you and…and…you must promise me that you will not—"

"Thirty seconds, Miss Marietta!" the stage director interrupted, speaking through the door.

"Be right there," Marietta called out and started to turn away.

"Wait!" said Sophia, and caught her arm. "What is it, dear? What's troubling my girl?"

"There's no time now. I'll tell you after the performance," said Marietta, patting Sophia's plump hand and exiting the dressing room.

*   *   *

At straight up nine o'clock, Cole walked into Pollock's Livery Stable. Once inside, he swung a leather gun belt around his slim hips and buckled it. He touched the handle of the holstered revolver and let his fingers dance over the belt's extra bullets.

He went into the stall where the black was stabled, reached into his breast pocket and drew out a cube of sugar. He fed it to the grateful beast.

As the horse crunched on the sugar lump, Cole leaned close and said, "I'm taking you out of here, boy, but you've got to be very quiet. No whinnying or neighing once we're outdoors."

The stallion shook its great head as if it understood, and Cole grinned and stroked its sleek jaw. He led the stallion out of the stable.

Strapped behind the cantle was the rolled-up blanket containing clothes for Marietta. Hanging from the saddle horn was a canteen filled with water and the loaded saddlebags were draped over the horse's flanks.

Cole had laid out his escape route in advance. Pollock's was down the hill and across the street from the Tivoli Opera House. He led the stallion farther on down the hill, away from town. When he was well past all the buildings and the illuminating gaslights, he guided the obedient stallion across the street and turned back toward town.

Under the cover of darkness, he moved along behind the buildings until he reached the back of the Tivoli Opera House. He loosely tethered the stallion and, making no noise in his soft leather moccasins, slipped around the side of the theater and up the alley. He silently approached the stage door.

Posted on either side of the door were the burly Burnett brothers. Just as expected. Cole knew he couldn't handle them both, so he stayed well hidden in the shadows and patiently waited for a break.

Sure enough, not more than a half hour passed before Jim Burnett said to his older brother, "Con, everything's pretty quiet around here tonight. Think I'll go inside for a drink of water."

"Don't be gone long," cautioned Con Burnett.

"No, I won't. Be back in a minute."

Jim Burnett went inside and Cole immediately seized his opportunity. He noiselessly slipped up behind Con Burnett and tapped him on the shoulder. Con automatically turned, mouth agape, eyes wide. Cole swiftly slammed a well-placed fist into the surprised man's right jaw. Burnett crumpled to the ground, unconscious.

Minutes later, the unsuspecting Jim Burnett came lumbering out the stage door. Cole tripped him, and when Jim stumbled and fell, Cole coldcocked him with the butt of his revolver. Like his brother, Jim was out cold.

Cole wasted no time.

He yanked the stage door open and rushed inside. He had timed it perfectly. The orchestra was now playing an interlude, and Marietta, having finished a lengthy aria, was exiting the stage to deafening applause.

She caught sight of Cole and her heart stopped. Before she could scream, he was to her. He grabbed her and clamped a hand firmly over her mouth. Her eyes wild, she struggled violently against him, but Cole had little trouble whisking her out the door.

He hauled her around the building, untethered the black and managed to get Marietta up across the saddle without taking his hand from her mouth. He swung up behind her and immediately put the black into motion.

The stallion swiftly carried the pair out of Central City without attracting any undue attention. When the city lights were behind them, Cole cautiously loosened his hand on Marietta's mouth and told her in a low, calming voice, "I am not going to hurt you, Marietta. You will not be harmed."

Her prompt reply was a vicious bite to his palm. When he jerked his hand away, she cursed him and vowed he would never get her to Galveston.

"You bastard! You sly, deceptive son of a bitch," she shouted as she clawed at his face, drawing blood. "You let me go this very instant, do you hear me! I command you, Texan! Let me go, damn you. You're wasting your time, you'll never get me to Galveston! Never, never, never!" She raged on as she beat on his chest and tried her best to tear his encircling arm from around her waist.

She threatened him, promising that Maltese would

come after her. "You don't know who you're dealing with, Heflin!" she hotly informed him. "The most powerful man in Colorado is mad about me! He'll never let you get away with kidnapping me. You'll hang for this!"

"And I'll hang if I don't do this," Cole said with a laugh.

"You're laughing? Dear God, you are insane," she screamed at him. "If I get the chance, I'll kill you. I will, I mean it! So help me, I'll kill you, you deranged fool."

She reached for his loaded revolver. He beat her to it. She tried to pry his fingers loose. They wouldn't budge. Thwarted, she promised, "I'll get my hands on the gun somehow and when I do I'll blow your stupid head off." Cole never even blinked.

Marietta was still swearing at him when, minutes after leaving Central City, they had dropped five hundred feet to the bustling mill town of Blackhawk, a mile below. On the outskirts, Cole drew up on the reins. The stallion immediately halted. Marietta quit swearing, stared at him, hopeful. Perhaps he had changed his mind, was going to let her go.

He had not.

Cole untied his black-and-gray bandanna, took it off, and before she knew his intent, he had gagged her with it.

"Sorry, Marietta, but you're much too loud. You can't be trusted to keep quiet."

She went into fresh fits of rage. She flailed her arms

and kicked her feet and screamed at the top of her lungs. But her loudest screams were muffled by the bandanna until they were no more than faint mewling sounds.

Cole calmly guided the black clear of the Blackhawk businesses. He skirted around behind the smelters and clapboard miners' dwellings, small modest cubes scattered across the pale gold and russet slopes along the gulch of North Clear Creek.

Her eyes flashing, her heart hammering, Marietta savagely elbowed her attacker, hoping to hurt him badly. She shook her head from side to side in an attempt to loosen the choking bandanna. She moaned. She grappled. She cried. She fought him with all her might.

It did no good.

Cole was as determined as she.

His jaw was bleeding from the furrowed marks left by her long, punishing nails. His stomach was tender from the continuous slamming of her sharp elbows into his exposed belly. His chest was bruised from the fierce pummeling of her balled fists.

He ignored the discomfort.

He held her fast with one arm wrapped firmly around her waist. But as he guided the surefooted stallion down onto the steep, treacherous path descending into Clear Creek Canyon, he knew that getting this red-haired wildcat back to Texas was going to be one hell of a long, unpleasant, arduous expedition.

Ten

The orchestra vamped.

The crowd grew restless.

The star soprano had not come back onstage.

The puzzled baritone kept glancing toward the wings, wondering why Marietta had not returned after her costume change. The other players looked at each other, baffled.

Backstage a frantic Andreas banged on the door to Marietta's dressing room,

"Where is she?" he demanded, looking past Sophia when the voice coach opened the door. "Where is our star? God in heaven, doesn't Marietta realize she is at least ten minutes late getting back onstage!"

"Late getting back on...?" Sophia repeated, dumbfounded. "But...but...she hasn't come offstage yet. Has she?"

"A good fifteen minutes ago," railed Andreas, wringing his hands, his face growing red.

Sophia felt her heart skip a beat. "Andreas, she hasn't been back to her dressing room. I haven't seen her since before the opera began. I thought she was still onstage!''

Andreas pressed a slender hand to his creased forehead. "Where on earth could she be? It makes no sense. She wouldn't just up and leave without...without... Help me look for her, Sophia. We must find her and get her onstage before the audience becomes unruly!''

Andreas turned and hurried down the corridor behind the stage's heavy backdrop where a row of dressing rooms stretched the length of the building's rear wall. Sophia was right behind him. Andreas pounded on doors. Sophia did the same. Startled players, some half-dressed, stuck their heads out, wondering what was going on.

"Is Marietta in here?" Andreas inquired at the first door.

"Have you seen Marietta?" Sophia asked at the next.

No one had.

Andreas and Sophia exchanged worried looks. "What shall we do?" asked Andreas, now completely distraught.

"I don't know, I can't imagine why...why..."

Sophia stopped speaking. Her throat tightened with alarm. She suddenly recalled how strange Marietta's mood had been before the opening curtain. She remembered asking what was wrong and Marietta had admitted that something was upsetting her. Marietta had said that she would talk about it after the performance had ended. Sophia grabbed Andreas's forearm and shared the vital information. He looked stricken.

"Something bad has happened to her," he said, his voice gone shrill. "She's gone! Someone has come in and taken her."

"No! No, that can't be," Sophia offered hopefully. "The Burnett brothers are outside, guarding the stage door. They wouldn't let anyone past. No one could get to her through them."

The artistic director's eyebrows rose, but he nodded. "Come, let's go out and question them."

Without another word, both turned and scurried toward the closed side door. Before they reached it, Maltese and his shadow, Lightnin', appeared backstage.

"Where is she?" Maltese demanded. "Where is Marietta? She should have been back onstage ten minutes ago. Her audience is waiting!"

"We don't know where she is," admitted Andreas.

"She never came to the dressing room between acts. We can't find her," said Sophia, her eyes quickly filling with tears.

Lightnin' was the first one out the stage door. There he saw both big men sprawled on the ground. It was instantly clear what had happened. Somebody had taken Marietta right under the Burnetts' worthless noses.

Con Burnett was just coming around. He sat up, rubbed his throbbing jaw and looked about, bewildered. Jim was still out, lying on his stomach, face in the dirt.

Furious, Lightnin' stepped forward, kicked Jim, stirring him, and at the same time reached down, grabbed the front of Con's shirt and backhanded him hard across the face.

"What the hell happened? Where is Marietta?"

"She missing?" asked Con, coming to his feet, wiping the blood from his split lip.

"You tell us," said Maltese, stepping around Lightnin'. "Where is she?" he shouted angrily at Con, the veins standing out on his forehead. "Marietta is gone! She is not inside the opera house. You're supposed to be guarding her. What has happened to my angel?"

"Oh, God, no," said Con, the terrible truth dawning.

Jim was shaking off the last traces of unconsciousness and rising unsteadily to his feet. The brothers were immediately peppered with questions from both Lightnin' and Maltese. But neither was sure what had happened. They just did not know. Jim swore he never saw anybody, that he was struck from behind when he came out the stage door.

"What were you doing inside?" asked Lightnin'. "You were supposed to stand outside this door throughout the opera! You weren't at your post!"

Jim hung his head. Con quickly spoke up, revealed that he had gotten one quick glance at his attacker.

"Tall man. Dark. Slim. Black hair. Clean shaven. Not a local or I'd have known him."

"The Texan," said Lightnin' resolutely, his beady eyes narrowing.

"Who?" asked Maltese, frantic. "Who did you say? You know the kidnapper?"

"No, but I know he took her."

Andreas and Sophia clung to each other, Sophia sobbing now, Andreas consoling her. Maltese paced anxiously, not sure what to do next. Lightnin' took quick command.

He began barking orders at the nervous Burnett boys. "You two have exactly fifteen minutes to get your horses and weapons and round up a half-dozen men to ride with us. We're going after her and we'd damn well better find her unharmed if you two morons want to see the sun rise tomorrow."

"Yes, sir," the brothers said and turned to hurry away, bumping into each other in their haste.

"You'll find her, won't you, Lightnin'?" Maltese asked, his voice thin, pleading. "You'll bring my sweet Marietta back to me?"

"You know I will," said Lightnin' and swung into action.

The twinkling lights of both Central City and Blackhawk had been left far behind. It was well after ten o'clock. A pale quarter moon had risen high above Clear Creek Canyon. But it sailed lazily in and out of thick, scattered clouds, intermittently casting the canyon into darkness.

Narrow, rocky, the trail down swiftly descended into the deep, steep-sided gorge where the cold waters of Clear Creek rushed over a bed of scattered boulders. It was a winding track that clung to the soaring rock walls high above the surging, splashing creek.

To travel the frightening trail in broad daylight took nerves of steel. To attempt it in darkness was downright foolhardy.

Cole had little choice. It was nighttime or never. So he kept a firm arm around his gagged, kicking cargo, and his eyes and mind on the treacherous path before them.

His jaw set, teeth clenched, he guided the black slowly around another switchback, well aware that they would have to drop another three thousand feet before they reached Denver.

If they reached Denver.

Cole glanced back over his shoulder as the pale moon moved out from behind a covering cloud. He squinted, saw no one. Heard nothing. He pulled up on the reins. The black stopped, blew and snorted, turned his head and looked back at Cole. Marietta, continuing to struggle, looked suspiciously at her stone-faced captor.

"There are no houses, no people for miles around now," Cole said. "If I take away your gag, there'll be no need to shout and scream. No one can hear you." He looked into her upturned face. "You'll be sensible and quiet?"

Marietta eagerly shook her head and answered with her eyes.

"Good girl," Cole praised, untying the bandanna and withdrawing it. He was immediately sorry that he had.

Once the bandanna was out of her mouth, Marietta spat and coughed and carried on as if she was dying. And as soon as she'd swallowed several times and licked her dry lips, she began to scream and curse him once more.

"You're going to be sorry you ever laid eyes on me, Heflin!" she raged.

"The same could be said for you," he replied calmly. "If you hadn't slipped off to have that clandestine lunch with me while—"

"You shut your mouth, you insolent bastard," she snarled. "None of this is my fault and no one will be blamed for it but you, you cad! You knave! You brute! You beast! You son of a bitch! You devil! You…you…bastard!"

"You're repeating yourself," Cole accused, cutting in as he touched the black's flanks with his moccasined feet and the black went again into motion.

"Don't you dare make fun of me," Marietta shouted at him. "The laugh will be on you once Maltese's men catch up with us."

"That isn't going to happen," Cole predicted, further infuriating her.

"Not happen? Why, you arrogant fool!" She raised a hand to slap his insolent face, but just then the black's sharp hoof struck a rock and sent it sailing over the trail's edge. The stone skittered and fell, striking solid granite, glancing off, and continuing to plunge downward. It seemed an eternity before the stone finally hit bottom far, far below.

Fear quickly replaced Marietta's wrath.

Instead of striking Cole as intended, she wrapped a trembling arm around his neck and clung to him as she peered cautiously over his shoulder and down into the deep, darkened chasm. She hadn't considered, until now, just how much danger they were in. She recalled her very first trip up to Central City and how terrified she had been riding inside the lumbering stagecoach.

But at least on that occasion there had been bright sunshine. Now it was dark and getting darker.

Clouds again obliterated the moon.

Marietta quickly fell silent. She was simply too frightened to speak or move. Her heart pounding, she automatically pressed closer to the broad, solid chest supporting her, her anger forgotten for the moment. Survival her only concern, she clutched Cole's shirtfront with her free hand, pressing her open palm against his heart. And was amazed to feel a slow, steady beating, as if he was not even nervous.

She peeked up at his dark face. His eyes were keenly alert but revealed no fear. His expression never changed as they wound around the constantly curving trail where one edge was bordered with soaring walls of rock. On the other side of the narrow trail, sheer drops into infinity were mere inches from where the horse's hooves struck each time it took a step. It would be nothing short of a miracle if they made it safely down. Dear God, she was in the care of a man who didn't have enough sense to be afraid.

"Nobody but a fool would take this road down at night," she finally dared to say, whispering past the lump of fear in her throat.

"That's Mr. Fool to you," Cole replied with a sardonic grin and continued to guide the stallion down the perilous path.

"You dare to make asinine jokes when any second we may plunge to our deaths?"

"That's not going to happen. You're as safe here in my arms as a babe is in her cradle."

"Safe? Safe! Are you crazy? This road twists and turns every inch of the way down and it's thirty-five miles to Denver. If the horse stumbles, we'll fall to our deaths and they'll find nothing but our mangled bodies."

"Want to turn back?" he teased.

"Don't you dare try to turn this beast," she shrieked, knowing they were at a point where turning would be incredibly dangerous if not impossible. "There isn't enough room for turning here, you moron."

"Ah, well, since we can't turn around, we best keep going. And you'd best hold on tight."

Marietta didn't argue. The road was becoming more perilous with every twist and turn. They moved into and out of the pale moonlight and a tense Marietta expected the stallion to step off into oblivion at any minute.

She was so frightened, she could no longer bear to look. She laid her head against Cole's shoulder and closed her eyes. She could hear the sound of the water gushing over the boulders far below. And the night birds calling from their perches high up in the canyon's deep crevices. And the steady, reassuring tempo of Cole's heart beating beneath her ear.

After what seemed a lifetime to Marietta, she felt the ground begin to flatten out beneath the horse's striking hooves. She tentatively opened her eyes. They had, she realized, reached one of those rare, welcome plateaus along the harrowing route. The valley had widened dramatically and a carpet of soft green grass stretched to the creek's edge, which was temporarily on the same level as the road.

Cole reined the black off the trail and into a thick sheltering forest of spruce and pine. He scouted until he found a spot where the cloaking trees would conceal them and a small tributary of the creek trickled past. Staying mounted, he carefully looked around, considering how safe and well hidden they would be here.

Confident he'd located a fairly secure citadel, Cole pulled up on the black, swung down and announced, "We'll camp here for the night."

"The minute my feet touch the ground, I'll run away," Marietta warned him.

"No, you won't," he calmly replied. He lifted her down and then turned his back on her.

"Oh yes I will!" she threatened, whirled around and took a few determined steps forward.

A lonesome wolf howled in the distance.

Marietta abruptly stopped.

Furious, but afraid to go off on foot in the darkness,

she sighed wearily and turned back. Eyes snapping with anger, she watched as Cole unstrapped a rolled-up blanket from behind the cantle and tossed it to the ground. Without so much as glancing her way, he unsaddled the big black and led it to the nearby shallow vein of the North Clear Creek. The stallion lowered its head and swilled the cold water gratefully.

When the horse was watered and loosely ground tethered so that it could crop the thick, rich grass, Cole sank to his knees and unrolled the blanket. He spread it on the grass and then stretched out across it. While Marietta watched, he covered himself with a second blanket and folded his hands beneath his head.

"Just what do you think you're doing?" Marietta demanded, hands on her hips.

"Fixing to get some sleep," he said. "And I suggest you do the same." He threw back one side of the covering blanket invitingly. "Won't you join me?"

"Never! Not in a million years!" she snapped, quick to set him straight.

"Suit yourself," he said with a yawn. Then he closed his eyes and went peacefully to sleep.

Eleven

Marietta stood there for a long minute staring at Cole, her lips parted in wonderment. She couldn't believe her eyes and she could hardly contain her excitement. Could it really be true? Had her big, bullying captor actually fallen asleep?

He had.

His eyes were closed and he was softly snoring! It was all Marietta could do to keep from laughing hysterically. The fool had already let down his guard and she would most assuredly take advantage of it.

While she'd been afraid to set out on foot, she wouldn't hesitate to ride the horse to freedom. She would, she plotted, wait just a few more minutes until she was absolutely certain that the Texan was in a deep, dreamless slumber. Then she would take the black and ride it right back up to Central City.

Taking no chances, Marietta waited patiently for several excruciatingly long, slow minutes to drag by. The man on the ground didn't stir, didn't move, slept on. She smiled, turned, lifted her skirts and tiptoed over to where the black was contentedly cropping grass. The stallion saw her coming, lifted its head and neighed to her.

"Shh!" Marietta whispered, making a mean face at him.

Cole cocked one eye open and said, "Not a chance, Marietta. Give it up and come get some rest."

"Thunderation!" she muttered.

She felt like crying but didn't. She would never allow the Texan to witness any weakness on her part. That, she was sure, would be a big mistake. She blinked back the unshed tears and sighed heavily. Dejectedly she turned around, sank onto the grassy ground and hugged her knees to her chest, glaring angrily at Cole.

"Come on over. Let's keep each other warm," Cole coaxed.

"I would rather lie down with a six-foot-long rattlesnake," she haughtily informed him.

"But, baby, I don't bite," he said. "I don't even have fangs."

"No," she retorted. "Just horns and a tail."

Cole chuckled.

Marietta bristled.

And shortly she began to tremble, her teeth chattering. Even in June, nights were cold at this high altitude and her silk, low-cut costume provided little protection against the elements. Chilled, frustrated and sleepy, Marietta finally gave in after swearing to herself that she would not.

She rose to her feet. Cole again threw back one

corner of the blanket. She gritted her teeth in resignation, went over and lay down by him, taking great care not to touch him. She turned onto her side, facing away from him, and exhaled with gratitude when the warm, covering blanket settled over her bare shoulders.

But her eyes widened and she stiffened, incensed, when Cole's long arm came around her. Try as she might to protest, she was rendered speechless when he drew her back against his hard, muscled frame.

Marietta swallowed. She bit her lip. She was alarmed by the way her heart had begun to beat erratically. She hoped against hope that he wouldn't know her pulse was racing, that she was greatly disturbed by his nearness. She emitted a little shriek of censure when his muscular forearm slid up from her waist and tightened around her midriff, directly below her breasts.

If not for that band of steel imprisoning her, she would have lunged away when he snuggled closer, intimately curving his body around hers, spoon fashion. Eyes wide, she didn't move and didn't make a sound. She was not sure how to handle this tricky situation.

She didn't realize she was holding her breath until Cole said softly, ''You can stop holding your breath, Marietta, I'm not going to hurt you.''

''I was not holding my breath,'' she hissed, and then she gasped for air.

''You okay?''

"I would be okay if you'd kindly unhand me," she snapped.

"Just trying to keep you warm," he replied and yawned as he took his arm from around her.

He turned over and stretched out on his back, taking his awesome body heat with him. Marietta remained as she was, lying on her side, facing away from him. She stayed in that position for several minutes before cautiously turning to peer over her shoulder and see if he was asleep.

He was.

He lay on his back, one arm flung up and folded beneath his head. Slowly, Marietta turned over so that she was lying on her left side, facing him. She scooted back, moving farther away from him, and felt the nip of the cold night air on her back. No matter. She'd rather freeze than get close to him again. So she lay there at the blanket's far edge with the cold night air on her back, staring at the dark man stretched out beside her.

Damn him.

He was slumbering like an innocent baby while she was wide awake and miserable. She would, she knew, never sleep. Never. The ground was hard. The air was cold. The night was dark. And she was a helpless captive. Or at least he thought her helpless, but she would show him come morning.

Moments passed and Marietta's eyelids grew droopy despite all her best efforts to remain awake. She was so cold and she was so sleepy. If she didn't get some rest she wouldn't be able to keep her wits about her and make her escape.

He was a sound sleeper. He'd never know it if she scooted over a little closer. Not so close she would touch him, but just close enough to get a little warmer. She was freezing and the covering top blanket wasn't wide enough.

Marietta very slowly, very carefully, inched a trifle nearer to the slumbering Cole. She stopped just short of actually touching him and was amazed by the warmth emanating from his body. She released a soft breath, closed her eyes, and was beginning to doze, when she felt his strong arms come around her. He drew her close against him, but she was simply too tired and drowsy to put up even a feeble protest.

So she sighed, inhaled deeply of his masculine scent, and fell asleep in the shelter of his arms.

It was nearing 1:00 a.m. when Lightnin' drew rein and held his hand up for the others to halt. He turned his mount about in a tight semicircle and, speaking low, addressed the men.

"This is the first level plateau on the way down," he said.

"That mean they'll be stopping here for the night?" asked Con Burnett.

"No, you fool," Lightnin' replied. "You have to outsmart your adversary, Con. You have to *think*. You should try it sometime."

"Sorry, Lightnin'," Con said, shamefaced.

"You can bet that the Texan *thinks*. And in so doing, he will suppose that we will be expecting them to camp here. Therefore, he won't do it. He'll ride on. And so will we."

Lightnin' turned his mount around and rode away. The others followed.

Cole and Marietta were awakened by the sound of drumming hoofbeats. Cole automatically covered Marietta's mouth with his hand and cautioned, "Stay still and quiet."

She didn't obey.

She tried to scream, but Cole's hand was clamped firmly over her mouth, pressing her lips against her teeth. She couldn't make a sound. She struggled violently against him, bowing her back, pushing on his chest, slamming the toes of her shoes into his shins.

And finally, viciously kneeing him in the groin, the assault instantly bringing tears to his eyes. But he didn't release her, never loosened his grip on her or made a sound.

Marietta was sure the riders were Maltese's men, looking for her. All she had to do was let them know where she was. She moaned and frantically strained against the suffering Cole, hoping to be seen or heard as the riders passed within a few short yards. But she was unable to alert them. When they had gone, when she could no longer hear the horses' hooves striking the ground, she slumped in defeat against Cole, her heart hammering, her breath short.

And was stunned when Cole's hand abruptly left her mouth and he forcefully flung her away from him. She wound up sprawled on her back, gaping at him.

But she quickly rallied, sat up and said smugly to the grimacing Cole, "Ah, too bad. Did I hurt you? I did, didn't I? Well, I'm glad. So there."

Cole thrashed around on the blanket, his hands now cupping his aching groin, his teeth clenched in pain.

When he could speak, he said with no emotion, "Do that again, I'll see to it you're sorry, not glad."

Marietta saw the beads of perspiration on his forehead and the pain etched on his face and believed him. She felt a twinge of remorse for hurting him, but didn't let on.

Instead, she said, "You won't get away with kidnapping me, Heflin. They were Maltese's men and they'll keep looking until they find me."

His pain beginning to subside, Cole sat up, took several deep breaths, then rose unsteadily to his feet. He stood just above, looking down at her with a mean expression on his face. She wondered, nervously, if he was going to strike her.

She winced in terror when he reached down and none too gently took her arm, hauling her swiftly to her feet.

He said, "They are not going to find you, Marietta. You're headed for Grandpa's house."

Twelve

"**I** am not! I've told you before and I'll say it again, you'll *never* get me to Texas. Never, never, never. I mean it, I will not go! Let me assure you that it's only a matter of time before...before—" Marietta stopped speaking when Cole took her arm and calmly maneuvered her off the spread blanket. He then stepped off himself, sank to his knees and began rolling up the bedding.

Marietta frowned and asked, "Now what are you doing? Are we to sleep on the hard, cold ground without the blankets?"

"We aren't going to sleep," he said. He lifted the rolled blankets, turned and walked toward the stallion.

Marietta followed, puzzled. "Why not? What are we going to do?"

"We're going to get back on the trail," he said. He handed her the rolled blankets, picked up the saddle and hoisted it up onto the black's back.

"Get back on the trail?" she repeated, incredulous. "Maltese's men just rode past looking for me! They're chasing us."

"I know," Cole said, tightening the saddle's cinch

beneath the stallion's belly. He put the bit in the black's mouth and made quick work of buckling the bridle's jaw strap. He turned, took the blankets from Marietta and placed them behind the cantle. Over his shoulder, he said, "Now we're going to chase them."

"Why on earth would we do that?"

"Because they are hunting for us up ahead—they believe that we're in front of them. They won't be looking for us behind them."

Marietta thought it over, knew that he was probably right. She said sarcastically, "You think you're pretty smart, don't you, Texan?"

"Smart enough," was his clipped reply. Cole drew the long leather reins up over the stallion's back, turned and said, "I'm sure that opera costume isn't very comfortable." He lifted the full saddlebags and told her, "I brought some clothes for you. Pants, a shirt, a pair of moccasins. Want to put them on before we ride?"

"I most certainly do not," she haughtily informed him. "If you think for one minute that I would ever take off one single article of clothing around you, you are sadly mistaken, mister!"

"I'll turn my back, won't look."

"I am not taking off this dress!"

"Fine. It's entirely up to you," he said. He draped the saddlebags over the horse's back and then turned to her. "Come here."

"No," she said stubbornly, wondering suddenly if he intended to tear off her clothes. He might. He was unpredictable and he was a lot bigger than she was. Marietta took a protective step backward.

Cole wrapped the reins around the saddle horn. Marietta cringed. He was to her in three long strides. Towering over her. Tall and intimidating. He said nothing, just plucked her from the ground with the greatest of ease, carried her to the waiting black and lifted her up across the saddle.

He swung up behind her and told her, "Baby, you can wear that cumbersome ball gown all the way to Galveston if you like. I couldn't care less."

"Why, of course not," she retorted. "The fact that I'm cold and miserable is of no importance to you. Is it?"

"Not really," Cole replied as he touched his heels to the black's flanks. "After all, it's your fault, not mine."

"My fault? *My* fault? Well, I never! What a ridiculous statement! You take me by brute force, carry me off into the dark, cold night, and then have the gall to tell me it's my fault that I'm freezing. Let me tell you something—"

"Tell me later," he interrupted and put the horse into a canter. "Lean back against me and get some rest."

"No," she said. "I certainly will not. In case you've failed to notice, I do not want to touch you and I do not want you touching me!"

"Again, that's your prerogative. But when you feel

like your back's breaking from sitting straight up, don't whine to me.''

''I never whine,'' she quickly defended herself.

But she was already tempted to complain. She was seated across the saddle, legs dangling, her position precarious. She constantly felt as if she might fall off the horse. She clung tenaciously to the saddle horn and leaned as far away from Cole as possible. Such stiff posture atop a moving horse was incredibly uncomfortable. But Marietta was determined that she would stay just like this no matter how miserable she was.

She forgot her misery for a moment when the trail once again started its steep descent. Her teeth clenched, she said a little prayer, promising the Almighty that if he would get her safely out of this dilemma, she would never, ever do another bad thing for the rest of her life.

The prayer finished, she stole a covert glance at Cole. He appeared to be totally relaxed and totally comfortable. She hated him for it. And for not caring about her discomfort. Damn him. Admitting that he didn't give a fig if she was cold and miserable. Which she most certainly was.

Marietta's teeth began to chatter. She attempted to clamp them firmly together, but it didn't work. They continued to chatter. She began to shiver from the frigid night air. She glared at Cole. Anybody with one ounce of human kindness would see that she was suffering and take pity on her.

He didn't.

He just guided the black down the narrow, rocky trail, slouching lazily in the saddle, paying her absolutely no mind.

For a time, her anger and the chill enveloping her kept Marietta awake and alert. But as the long night dragged on, she became more and more weary. Her fingers were numb from clinging to the saddle horn. Her back was absolutely breaking. Try as she might, she couldn't keep her chin from sagging to her chest, nor her eyes from slipping closed.

But she opened her eyes and jerked her head up when Cole abruptly pulled up on the black. The big beast halted. Marietta was horrified when Cole reached down and jerked her long skirts up past her knees. Dear Lord, he was going to ravish her right here atop the stallion!

"Don't flatter yourself," Cole drawled, knowing what was running through her mind.

He then deftly turned her about and urged a slender leg over the horse, seating her astride the saddle. Marietta was struggling to shove her raised skirts down, when Cole cupped her shoulders and gently drew her back against him. She couldn't keep from sighing. With gratitude. His long arms safely enclosing her and his solid chest supporting her aching back were pure heaven.

Marietta sighed again, squirmed a little, settled back, relaxed.

And fell asleep.

It was Cole's turn to sigh with relief. He liked her much better asleep than awake. She was a handful and no denying it.

Just then a strand of flaming-red hair came loose from the oyster-shell comb that held the heavy tresses in place atop her head. The silky lock blew across Cole's face, tickled his lips and nose. He automatically inhaled deeply. The pleasing scent of the subtly perfumed hair filled his nostrils.

Cole exhaled.

Then immediately frowned and reaching up, swept the intrusive lock aside before giving the sleeping Marietta a sharp look.

He gritted his teeth and felt a muscle dance in his jaw. He would, he silently swore to himself, get this beautiful bundle of feminine trouble home to her waiting grandfather without laying a hand on her. So help him God.

When the first gray light of the summer dawn streaked across the cloudless sky, Cole and Marietta had made it all the way down out of the mountains. They had not encountered Maltese's men or any other misfortune.

On level ground at last, they were approaching the little mining community of Golden, nestled at the eastern base of the Front Range.

Marietta began to stir.

Cole grimaced.

No more peace and quiet. How long, he idly asked

himself, would it take before she started grumbling. Yawning and rubbing her eyes, Marietta looked sleepily around, scowled and wondered where she was and what she was doing out here on horseback at dawn. And then remembered. Everything.

She anxiously leaned away from Cole, looked over her shoulder and snapped, "I will not put up with any more of your nonsense, Texan. I want you to let me go!"

"I'd love to, but I can't. I gave my word to your grandfather that I'd bring you home."

"How much did he pay you? Maltese will double it. Take me back to Central City. Tell my grandfather you couldn't find me. That I wasn't there."

"Why, now, that would be a lie, wouldn't it?"

"As if you never lie. Really! Do you expect me to believe that of an unscrupulous man like you?"

"Believe anything you choose, but understand this, princess. If I never do anything else in my life, I am going to deliver you to your grandfather in Galveston."

"Oh, you are impossible," she declared, knowing there was no reaching him.

At the edge of the dense forest, on the banks of the gently flowing North Clear Creek, Cole drew rein, dismounted. He reached for Marietta. She drew away and wildly kicked her feet against the stallion's belly, meaning to flee. But Cole held the reins. The black didn't budge. And that angered Marietta. Thwarted, she cursed the stallion and she cursed Cole. Cole let her rave, allowed her to blow her top for a while.

Then finally said, "That's enough, Marietta. Get down off the horse or I'll get you down."

"Don't you touch me!" Marietta warned, throwing her leg over and dropping to the ground. "And just why are we stopping out here? Why don't we ride into town?"

"I'm going to ride into town."

"And I'm not?"

"No, you're going to stay here."

She tilted her head to one side and looked up at him. "So you're going to leave me here alone?"

"I am."

"And you expect me to still be here when you return?" She shook her head and regarded him as though he were dimwitted.

"You'll be here," he said, unconcerned.

"Don't bet on it, Texan," she declared with a smirk. But the smirk left her face when she saw him take a coiled lasso from the saddle. Eyes gone wide, she said, "No! You wouldn't do that. You wouldn't tie me up." She backed away from him.

He followed. "You leave me no choice, Marietta. If you could be trusted to keep quiet, why then I'd gladly take you into town with me."

"I will. I promise. I won't make a sound, won't say a word."

"Why is it that I don't believe you?" he asked as if not knowing the answer.

Marietta angrily whirled about and started to dash away, but Cole caught her skirts and reeled her back in. She fought him furiously for as long as she could lift her rapidly tiring arms. Soon out of breath and perspiring with exertion, she gave up and slumped against him.

Cole patted her back in a brotherly fashion and told her, "I won't be gone long."

"Mmm," she murmured, the sound muffled against his shirtfront.

"Will you miss me?" he teased.

Her head snapped up. Her face a study in wrath, she attempted to push him away, but he held her fast.

Minutes later Cole rode away, leaving her tied securely to the thick trunk of a huge sheltering evergreen with a promise that he would be back soon. Marietta worked at getting her hands free of their bonds and prayed that Maltese's men would find her while Cole was gone.

They did not.

Nor did anyone else.

For several long minutes she screamed and shouted for help before giving up. Within an hour, Cole returned, leading a saddled black-and-white-spotted piebald gelding. Marietta felt her heart leap inside her breast. She was an excellent horsewoman. If she were allowed to ride the gelding, she could escape her cruel captor.

Cole dismounted, came over and crouched beside

Marietta. He said, "I bought a gentle gelding for you to ride."

"That's the ugliest horse I have ever seen in my life," she said. "Looks just like you."

Cole ignored the barb and looked pointedly at her wrinkled, low-cut gown as he untied her hands. "You ready to change into the riding clothes now?"

Marietta quickly decided it would be wise to start holding her tongue and appear more docile. She smiled at Cole and said, "Yes, I am. And thank you for the horse."

"You're very welcome." Cole drew her to her feet. "I'll get the clothes. You can change behind this tree."

Rubbing her raw wrists, Marietta nodded.

With the shirt and pants over her arm and the moccasins in her hand, she went around behind the towering, lush-limbed evergreen. Already forgetting her decision to be more agreeable, she warned Cole that he'd better not spy on her if knew what was good for him.

And then, to her frustration, she found that she could not get to the tiny hooks going down the back of her dress. She reached and worked and tussled and strained and muttered to herself.

"Everything all right?" Cole called out, knowing exactly what the problem was, expecting her to enlist his help at any minute.

"Everything's just fine, thank you very much!" she shouted.

Several minutes passed.

Finally Marietta dropped her arms to her sides and huffed loudly. It was futile. She could not get out of the costume.

"Heflin, I need help with this danged dress. Come here!" His full lips stretching into a devilish grin, Cole stayed right where he was. Marietta waited, exhaling heavily. "Did you hear me? I said come here!"

"You didn't say please," Cole replied.

"Oh, for heaven's sake. The day won't come when I'll say 'please' to you."

Her face bloodred with anger, Marietta began violently yanking on the dress, determined to get it off and not caring if she tore it. Cole appeared, turned her around, brushed her hands away and easily unfastened the tiny hooks.

The gown now open down the back, he said, "Step out of the dress and I'll fold it and put it with our gear."

"Why don't we just leave it here?" she casually suggested, sure it would be the smart thing to do. Lightnin' and his men would find the dress and know they'd been here.

Cole knew what was going through her mind. He said, "Sure. Leave it if you like, but it will do no good. You're forgetting, Lightnin' and the boys are ahead of us. By the time they turn back and find the dress, we'll be halfway to Texas."

Holding her open dress up with one hand, Marietta

whirled to face him. Her chin lifted in defiance, she told him, "Lightnin' will not turn back. He will find you!"

"He will find me ready."

Thirteen

When the sun came up in Central City, a haggard, sleep-deprived Maltese was wearily pacing back and forth in the upstairs sitting room of Marietta's private quarters. He had been pacing off and on all night. When he wasn't, he was crossing to the tall front windows to push back the heavy curtains and peer out. Eagerly, he looked down Eureka Street, hoping to see his beloved come riding up the road and into his waiting arms.

Sophia, twisting a tear-dampened handkerchief in her plump fingers, sat on the rose-and-gold brocade sofa watching Maltese walk the floor. Both he and Andreas had urged her to go home and get some rest, but Sophia refused. She wanted to be here when her dear Marietta returned.

"They will find her? She will come back, won't she?" she asked again and again.

"Of course she will," Andreas assured her. "Lightnin' will find her."

Shortly after Marietta's disappearance, Sophia had told Maltese about the singer's strange behavior just prior to the curtain rising. She confided that Marietta had seemed unusually anxious, as if she had a premonition that something like this was going to happen.

Maltese had questioned Sophia at length after her disturbing revelation. Had Marietta mentioned any reason for being nervous? Had she met someone who might want to harm her? A deranged fan perhaps?

Con Burnett had gotten a glimpse of the dark stranger who took Marietta. Lightnin' had said that a Texan fitting that description was in town. No one knew why he was in Central City. Could it be that Marietta knew the Texan from her past? Could it be that she was secretly planning to run away with another man? If that were the case, Maltese no longer wanted to live!

"No. No. No" was Sophia's answer to all of Maltese's questions. "Marietta would never have run away. She loved the opera, it was her life."

At that, Maltese bristled. "I would hope that perhaps I am as important to her as the opera."

"Oh, yes," Sophia amended. "She is very fond of you, Maltese."

"And I worship her," said the distraught multimillionaire.

Tears suddenly sprang to his eyes and Maltese excused himself. Needing to be alone, he hurried into Marietta's bedroom and closed the door behind him. For a moment he stood quietly leaning back against the door, trembling with rising despair.

Then all at once his gaze fell on a delicate pair of

satin high-heeled bedroom slippers. One slipper lay on its side, the other stood straight up on its slender heel. Marietta had apparently kicked off the slippers and left them there.

Maltese's heart raced in his chest. He crossed the room, sank wearily onto a comfortable chaise lounge and reaching down picked up one of the small pink slippers.

He sat staring fixedly at the exquisite footwear, imagining Marietta's dainty naked foot slipping seductively into it. Impulsively, he raised the slipper to his lips, pressed eager kisses to the heel, the toe, the instep. He rubbed the slipper against his cheek, again and again.

Exhausted, he lay back and stretched out on the long chaise lounge to rest for a minute. Brushing the toe of the satin bedroom slipper back and forth across his mouth, Maltese experienced a sweet mixture of excitement and relaxation.

His hand, firmly gripping the shoe, slipped down to his chest. Maltese sighed and drifted off to sleep.

"Wake up, damn you!"

"I wasn't asleep."

"Yes you were, Jim," accused Lightnin'. "You were dozing in the saddle, about to fall off your horse."

"Sorry," Jim Burnett apologized.

"Listen to me, all of you," Lightnin' said, pulling up on his paint stallion. "I know you're tired, so am

I, but we must press on. I told you that we will not stop until we find Marietta. And that's exactly what we're going to do. Have I made myself clear?''

No one said a word.

It was midmorning.

The men had ridden all night. They had arrived in Golden shortly before sunrise. They had found the little town already astir, many early risers on the streets. The riders had fanned out, questioned anyone they saw, searched for any trace of the missing Marietta.

No one had seen or heard a thing.

Lightnin' was worried.

He had known from the start that if the Texan managed to get Marietta down out of the mountains, it would be almost impossible to find them. He was baffled. He couldn't believe that he hadn't been able to overtake the pair on the one route down. Throughout the night, he and his men had stopped only briefly to water and rest their winded mounts each time they had reached a plateau. All the way down they had kept a careful lookout, but had seen no signs of the two.

It made no sense. They should have overtaken the pair somewhere along the narrow, twisting trail. The fine hair rose on the nape of Lightnin's neck. If he couldn't find Marietta, he would have to answer to Maltese. If he failed Maltese, Maltese would fire him on the spot. No more generous salary and fancy living accommodations. No more pretty women and fine Kentucky bourbon to enjoy in his free time.

Now at shortly after 10:00 a.m., Lightnin' and the men were nearing the outskirts of Denver. Denver was a big, sprawling city. Even if Marietta and the Texan were there, it would be like hunting for a needle in a haystack. No matter. If the pair were in Denver, he would smoke them out.

He *had* to find that spirited red-haired singer or pay the consequences.

Cole and Marietta were not in Denver. Had never been in Denver. They had continued to trail Lightnin' and his riders at a safe distance, but Cole rightly figured that Lightnin' would look for them in Denver. So he avoided the city, much to Marietta's chagrin.

Once the two left Golden, Cole headed due south. This despite the fact that by doing so they would once again be riding into timbered, mountainous terrain. While it would have been easier on them to ride through Denver and then head directly out onto the plains, it wouldn't have been as safe.

So now, at straight up noon, Cole and Marietta were well south of Denver and the coolness of the night was long gone. The landscape was shimmering with the fierce heat of June. Marietta was hot and miserable and didn't hesitate to let Cole know it. He, too, was hot and tired. He had not yet slept a wink.

When he suggested they stop to eat and rest, Marietta nodded. And immediately began to scheme. He had been up all night; he had to sleep sometime. Nobody could stay awake forever. She would, after they'd had lunch, suggest that he take a much-needed nap. And then, while he slept, she would escape.

Cole chose an ideal place to stop. A lush meadow in the rugged foothills of the great western mountains where soaring snowcapped peaks rose to meet clear blue sky. Dark-green forest covered the slopes and a clear rushing stream spilled down from the rocky summits. Summer grass rippled in the slight breeze and tall verdant pines sweetened the air and provided ample shade.

"This a fine place to rest?" Cole asked, swinging down off the black.

Marietta shrugged slender shoulders. "It's all right, I suppose."

Cole shook his head. She was without doubt the most disagreeable woman he had ever had the displeasure of meeting.

When the horses were unsaddled and left to graze, Cole took off his gun belt, placed it safely out of her reach. He took food from his saddlebags and began to prepare their meal. When he handed the tin plate to Marietta, she looked at it and frowned.

"What is this?" she asked, making a face.

"Jerked beef. Beans. Crackers."

"And you actually believe that I would eat this?"

"Do or don't," he said and leveled a forkful of beans into his mouth.

"I cannot eat this food," she said and set her plate down.

"Cannot or will not?" he asked.

"Very well, I will not. And you can't make me."

"Why, I wouldn't dream of trying to make you," he said. "When you get hungry enough, you'll eat."

Cole finished his plate of food and reached for hers. "May I?" he asked, and not waiting for an answer, hungrily devoured everything on her plate. Marietta scowled at him.

The meal finished, Cole sighed and patted his full belly. He drew a slightly crushed cigar out of his breast pocket and lit up. He blew a perfect smoke ring and said, "I need a nap, how about you?"

"What do you think?" she replied hatefully.

"Why don't you roll out the blankets so we can lie down."

"Do it yourself" was her sharp reply and one that he would hear many times in the coming days.

For now, Cole didn't argue. He leisurely finished his cigar, unrolled the blankets and spread them beneath a fragrant pine. Marietta's lips fell open with alarm when he casually unbuckled his belt. She tensed when he unbuttoned the top button of his dark twill trousers.

Her eyes round, she screeched, "Are you taking off your pants?"

Cole grinned. "I will if you will."

"Don't you dare!"

"Aw, relax, Marietta. I ate too much and I'm just

getting comfortable for my nap.'' He lay down on the blankets, patted the space beside him. ''Coming?''

Her lips now compressed into a thin line, Marietta rose to her feet. She knew that the only way to get him to go to sleep was to lie down beside him and pretend that she was sleeping. So, distasteful as it was to get near him, she walked over to the blankets, sank to her knees and lay on her side, facing away from him.

She braced herself, fully expecting his intrusive arm to come around her. When it didn't, she was greatly relieved. She relaxed and soon found, to her dismay, that she was very, very sleepy.

She could hardly hold her eyes open, but she forced herself to stay awake. This was her chance to get away and she meant to take it. Marietta waited impatiently. Finally, when she could tell by Cole's deep, slow breathing that he was sleeping, she made her move.

Then yelped in horror when his hand shot out and firmly gripped the waistband of her trousers, yanking her back. ''Going somewhere?'' he asked.

''Get your hand out of my pants!'' she hotly ordered, trying desperately to pull free.

''If I do, will you behave yourself?''

''Turn me loose, damn you.''

Cole released her trousers, but slipped an arm around her. ''Hush now,'' he said. ''Be good and I will too.''

"You don't know the meaning of the word," she huffed.

But when he took his arm away, she gave in to exhaustion. She was sleepy, so very sleepy. Soon she was asleep.

So was he.

Cole awakened before Marietta.

Turning his head, he saw that she was still sleeping. He rolled up into a sitting position, ran his hands through his hair and rubbed his eyes and face. Then raised his knees and draped his forearms atop them. He looked down at Marietta and lost his breath.

Her flaming-red hair was in total disarray. Wayward locks had escaped the restraining comb and curled appealingly around her beautiful face. Her large, emerald eyes were closed, the long dark lashes resting in twin crescents on her pale-apricot cheeks. Relaxed in slumber, her mouth was curved and generous and voluptuous.

Her tall, slender body was sheer perfection. Full, round breasts pressing against the white fabric of her shirt. A waist so small his hands could easily span it. Flaring hips and flat stomach appealingly delineated in the chamois trousers.

His gaze guiltily lowered to touch the front arch of her pelvis where her long legs met. He stared, narroweyed, at her pubis region, becomingly contoured in the snug pants. Heat swiftly enveloped him.

Cole looked away, silently cursing her.

She was that irresistible combination of childlike

innocence and provocative guile. She was all that was desirable in a woman. No wonder she made Maltese drool and give her anything she wanted.

Thank God he himself wasn't some lonely middle-aged man or green boy that she could turn inside out.

Fourteen

"Let's stop here."

"No. Too early. The sun's still high. We'll stop in a couple of hours."

Marietta drew rein. "I said I want to stop!"

"We're not stopping," Cole replied, continuing to ride on.

"My back aches," Marietta called after him.

"So you mentioned," he said. "At least a dozen times in the past hour."

Marietta sighed irritably, but put the piebald mare back in motion. When she drew alongside, she glared at Cole and said, "You are mean and spiteful, Cole Heflin, and I hate you."

"Baby, I don't care," Cole said and meant it.

Cole exhaled heavily. He couldn't believe it had been only four days since he had spirited the fiery Marietta out of Central City. It seemed more like a lifetime.

In that short period of time he had learned that the red-haired opera singer had the hottest temper of any woman he had ever known. Everything he did or said set her off. If she had thrown one fit, she had thrown a dozen.

She was a pushy, pampered beauty who had never slept outdoors on the hard ground. Or cooked over a campfire. Or bathed in a cold mountain stream. Nor, since she had blossomed into a stunningly beautiful woman, had she been in the company of anyone who hadn't immediately catered to her.

She tried to add him to that coddling number, but he wasn't buying it. Cole catered to no one. It annoyed the hell out of him that she would expect him to humor and indulge her as if she was royalty and he her faithful servant.

When he refused to toe the line, she heatedly threatened him, promising to do him great bodily harm the minute she got the chance.

Cole was not concerned.

She was not the first woman who had sworn she hated him and had threatened to kill him. He well remembered a brunette beauty who had, years ago, nearly made good on her promise. He couldn't recall the lovely lady's name or what the fierce argument had been about. All he remembered was that after a long night of wild, raunchy lovemaking, the dark-haired, dark-eyed spitfire had come at him with a knife in a Fort Worth hotel room. He had been forced to grab his clothes and flee—buck naked—out a second-story window.

Marietta was headstrong and stubborn, but he could

handle the spoiled opera singer. He was just as stubborn and headstrong as she was.

She was used to ordering people around. Took it as her due to be promptly and cheerfully obeyed. Naturally she attempted to boss Cole around.

Big mistake.

Cole Heflin allowed no one to boss him around. Especially not a whining, bothersome woman.

This red-haired, green-eyed Marietta was vain, spoiled, egotistical, selfish, beautiful and would, he firmly believed, benefit from a dose of long-overdue discipline. More than once when she had pushed him as far as she could, he found himself wishing that she was—just for a minute—a man so that he could throw a couple of well-aimed punches at her smug face.

But he never let on that she had even faintly upset him, never allowed her to suspect that she *could* anger him. He never raised his hand or his voice to her. Never paid one bit of attention to her numerous explosions.

Never rose to the bait.

Cole's total and consistent indifference made the hot-tempered Marietta all the angrier. She could not understand how he could be so consistently stoic and unresponsive. No matter what she did or said, he was unmoved.

Unreachable.

But strangely enough, while his constant coldness frustrated her, it also fascinated her. She was both puzzled and provoked by his unfailingly impassive manner. To her astonishment and chagrin, Marietta found herself mysteriously attracted to this inflexible, cocksure, infuriating, ruggedly handsome Texan.

And she wondered why on earth the attraction was not mutual.

Marietta was fully aware of her feminine charms and was so accustomed to having men fawn over her that Cole's I-don't-give-a-damn attitude surprised and intrigued her. She found herself trying to get his attention, to make him respond to her as a woman. After all, she had yet to meet a man she couldn't enchant.

Cole Heflin was different from any man she'd ever known.

But surely he was not *that* different. This darkly handsome Texan was definitely all male, so she could undoubtedly captivate him if she set her mind to it.

And when she did, when he had totally succumbed to her allure, she could then easily persuade him to let her go. It was quite simple really. She would just treat him the way she treated Maltese and all her past admirers. Tickle him under the chin and flutter her eyelashes and make him think—if he were fortunate—she might possibly favor him with a kiss or two.

And when he was in her thrall, he would see things her way. She would convince him that she was a star on the rise and the stage was where she belonged.

Her career in opera meant everything to her. The production at the Tivoli could not go on without her.

Marietta mulled over her plan as the two of them rode knee to knee under the broiling June sun. She set aside her discomfort. Momentarily forgot that her shirt was wet with perspiration and sticking to her back. Or that her throat was dust dry and that she had a nagging headache.

She had been using the wrong approach entirely. She would, she decided, set out on the crusade to get Cole's attention. The right kind of attention. She would stop cursing and screaming. Stop complaining and giving in to fits of anger. Take great care to be pleasant and good company. She would be totally sweet and agreeable.

Starting now.

For the rest of the afternoon Marietta went out of her way to make her riding companion like her. She smiled at Cole often, frequently turning on that dazzling, dimpling smile that made most men go weak in the knees. She teased and flattered and flirted with him. She did everything she could think of to make him respond to her the way other men always had.

Nothing happened.

She might have been a man for all he cared. She was exasperated that he had not behaved as any other red-blooded man would. Hadn't shown any sign of weakness whatsoever. Hadn't melted with desire when she had played the coquette for his benefit.

Disappointed, Marietta promptly changed her tactics.

She felt that if she could get a rise out of him, make him react in a volatile manner, she would be assured that he actually was attracted to her and just didn't want her to know it.

Marietta flashed a look of pure hatred in Cole's direction. She decided she'd pick a fight with him. She insulted him, called him names, accused him of being a coward. She belittled him. She cursed him. She did everything she could think of to make him angry.

It didn't work.

As coolly as if he were saying good-morning, Cole finally turned in the saddle, fixed her with those startling sky blue eyes, and unemotionally said, "Behave yourself, Marietta."

That was it.

That's all the response she got.

By now Marietta was so angry and frustrated she began to cry. But her anguished tears didn't move her impervious companion. Not one whit. Cole never even noticed she was crying. Or if he did, he didn't care.

Marietta sniffed back her tears, incredulous. She found it absolutely impossible to believe that she could *not* charm Cole Heflin.

One of the men Marietta *had* greatly charmed, Taylor Maltese, was frantic with worry. He had not left

Marietta's private quarters since her disappearance, had hardly eaten or slept. When he did wearily doze for a few minutes at a time, he lay on her bed, clutching one of her shoes to his chest.

Maltese realized that the longer Marietta was gone, the less chance there was of finding her. And even if she should be found, what shape would she be in? What might her cruel abductor have done to her by now? The thought of some vile, depraved man laying hands on his beloved sickened Maltese.

His aching heart leaped with joy and hope when, four days after Marietta had been taken, he looked out the front window to see the posse of men riding up Eureka Street at a gallop.

But his hopes were quickly dashed when big Con Burnett, shamefaced, admitted that he, his brother and the other riders had called off the hunt and come home empty-handed. Angry that the bumbling Burnett brothers had allowed Marietta to be kidnapped, Maltese was furious with the gigantic man filling the doorway.

"I told you not to come back without Marietta!" Maltese thundered. "Damn you to hell! Where is she? Where is my darling?"

"We rode for three days and nights and couldn't find any sign of her," said Conlin Burnett. "No one has seen her. She's disappeared without a trace. I'm sorry."

"Sorry? You're sorry!" Maltese reached out, grabbed the taller man by the collar and said, "I'll make you sorry if you don't get right back in the saddle and go after her, you hear me!''

''It's no use, Maltese. No telling where they are by now.''

''You're fired, both of you!'' Maltese said, a vein standing out on his forehead. He released his hold on Conlin. ''Get out of Central City! Get out of Colorado!''

''Yes, sir,'' said a meek Con Burnett. He started to leave, turned back and said, ''Lightnin', he didn't come back. He's still out there hunting for Marietta. Maybe he will find her.''

''Get out of my sight!''

Fifteen

Cole pulled up on the reins. He leaned forward in his stirrups as his horse fidgeted and tossed his head. Cole rolled his tired shoulders and looked around.

It was past time to stop and make camp, but he saw no signs of water. He exhaled wearily and mulled over the situation. He didn't feel like riding any farther and he knew Marietta was exhausted.

They had watered the horses and filled the canteens at the last rest stop. The horses could make it until tomorrow and so could they.

"We'll stop here," he announced, turned his head and looked at Marietta.

Marietta shrugged, but gave no reply.

Cole said, "There's no water here, no brook or stream of any kind."

Again she shrugged, then immediately brightened, smiled and said, "Doesn't matter. Let's stop. It's a lovely place and we're both tired."

"Good enough," Cole said, but his eyes narrowed and his eyebrows knitted. She was suddenly too agreeable to suit him. Something was up. She intended to pull something. God knew what.

Marietta's mind was racing. She had, for the past hour, been wondering how she could snare Cole Heflin. How best to spin her web of feminine enticement around him. How could she tease and tempt him until he was fully under her spell?

Now he had innocently handed her the answer. She knew just how she was going to make him an obedient soldier in her army of admirers. Marietta was nothing if not resourceful. If the unresponsive Cole Heflin assumed she was finished with him, he was sadly mistaken.

Marietta dismounted and looked around. She was pleased with this high, hidden mountain paradise. It was perfect. Soft green grass. Tall sheltering pines and leafy conifers. An incredible view of the wide valley far below.

And, best of all, no high-country tarn or splashing waterfall or babbling brook. No water of any kind. Only the two canteens they had filled three hours ago. Plenty for her plan.

"Goodness," she said, and when she had drawn Cole's attention, she casually unbuttoned the top two buttons of her shirt. She pulled the collar apart, revealing her pale, dewy throat. "I'm *sooo* hot. Sticky hot all over."

"You'll cool off as soon as the sun goes down," he replied.

But you won't, she silently promised.

Cole turned away, went about unsaddling the mounts and making camp. When the horses were contentedly grazing, he began gathering firewood. To his amazement, Marietta offered to help.

Marietta could hardly wait for supper to be over. Determined to be sweet and agreeable, she ate the unappetizing food Cole handed her without complaint.

Her change in temperament made Cole nervous. He looked at her suspiciously. He would have to keep a constant eye on her.

The meal finished, Marietta cheerfully wiped the plates clean. Then she stretched, sighed dramatically and said, "Lord, I need a nice, refreshing bath."

Cole shook his head. "No bath tonight."

"But I'm all gritty and dirty."

"I told you, there's no water here."

"I know you did, but—"

Cole interrupted, "I suggested a bath last night."

"You did," she said meekly.

"And you refused. You'll have to wait until tomorrow night. I'll say it again, there is no water here."

Marietta was undeterred. "Both canteens are full."

"That's for drinking. Who knows how far we'll have to ride before we can refill them."

Marietta turned the full force of her smile on him and said, "I thought perhaps I could just take a little sponge bath." Cole frowned and rolled his eyes heavenward. She continued, "I wouldn't use much water, I promise. I could just pour a tiny little bit out into an empty tin plate. That's all. Please say yes. Just look at me, I'm drenched with perspiration."

"Go head," he finally agreed, "but don't use more than one cupful of water."

Marietta sprang to her feet. "Thank you, Cole." He cocked an eyebrow. She had never called him Cole. Pointing, she said, "If you would get your coiled lasso and stretch it out between those two aspen trees there and tie the ends to—"

"Why would I do that?"

She smiled, "I will explain. Once you've strung the rope and tied it between the trees, I could toss the blanket over it. That way I'd have a dressing screen to stand behind while I bathe."

"Why don't you just go over behind the trees?"

"It will soon be turning dark," she explained, her large emerald eyes soft and beseeching. "I'd be afraid out there by myself. Who knows, there might be hostile Indians in the area."

"*You* afraid?" he said sarcastically. "Jesus. Pity the poor savage that gets his hands on you."

"Oh, Cole, please."

"You're a lot of trouble," Cole said, but rose to his feet and went for the rope and blanket.

Minutes later a pleased-with-herself Marietta slipped behind the hung blanket, ready to disrobe. And to bring the impassive Cole Heflin to his knees.

The sun was beginning to set, but it's fiery glow lingered to bathe everything in an ambient rosy light. Ideal. She couldn't have planned it any better. Her bare shoulders would be luminous in the dying sunlight.

His back resting against a sturdy conifer trunk, Cole sat with his legs stretched out and crossed at the ankles. He calmly smoked a cigar, purposely paying Marietta no attention and trying to forget that an incredibly beautiful woman was taking off her clothes not ten feet away.

He was not entirely successful.

Marietta was delighted to find that the blanket struck her well below the shoulders. She finished unbuttoning her soiled white shirt. As she tossed it over the blanket, she said Cole's name so that he would look at her. She then cleverly engaged him in conversation as she unhooked her camisole and slipped it off.

"Isn't this one of the most beautiful spots on earth?" she said and, as she had done behind the screen as Maltese had watched, Marietta lifted her tangled hair atop her head and sighed. "Ah, that's so much cooler," she commented, knowing that the movement of her raised arms lifted her bare breasts until the rising swell was exposed above the blanket. "I swear, sometimes I don't know why we have to wear clothes at all, do you, Cole?"

He didn't answer.

Marietta moved her arms higher and slowly raised on tiptoe so that only her pale pink nipples were concealed behind the covering blanket.

To her amazement, Cole registered no response.

None whatsoever.

She released her hair, reached down and anxiously unbuttoned her snug trousers. She then made a big production of shimmying out of the soft chamois pants, thrusting a hip this way, then that, bumping up against the blanket. On purpose. And as she did so, she shared with her disinterested companion the intimate fact that she wore nothing beneath the trousers.

Laughing merrily, Marietta confided, "You know, when I changed into these riding clothes back there outside Golden, I made every attempt to get these tight trousers up over my lacy pantalets."

No reply from Cole.

Marietta frowned. "Did you hear me, Cole? I said that I couldn't—"

"I heard you."

"Well, anyhow, it was just impossible. I simply could not get the trousers up over my underwear." She paused, sighed and said, "So do you know what I had to do?"

"Let me guess," was his cool reply.

"I had to discard the pantalets." She threw back her head then and laughed gaily. "I have ridden all this way with nothing between me and these snug-fitting trousers."

Cole swallowed hard, but remained outwardly composed. He drew on his cigar, slowly blowing out the smoke. He continued to sit there in an attitude of total indifference.

"There," Marietta announced as she tossed the

chamois pants atop her discarded blouse. "Ah, heaven, absolute heaven. I am now as bare as the day I was born."

Cole's teeth clamped down hard on his cigar. He leaned his head back against the tree trunk and lowered his eyelids. But she wouldn't let it go. Wouldn't leave him alone. Damn her.

"Oh, dear me," Marietta said suddenly, as if surprised. "Can you believe me? Here I am totally naked and ready to take a nice cool bath and I forgot to bring a cloth with me to wash with."

"Use your hand," Cole said, annoyed.

"Don't be silly, Cole," she laughingly scolded. Then sweetly, "Could you possibly help me out? Do you have a handkerchief I could borrow?"

"No."

"Well, then, would you be an angel and loan me your neckerchief?"

Cole gritted his even, white teeth. He rose to his feet, dropped his smoked-down cigar and crushed it out beneath the heel of his moccasin. He untied the bandanna, slipped it from around his throat. His firm jaw set, he crossed to Marietta. He held out the silk neck wear. She took it, hoping that he would continue to hold on to it for a moment. That the two of them would hold either end of the neckerchief and look into each other's eyes for a magical moment.

Cole immediately released the scarf.

"Thank you very much," she said.

"Don't mention it," Cole replied before turning and walking away.

Marietta began her bath. She bent and dipped the neckerchief in the tin plate of water and brought it dripping up to her throat.

"Mmm," she moaned, tilting her head back. "That feels wonderful. Oh, my," she murmured and let the soaked silk cloth slip slowly down from her throat to her chest.

Marietta continued to sensuously slide the soaking silk over her nude body, sighing and gasping and carrying on for Cole's benefit. She kept him informed of just which part of her heated body she was presently cleansing. And she told him just how splendid it felt to have that sopping-wet silk—the very same one he had worn around his throat—gliding over her hot, tingling flesh.

To no avail.

Marietta was now wet all over.

Her pale skin glistened in the dying light.

She was wet and naked behind the blanket. Cole should have been breathing heavily by now. He should have been wanting her so badly he would be suffering in sweet agony. He should have been staring intently at her, his face bathed in perspiration, his heart racing in his chest, his lean body tensed, passion smoldering in the depths of his eyes.

Instead, Cole was, to Marietta's shocked dismay, totally detached. Just as always. She waited for him to react, to speak, to say something, but she waited in vain. He was as taciturn as ever, simply ignoring her. She could have yanked down the covering blanket and he wouldn't have turned his head. She could have walked right up to him, gleaming wet and vulnerably naked, and he wouldn't have bothered to look up!

Marietta was incensed and mortified.

Feeling foolish and rebuffed, she couldn't wait to get her clothes back on. And she swore to herself that she would *never* take them off in his presence again.

Marietta could not sleep.

She had not said a word to Cole since her failed attempt to captivate him by taking the sponge bath.

Bedtime had come and gone, but she lay alone on the blanket. When she went to bed, Cole had said he was not sleepy, had stayed up. Was still up. Now as it grew late—well past midnight—Marietta remained awake. She was wide awake. She found herself in a strange state of anxious excitement, a feeling that was foreign and frightening to her.

Cole Heflin was responsible.

Her head turned in his direction, Marietta lay on her back and spied on him from beneath lowered lashes. Bare-chested and barefoot, he paced back and forth like a dangerous panther in heat, his strong shoulders and naked torso gleaming with a sheen of perspiration. The flames of the dying campfire licked at his smooth bronzed flesh and cast shadows over his ruggedly handsome face.

Marietta's heart beat heavily as she guiltily gazed at him, admiring his striking physique. She was mesmerized by his smoldering, masculine good looks. He was a perfect physical specimen with his leanly muscled arms and broad shoulders.

Much as she despised him, she was unable to take her eyes off him. And she caught herself wondering how it would feel to have those long, powerful arms around her, holding her tight. Would it be thrilling beyond compare to be pressed against that bare, gleaming chest?

At the prospect, Marietta felt her nipples tighten into points of sensation, felt her belly contract sharply. She clutched at the blanket beneath her and ordered herself to calm down, to look away from him.

But she didn't do it.

Couldn't do it.

She continued to watch Cole. She shivered with a mixture of fear and fascination. There was an erotic aura about him, as if he had made love to dozens of women. She would bet anything that he had. And that those women had swooned with ecstasy when they were in his arms because he was such an exciting lover.

Marietta was excited just watching him pace back and forth. She told herself it was not entirely her fault. It was natural that she would be drawn to such a magnificent figure of power and sensuality. His physical beauty and superb animal strength were impossible to ignore. She was far from civilization in a primitive environment and in danger of falling under the spell of this erotically attractive man.

Marietta frowned.

This wasn't the way she had planned it! He should have been falling under *her* spell. What on earth was wrong with him?

He couldn't possibly be so magnetic, such a figure of power and sensuality, if he was not a hot-blooded man. There had to be a fiery nature beneath that impassive exterior. And she could well imagine what he might be like if that blazing passion should ever be unleashed.

Marietta trembled at the thought.

Sixteen

Cole continued to pace restlessly before the dying fire.

It was late, but he wasn't sleepy. He did not dare lie down. Couldn't trust himself to stretch out beside this tempting Jezebel who had driven him half-crazy by slowly taking off her clothes a few feet from him.

His blood was up.

Had been up since she had stripped down to the skin and rubbed his wet bandanna all over her bare flesh. He had suffered as he sat there trying to keep his eyes and his mind off her. More than once he had been tempted to yank down the blanket and draw her, wet and naked, into his arms and kiss her senseless.

Jesus, how he had wanted her.

Wanted her still.

But he'd be damned if he'd let her know it. He was on to her. Marietta was a mean, selfish little bitch, bent on making a slavering fool of him. Well, lots of good old-fashioned luck to her. She wasn't *quite* as irresistible as she supposed. Nor was he as easily seduced as she assumed.

Cole stopped pacing.

He withdrew the still-damp bandanna from his hip pocket and held it in the palm of his hand. He glanced toward the blanket where Marietta lay. She was asleep. Finally.

Cole's bare shoulders sagged with relief. He guiltily raised the silk bandanna to his face and inhaled deeply, hoping to catch Marietta's unique scent. He breathed in. He shuddered, recalling where the slick fabric had been.

Against her wet bare flesh. Touching her, washing her. All over. Cole closed his eyes and impulsively pressed the silk to his lips. He kissed it, brushing his closed mouth lightly against it. He parted his lips slightly. He put out the tip of his tongue and licked at the damp material. He opened his mouth wider. He sucked a small portion of neckerchief inside.

Then abruptly jerked the bandanna out of his mouth and stuffed it back into his pocket. He stalked over to the blanket, stood just above, staring down at the sleeping Marietta. He was angry with her. She had kept him awake for hours when he badly needed his rest. Damn her.

Cole exhaled irritably, lifted a hand and rubbed the back of his neck. He yawned. Finally, he was growing sleepy. He sank to his knees on the blanket and stretched out beside Marietta. Close, but not touching. He released a long sigh of exhaustion, closed his burning, bloodshot eyes and instantly fell asleep.

* * *

Disappointed that she had been unable to captivate him, Marietta was unusually disagreeable for the next couple of days. She complained. She ridiculed. She criticized. She was going at him hot and heavy one noontime just after they had stopped to rest. They had been there but a few short minutes when, to Marietta's puzzlement, Cole, without saying a word, rose and casually walked over to the black stallion. He swung up into the saddle and unceremoniously rode away, leaving her behind.

Marietta frowned.

She got to her feet and stood there baffled for a minute. Then she began running after him on foot.

"What in blazes do you think you're doing? Where are you going?"

"To Texas," he calmly replied.

"Well...well, wait! What...what about me?"

"You'll have to find a new sparring partner, I'm worn out."

"But you can't just leave me in the middle of nowhere! I don't know where we are."

"That," he said, "is your misfortune."

And on he rode.

Marietta's anger was immediately replaced with panic. Without him, she would be lost in this dense mountain wilderness. She couldn't even discern directions, had no idea how to get to a city. She might never find her way out, might die here alone.

Truly frightened, Marietta stopped running beside Cole. Out of breath, heart racing, she ran back to camp and hastily gathered up the gear. She anxiously mounted the piebald mare and galloped after Cole.

When she finally overtook him, she opened her mouth to speak, but he silenced her with a look.

She fretted in silence for the rest of the day and plotted how she would escape once they were nearer to civilization. She had made up her mind. She was going to get away from this callous bastard one way or another.

When they stopped for the night, Cole knew that Marietta was quietly seething, but he didn't care. She was so angry she wouldn't speak to him? Good. The silence was blessed. He hoped it lasted.

As he drifted peacefully off to sleep that night his last thought was that it would suit him fine if he didn't hear another peep out of her the rest of the way to Galveston.

An hour after he had drifted off to sleep, Cole was awakened by the distinctive sound of a revolver being cocked. Very close. Cole didn't move. He opened his eyes only a slit and saw, framed in the pale moonlight, the scar-faced Lightnin' standing above, grinning evilly.

Cole pretended to remain fast asleep.

Marietta stirred and Lightnin's gaze shifted to her. Quick as a cat, Cole lunged up, surprising the distracted Lightnin' and knocking him off his feet. The gun was still in Lightnin's hand. The two men began a fierce battle, rolling around on the ground, grunting and fighting for possession of the revolver.

Marietta leaped up, her heart in her throat, hands pressed to her cheeks, just beginning to grasp what was happening. Lightnin' had finally found her. Thank God! Thank God! He had tracked them down at last, just as she'd prayed he would. Excited and relieved, she watched the two men scuffle, each fighting fiercely for possession of the revolver.

After several long minutes of tussling, Cole managed to wrestle the revolver from Lightnin's hand. The weapon slid across the grassy ground and into the shadows.

Marietta saw that Lightnin' had lost the gun, but she wasn't too worried. Lightnin' was as tough as they came. He would surely be triumphant in this fight. He would soon best the Texan and before the night was over she'd be on her way back to Central City and the stage.

But to Marietta's surprise and disappointment, the bitter struggle continued. And continued. By now she was wincing and covering her mouth each time another loud, punishing blow was landed on either of their faces. Both men were bloodied. Both were groaning in pain. Both were gasping for breath.

But they kept fighting.

And fighting.

Hopping around above the battling pair now, Marietta watched wide-eyed and grimacing. She was becoming increasingly more worried. If they didn't stop hitting each other, somebody was going to be badly hurt, perhaps even killed.

An odd mixture of fear and relief warring within her, she began to pray that Cole would give up. Or that Lightnin' would knock Cole out and the bloody fight would end without the Texan being too badly injured.

Marietta involuntarily screamed when she saw the flash of a blade appear. It was Lightnin' who wielded the knife. He was going to stab Cole. Lightnin' meant to kill Cole!

The tendons standing out in Cole's throat, he managed to grip Lightnin's wrist and stay his hand. He fought to shake the knife loose. Lightnin' fought just as hard to free his hand and stab Cole.

"My gun, Marietta! Get my gun," called the hard-breathing Cole as he struggled to keep the knife's blade away from his chest.

"Get the gun, Marietta," ordered the equally winded Lightnin'. "Kill this kidnapping bastard!"

Her heart racing, Marietta stood rooted to the spot, unable to move, as the two men stayed locked in a death struggle. She was paralyzed with indecision. Couldn't help either man. Didn't know which one she really wanted to help.

But then she saw the long, sharp knife blade inch closer to Cole's heart.

That did it.

She looked frantically around and found a large rock. Picking it up she hurried to the two wrestling men, waited for a clear opportunity and brought the rock down squarely atop Lightnin's head.

He instantly collapsed atop the hard-breathing Cole, the deadly knife slipping from his open fingers. Cole shoved the unconscious man away and struggled to sit up. Marietta fell to her knees beside him, her face a study in concern.

She put her arm around Cole's bare shoulders while he sat there and fought to get his breath. His chest was heaving and sweat glistened on his bloodied, battered face. Grateful she had saved his life, Cole sagged tiredly against Marietta.

"Cole, oh, Cole," she said, and impulsively lifted the long tail of her white shirt up to wipe his face. "Are you all right? Are you badly hurt? Is there anything I can do?"

Cole finally caught his breath. He looked at her and his rapidly swelling lips stretched into an impish grin.

"Why, darlin'," he said, "I didn't know you cared."

Same old arrogant Heflin. Incensed, Marietta immediately released him, shot to her feet and said, "I *don't* care, you fool!"

She fumed as she watched Cole loosely tie the unconscious Lightnin' to a tree, purposely leaving the rope slack so that once Lightnin' came to, he could easily free himself.

Marietta was still berating herself when she and Cole rode away from the plateau, leaving Lightnin' behind, sans guns, sans bowie knife, sans horse.

Angry with Cole, angrier with herself for helping him instead of Lightnin', Marietta was nonetheless too tired to object when, a couple of hours later, Cole suggested they stop again and get some rest. She didn't even protest when Cole stripped off his shirt and stretched out close beside her.

But before she drifted off to sleep, she silently told herself that she was going to get away from him one way or the other.

Cole awakened with a start from a horrible nightmare. He bolted up and put his hands over his ears, attempting to shut out the dreadful noise of the lingering dream.

It didn't work.

The loud, scary sound was still ringing in his ears, setting his nerves on edge, causing his teeth to grind.

Grimacing, he leaped up, looked all around, unsure what was happening, not knowing where the ghastly sound was coming from.

Then, in the bright morning sunlight, he caught sight of Marietta. And he realized that he had not been having a terrible nightmare. The bad dream was all too real. The discordant sounds were coming from her. She was standing a few feet from him, singing loudly, arms outstretched, as if she were performing for a large audience.

Marietta reached for a high note and Cole promptly got a headache. He scowled at her, wishing to high heaven she would shut up.

She did not.

Marietta had no idea that her singing was bothersome to him. She supposed that Cole enjoyed hearing her sing. Everyone else did. So she continued to practice the scales, happily oblivious to Cole's distress.

Making a face, Cole turned away, silently cursing her and her jarring singing voice. He walked directly to the cold spring that rushed through their camp. Crouching down on his heels, he scooped up a double handful of water and drank thirstily. Then he dipped again and splashed it on his bruised face and bare chest.

Behind him the unpleasant serenade continued.

Cole leaned down and fully ducked his head beneath the water, trying to escape the sound that was worse than chalk on a blackboard. Head and ears submerged, he could still hear her.

Cole raised his head, ran his hands through his wet hair and over his face and chest. He closed his eyes, rubbed the moisture from his dark eyelashes.

Behind him, Marietta continued to sing. Cole rolled his eyes heavenward and considered drowning himself. Jesus, it wasn't enough that she griped and complained and argued and tried to seduce him, now she had decided to torture him with that earsplitting vocalizing.

Marietta went on singing. Loudly. Enthusiastically. With heartfelt passion. She had given it a great deal of thought and had decided that, distasteful as it would be, the only way out of this terrible predicament she found herself in was to seduce Cole Heflin. Do whatever it took to make him want her so completely he could no longer resist.

Cole's continuing chilly demeanor had made her all the more determined to have him fall under her spell. She had failed with her impromptu bath behind the blanket, but she had not given up. She would figure out a way to get the best of him.

She thought back to the dozens of men who had cheered and applauded when she had graced the stage of the Tivoli Opera House. Her singing had inspired and enchanted them, had caused them to whistle and swoon and toss roses at her feet. Wouldn't the same thing work on the Texan?

It would.

Marietta reached for another high note as Cole turned to face her. Seeing the pained expression on his face, she stopped singing. "You're hurting, aren't you?" she asked as she walked toward him.

"You can say that again," he replied truthfully, but she misunderstood.

"Is it your split lip or your swollen jaw?"

"Both," he replied with a shrug.

"Or could it be this," she said and, catching him by surprise, reached out and laid a soft, warm hand on his naked chest where the flesh directly above his heart was bruised and discolored.

At her gentle touch, Cole felt a quick rush of sexual excitement. He brushed her hand away and turned his back on her.

"Sing some more, Marietta," he said, knowing that would quickly dampen his desire. "I do so like to hear you sing."

"Really?" she asked, eyes shining.

"You have no idea," he said and picked up his chambray shirt.

Marietta was thrilled. Her singing had had the desired effect. She would use it as her chief tool to tempt him. And once she had seduced him, had given herself to him, he would surely be in love with her. So much in love he would not force her to go to Galveston. He would take her wherever she wanted to go. And she wanted to go back to Central City and the opera!

Marietta inwardly shuddered at the prospect of allowing Cole to actually make love to her. She didn't really know what to expect. Wasn't sure she would know what she was supposed to do when the time came. She hoped that he would know.

She was worried. She wondered if it would be terribly unpleasant. So unpleasant that she couldn't make herself go through with it.

She had to.

There was no other choice. If she was ever to be free of him, then she would have to let Cole make love to her. It would, she knew, be quite a sacrifice on her part.

But it would be worth it.

Seventeen

Marietta went to work on Cole.

Immediately and thoroughly.

She turned on the full force of her feminine charms, determined to spin her web around him. She was sweet and charming as they rode knee to knee that afternoon, asking intelligent questions, listening with interest as he pointed out various landmarks.

It was a beautiful late-June day. The sun was brilliant overhead, but at this altitude it was not boiling hot. Off to the west, sailing above the mountain peaks, great cumulus clouds were charged with lightning and thunder, threatening an afternoon shower.

Marietta laughed gaily as the meadowlarks and canyon wrens sang as clear as angels. And she pulled up on her mare and stared in awe when Cole pointed to a huge golden bobcat lying on a ledge above, casually sunning himself. The big cat slowly turned his head and stared down on them, his yellow eyes aglow.

"Will he hurt us?" Marietta whispered, reaching out and laying a hand on Cole's forearm.

"Only if he's hungry."

"Is he?" she asked, her eyes widening with alarm.

"No. It's summertime. He's fat and lazy."

The sleek cat finally stirred himself, languidly rose on all fours, stretched and yawned. He lowered his massive head and gazed down on them again as if bored. Then abruptly, he turned and, with exceptionally fluid grace, vanished into the forest.

Marietta and Cole smiled at each other and rode on.

The clouds soon thickened. The sound of distant thunder rumbled down out of the mountains. The blue sky darkened, turned gray, then an ominous black.

"We better find a place to wait out the coming thunderstorm," Cole said.

"Sounds like a good idea," Marietta replied, pushing a juniper branch out of her way.

Marietta's heart began to beat faster. It was going to rain and rain hard. Perhaps all afternoon. And while it rained, she and Cole would be forced to share close quarters somewhere to wait out the storm. Perfect! She could think of an ideal way to pass the time.

Marietta glanced at Cole from beneath lowered lashes. He was not looking at her. His eyes narrowed, he was scanning the timbered slopes, looking for a place to elude the storm. He didn't locate suitable shelter quite soon enough.

There was a sudden rush of wind in the pines above and the rain began to fall. All at once the storm engulfed the mountains as the clouds closed in and the winds rose and strengthened. Bolts of lightning and claps of thunder arrived simultaneously.

The heavy air cooled instantly.

In the blink of an eye it had become a dark and chilly afternoon in the rugged foothills of the Rockies. Huge drops of rain fell in sheets, blinding the two of them and quickly saturating their clothes.

"Up there," Cole shouted as he pointed. "A canyon cave thirty yards ahead."

"I can't see it," Marietta called back, attempting to blink away the peppering rain.

"Follow me," Cole shouted as he kicked the black and led the way.

In minutes they reached their destination, dismounted and, leading the horses inside with them, swiftly took shelter inside a dry stone cavern. While Cole tethered the nervous creatures to jutting spires of stone, Marietta explored. The cave appeared to be quite deep, winding back into the solid mountain of rock.

Marietta ventured only a few yards, found a small, dry, cozy room and called out to Cole, her voice echoing in the cavern. He promptly joined her.

"How's this?" she asked, turning about in a circle, arms extended.

"Fine," he said, squinting in the semidarkness, ducking so as not to bump his head.

They looked at each other then, noting that they were both drenched to the skin. But it was Marietta who mentioned it.

"We're absolutely soaked," she said, plucking at the wet fabric of her shirt, pulling it away from her damp skin.

"So we are," Cole said and quickly turned away.

Marietta took the few short steps toward him. She touched his shoulder and asked, "Don't you think that we...ah...should get out of these wet clothes?"

Cole swallowed hard. He faced her. "No. In this summertime heat our clothes will dry out in nothing flat."

"I suppose," she said.

Marietta looked around, chose a spot where the stone floor and the gently sloping wall were both totally smooth. She sat down, leaned back, looked up, smiled and invited Cole to join her.

Cole declined. He took off his gun belt, laid it aside, then dropped onto the stone floor directly across from Marietta. He leaned back, raised one knee and rested a forearm atop it.

And knew immediately that he had made a major mistake. If he had done as she had asked and sat down beside her, he wouldn't be looking at her. As it was, he was staring straight at her.

And what a sight she was.

Her glorious red hair was appealingly damp and tangled, the long gleaming locks falling over her shoulders and curling around her shiny face. The shirt she wore was soaked and plastered to her body. Her full breasts were clearly contoured, the chilled nipples thrusting out in twin points of temptation, their pale-pink hue visible through the thin, wet fabric.

Every bit as wet as her shirt, her trousers clung to her hips and flat stomach and long legs like a second skin. As he had done, she had raised one leg and stretched the other out before her. It was a totally innocent action, but the movement drew his attention to her groin. He suddenly recalled her saying that she wore nothing beneath the trousers.

He believed her.

All too clearly he could see the seam of the wet trousers seek and sink into the natural seam of her lush woman's body. That well-defined, delicate crevice between her legs guarding the ultrasensitive feminine flesh he yearned to touch and taste.

Cole was instantly choked with desire. He tried, but failed, to look away. He couldn't take his eyes off Marietta. His low-lidded gaze stayed riveted on her. Never had she been more beautiful, more vulnerable, more desirable. Never had he wanted her more than at this minute. His mind told him no—good God no—but his body refused to listen. His sudden, fully formed erection was restrained only by the confines of his tight, wet trousers. Anxiously, he draped a concealing arm over his surging groin. He clamped his teeth together. He shuddered and fought the overwhelming primal urge to take her. To pull her to him and strip the wet clothes away. He had to think of something fast or he'd be lost.

"Marietta," he said, his voice strained, the pulse in his tanned throat pounding.

"Yes?" she replied, barely able to breathe, certain the time had come, that he would beckon her to him and take her in his arms.

"Will you...?"

"Yes, oh, yes, I will, Cole," she said breathlessly and started to rise.

"No," he replied, stopping her. "Stay where you are. And sing. Sing to me."

"Sing?"

"Yes, sing. I want to hear you sing," he ground out. "And hurry."

Marietta made a face. She shook her head in puzzlement. Surely he was teasing.

"You're certain that's what you really want from me, Cole?" she asked playfully.

"Positive," he managed to say. "Sing, woman. Now."

Flattered, supposing this could be part of their prelude to lovemaking, Marietta licked her lips, opened her mouth and started singing. In seconds, Cole released a long breath of relief. He felt his tense body relax, felt his stirring erection ease and go down.

When the sudden summer storm finally ended, Cole had a nagging headache. But he hadn't laid a hand on Marietta. He was proud of himself. He had spent a chilly, rainy afternoon in a cave with Marietta a few short feet away in wet, revealing clothes and nothing had happened. He knew that he would be safe from now on. He had found the armor to protect himself against her. She had supplied it.

Bless her.

Eighteen

Three days had gone by since the rainy afternoon in the cave. Nothing had happened then. Nothing had happened since. Marietta had tried everything she could think of to make Cole Heflin want her. She brushed up against him any chance she got, hoping the physical contact would have the desired effect.

She had, on more than one occasion, managed to get close enough to press a soft breast against his arm or shoulder. If he even noticed, he had never let on.

Marietta was bewildered. Completely at a loss. She had used just about every weapon in her arsenal to make him knuckle under. Without success. She was unable to understand Cole's continued coldness. And she had begun to wonder if she had lost her allure. It could well be. She had no mirror out here. Perhaps she looked ugly and unattractive. Maybe the sight of her repulsed him.

She knew one thing, Heflin didn't look all that handsome anymore himself. He hadn't shaved since before his fight with Lightnin' and the growth of his heavy black beard made him look mean and scary.

At the same time, his aggravating, cocksure manner

and commanding masculinity had an effect on her, made her shiver inside. She couldn't seem to make him shiver. Nor could she make him angry. She couldn't make him respond to her in any way. Apparently Cole Heflin was incapable of feeling anything. He was made of cold hard steel, not flesh and blood.

Heat shimmered in palpable waves, blurring the horizon. It was early afternoon. Finally they had turned due east. They were dropping steadily down out of the craggy, juniper-dotted foothills and closer to a long green valley. Across the valley rose another narrow ridge of jutting timbered hills.

"Will we have to traverse that low-lying range?" Marietta asked, pointing.

"Yes, but it won't take long. By tomorrow evening we should be on the other side."

"Mmm," she murmured. "How far are we from the next town?"

"Ten miles or so. We'll be just south of Colorado Springs once we cross that pass between the two highest promontories."

Marietta nodded, said no more. She had—though it was terribly insulting to her pride—realized that she could not captivate Heflin. He had made it clear that he was not attracted to her, had no desire to even kiss her, much less make love to her. Since that was the case, the only thing to do was to escape as soon as possible. Get away from him once and for all.

And this was her chance. She was an experienced rider. She could easily make it across the wide valley, then up and over those jagged eastern ridges and down into Colorado Springs.

He wouldn't be able to catch her. Not if she took him totally by surprise, caught him napping. That's what she would do. Wait for just the right moment, then make a mad dash for freedom. Leave the arrogant bastard in her dust.

Another hour went by.

They weren't far now from the level ground of the valley. Marietta wasted no more time. She glanced at Cole. He was slouched in the saddle, looking straight ahead, not at her. She abruptly dug her heels into the startled mare's flanks and the mount lunged forward.

Marietta leaned low over the mare's neck and slapped the reins from side to side. Pebbles loosened and scattered beneath the animal's striking hooves as horse and rider raced down the incline.

Marietta never looked back. But she soon heard the thunder of hooves and knew that Cole was rapidly closing in. In minutes the powerful black had overtaken the galloping mare and a clearly irate Cole drew alongside, grabbed the mare's reins and yanked the animal to a dirt-flinging halt.

Cole threw a long leg over, dropped to the ground, came around and hauled Marietta down out of the saddle. He was angry, his bearded face set, his indigo eyes snapping with fury. His hand tightly encircling her upper arm, Cole shoved Marietta up against the winded mare.

He took her chin roughly in his hand, tilted her head back, made her look up at him and said, "Damn you, don't you ever try anything like that again! You hear me? You can't get away from me, can't outsmart me, so stop trying. You, sweetheart, are going to Texas, like it or not. I am taking you to your Grandpa in Galveston if I have to drag you every step of the way by the scruff of your neck!"

His eyes were feverish and his lean frame vibrated with anger against her trembling body. Half-afraid of him, Marietta nonetheless experienced a delicious feeling of triumph. His broad chest, pressed against her breasts, was rising and falling rapidly with his excited breaths and his hard thighs had her pinned against the horse's heaving belly.

He continued to hold her chin firmly between thumb and forefinger and his voice was hot, not cold, when he said, "Damn you, woman, I've had about enough of your nonsense. Either start behaving or suffer the consequences, because I am out of patience. I know your kind, baby, you're dime a dozen and I can beat you at any game you want to play. You aren't the first conniving female to think you can get the best of me, but it isn't going to happen. You can't escape me nor can you seduce me, trust me on that. You're nothing more than a spoiled little witch bent on annoying the hell out of me and I am tired to death of you and your shenanigans. You understand me?"

Staring up into his angry face, Marietta tried to speak but couldn't. He was holding her cheeks and mouth too tightly in the vise of his hand. So she made an attempt to nod, her eyes wide.

"Answer me, dammit!" Cole commanded, "before I lose my temper."

Marietta's eyes grew wider. Her heart thumped against her ribs. She clawed at his hand, trying to swallow. "Y-yes," she finally managed to say.

Cole released her chin, but kept her pinned to the mare with his unyielding body. "Yes, what?" he snarled.

Again she anxiously swallowed, attempting to get some saliva into her dry mouth. "Yes, I understand, Cole. I won't give you any more trouble."

"See that you don't," he said. He released her and stepped back so quickly that she lost her balance and fell to her knees.

Cole didn't help her up. His back was already turned on her. So he never saw Marietta's exultant smile as she got to her feet and dusted herself off. He thought he had won the battle of wills.

She knew better.

She was the victor.

His surrender was imminent.

At long last she had succeeded in making the impervious Mr.-God-Almighty-Heflin angry. Really, really angry.

Couldn't she make him want her with that same brand of fiery passion? Of course she could.

* * *

Late that same afternoon they had crossed the wide green valley and reached the last line of jagged foothills marching north to south. They made camp near a winding snow-fed brook bordered by tall evergreens, verdant pines and thick weeping willows.

As soon as they had unloaded the gear, Cole left Marietta alone. Without a word he took a towel, his razor, a bar of soap and disappeared into the woods.

He wasn't worried that she would try to escape. She had, he was sure, learned her lesson and would give him no more trouble. The rest of the journey should prove uneventful.

Cole returned to the campsite shortly, clean shaven, his raven hair damp and glistening, his shirt unbuttoned down his dark chest. Marietta looked up at him and felt her heart skip a beat.

It was, she realized, not going to be all that unpleasant to make love to him. His face, devoid of the thick dark whiskers, was smooth and handsome and his broad, bare chest, revealed in the open shirt, was nothing short of magnificent.

"You take a bath?" Marietta asked.

"I did," Cole said and went about gathering firewood.

"You enjoy it?"

"I did," he said again.

"I need a bath myself," Marietta informed him. Cole said nothing. His back to her, he continued to gather wood. Marietta rose, stretched and announced,

"Yes, sir, I think I'll just go take myself a nice refreshing bath like you did."

Over his shoulder, he said, "Go ahead. But don't get too far out of my sight."

She smiled and teased, "You won't peek, will you, Cole?"

He finally turned, glanced at her and said, "I have no desire to spy on you, Marietta."

"I'm sure relieved to hear that," she replied and smiled at him. "Now I'll feel quite safe and can take my time."

"Don't take too much time," he warned. "You do and I'll come after you."

"Promise?" she kidded, took a blanket, the soap and towel, and headed for the stream.

Cole finished gathering wood. He built a fire. He laid out their evening meal. He sat down to wait for Marietta.

Cole waited.

And waited.

He became more alarmed with each passing minute. He finally rose to his feet. She had been gone too long. Way too long. Almost an hour. Jesus, maybe she had drowned. The current was swift from the recent rains. Perhaps she couldn't swim. He should never have allowed her to go off alone.

Cole's heart began to hammer in his chest. He started running. He raced headlong into the stand of tall weeping willows where she had disappeared.

"Marietta! Marietta!" he shouted frantically, slapping greenery out of his way.

No answer.

Panic seized Cole.

"Marietta!" he shouted, cupping his hands to his mouth. "Please, Marietta, answer me! Oh, God, where are you? Answer me!"

"Were you looking for me?" came a soft feminine voice from close by.

Cole crashed to a stop, turned his head and saw her. She was seated on a blanket spread out on the grass. Her damp red hair was blazing in the dying summer sunlight. She was naked to the waist. Her pale, high breasts were full and perfectly shaped, the satiny nipples large and soft. How long, he idly wondered, would it take him to awaken those sleeping nipples?

His hot gaze slid lower.

Marietta still had on her leather riding pants, but the trousers were unbuttoned down her bare belly. She was leaning back on stiffened arms with her long legs stretched out before her. Her feet were bare.

She was the loveliest woman Cole had ever seen.

He swallowed hard when he glimpsed the wisp of fiery red curls against pale ivory flesh appealingly exposed in the open vee of her unbuttoned leather trousers.

Even as he approached her, Cole struggled to resist. He couldn't touch her, he couldn't. She was Maxwell Lacey's granddaughter, for God sake. Maxwell Lacey had saved him from the gallows and he had paid him a fortune. He couldn't repay the old gentleman by seducing his misbehaving granddaughter.

Unbuttoning his shirt as he knelt on one knee beside the half-naked, naughty Marietta, Cole's last logical thought was, *Ah, what the hell, the old man will likely be dead before we ever get to Galveston.*

Cole put his hand to the crown of Marietta's flaming red-gold hair and said in a low, caressing voice, "I intend to take off your britches, Marietta. If you don't want me to, stop me now while I still can."

Nineteen

Marietta did not reply.

She smiled catlike, the answer clearly written in her flashing emerald eyes. The trap had been set and was about to be sprung.

Cole gazed at Marietta for a long, tense moment, then drew her up and gently pressed her against his raised knee. With his hand still in her hair, he urged her head back slightly, leaned down, started to kiss her, but paused when his lips were a scant inch from her own.

In a voice that sounded like a caress, but drawling a little more than usual, Cole said softly, "Tell me, Marietta. Tell me you want me to kiss you."

Her heart now beginning to race beneath her naked breasts, Marietta gulped anxiously for air, then whispered, "Yes, I do, Cole. I want you to kiss—"

Before she could finish the sentence, Cole kissed her.

And what a kiss it was.

Squirming against him, her left breast brushing his naked chest, Marietta couldn't believe that a mere kiss could be so incredibly exciting. No one, absolutely no one, had ever kissed her the way Cole Heflin was kissing her now.

She hadn't expected this, wasn't prepared to get involved, to be so thrilled by his touch. She hadn't intended to let herself actually become engrossed in the lovemaking. She had meant to hold herself apart, to not truly surrender to his passion, to only pretend.

The troubled thought ran through her mind that this unexpected excitement, this sensual awakening, was not in her well-laid plans. Heflin was supposed to be the one aroused, not her. She had given it a great deal of thought before coming to the decision that allowing Cole to make love to her was a necessary evil. Simply the means to an end. For one reason and one reason only.

But just what was that reason? Marietta wondered now as Cole deepened the kiss, his hot mouth open on hers, his tongue dipping inside to touch and taste and thrill her. Marietta tingled with rising pleasure and promptly forgot everything, save how wonderful it felt to have Cole's marvelous mouth moving so persuasively on hers.

As the slow, hot kiss continued, Cole's warm hand lifted to cup a soft, pale breast. He slowly rubbed his thumb back and forth over the rapidly stiffening nipple. Marietta shivered at his touch, made a little whimpering sound deep in her throat and finally tore her burning lips from his.

Cole raised his dark head, but his caressing hand stayed at her breast, his thumb continuing to tease and pluck at the sensitive nipple. Fighting for breath, her heart hammering, Marietta knew in that instant that she had made a mistake. Had miscalculated her formidable foe.

She looked into Cole's heavily lidded, sleepily sensual eyes and was suddenly quite frightened. He stared at her and she felt a fierce animal power emanating from him, fully enveloping her, rendering her defenseless. She trembled. She should never have allowed things to go this far. She was in imminent danger and it was her fault. Perhaps she should just tell him she had changed her mind.

"Cole," she began, her eyes closing, "I don't think we should...that is, I...I..."

"Hmm," he murmured, agilely swung around, threw a leg across Marietta and sank down astride her thighs.

He took hold of her shoulders, drew her up into his close embrace and slowly kissed her closed eyes, her face, her throat, his heated lips moving down until he reached the swell of her breast. Marietta's eyes opened and she again feebly tried to protest.

"Cole, we really can't..."

Her words trailed away as his head moved down her chest until his lips closed over her left nipple. Her breath caught in her throat and she raised her hands to push him away. She slid her slender fingers into the thick hair at the sides of his head.

But she didn't push him away.

She couldn't.

His tantalizing tongue was licking her responsive nipple and it felt so heavenly she decided to let him continue. Just for a second or two. Then she'd make him stop.

"Ohhhh, my," she murmured, her eyes closing again when his teeth playfully raked back and forth, nibbling at the pebble-hard nipple. Her fingers automatically tightened in his hair.

"Cole," she breathed his name when he began to suck on the nipple, his jaws flexing, lips pulling vigorously.

Marietta's eyes opened and she gazed down on the head at her breast. It was an erotic sight to watch him suckle her, his handsome face dark against the paleness of her breast. His beautiful blue eyes were closed, the long dark lashes fluttering restlessly. He had a hand beneath her breast, lifting it to his lips, his lean, tanned fingers gently kneading the soft flesh.

For a delicious moment it was as if Marietta were outside herself, watching. She was intensely aroused by what she saw. The two of them, naked to the waist together on a blanket under a dying red sun. Cole seated astride her, his weight supported on his bent knees, his mouth on her breast.

Cole gave Marietta's nipple one last plucking kiss, raised his head and looked into her widened eyes. He put a hand to the side of her throat, his thumb beneath her chin.

"Kiss me, darlin'," he urged. "Kiss me like you mean it."

Marietta raised her arms up around his neck, lifted her face for his kiss and again closed her eyes, waiting. Cole didn't kiss her. A long minute passed. Marietta opened her eyes and gave him a questioning look.

"Don't you want to kiss me?" she asked.

"No," he said. "I want you to kiss me."

She shrugged, pulled his head down and eagerly pressed her lips to his. Cole allowed her to control the kiss for a moment or too. Then he took over. The enveloping hotness of his mouth closed commandingly over Marietta's and he sucked the very breath from her lungs. Then gave it back to her.

They kissed several times, seated like that and with each kiss both became increasingly feverish with desire, eager to have more, to know each other completely. It was during one of those long, heated kisses that they changed positions. Deftly, with Marietta hardly realizing what was happening, Cole managed to roll the two of them over until he was lying flat on his back and she was seated atop him.

Another lengthy, ardent kiss finally ended and Marietta was surprised to find herself astride Cole. She slowly sat up. She looked at him and realized that his sleepy-eyed gaze was focused on the vee of her open trousers. She automatically lowered protective hands to cover herself.

"No, baby," he said, brushing her hands aside. "Don't. Come here." Cole drew Marietta back down onto his chest, placed her head on his shoulder and murmured into her ear, "Remember I told you I was going to take your britches off?" Marietta nodded against his bare shoulder but said nothing. "Marietta?"

"Yes?"

"Say it. Tell me you want me to take off your pants and make love to you."

A long minute passed in silence. Finally, she managed to say, "Yes, all right."

"Yes, all right, what?" he said.

"I...I...you know."

"No, sweetheart, that's not good enough," he told her. "I want to be sure you know exactly what I intend to do and that you want me to do it."

He fell silent then, let her think it over. Marietta realized he was giving her the opportunity to change her mind. She could say no, get up and button her britches. But, how could she possibly make such a decision when she was lying here against his hot, hard body? Her breasts were flattened on his broad, bare chest, the crisp dark hair tickling her sensitive nipples. If that were not enough, she was seated astride him, her trousered legs open directly atop his pelvis.

Through the shielding fabric of both her trousers and his, she could feel the hot throbbing power of his erection. And she could feel the answering pulsating of her own body.

"Cole," she whispered, her lips against his throat, "I want you to take off my pants. I want you to make love to me. I want to make love to you."

Cole turned his head and kissed her. A long, slow, fervent kiss. During that kiss, Cole gently urged Marietta over onto her side and he rolled onto his. He lay facing her, stroking her hair, allowing her a moment to calm down, to put aside any lingering anxiety. When her nervous breathing had slowed, when she was tranquilly stroking his chest, his shoulders, Cole slipped a warm hand down inside Marietta's open trousers.

He watched her beautiful face change expressions as his fingers brushed lightly through the crisp red curls to gently, possessively cup her. For a long moment Cole did no more than that. Just held her as if she were a fragile work of art and all the while he looked into her eyes, reading every emotion she was experiencing.

Marietta felt as if she was bewitched. It was heaven to lie looking into the sky blue eyes of this dark, compelling man while his warm, gentle hand lay lightly enclosing the most intimate part of her body, that part that no man had ever touched before. She supposed she should be shocked and outraged. Should tell him that she had not expected, nor did she approve of him examining her with his hand.

Instead, she felt herself involuntarily begin to squirm and thrust her hips forward. She flushed at the realization that she actually longed to feel his long, tanned fingers touch her even more intimately. Would they? She didn't know. She dared not ask.

Cole could easily read Marietta's thoughts. Her

body was signaling her desires. She was ready. She wanted him to touch her more aggressively, needed it, was asking for it.

Cole gladly gave it to her.

Continuing to lie on his side facing her, Cole eased up, balanced his weight on a bent elbow and watched Marietta closely as he deftly parted the fiery curls partially concealed in the open trousers. Marietta was looking directly at his face. She caught her lower lip between her teeth and blushed hotly. She couldn't keep from glancing down when she felt the tip of Cole's middle finger touch her where she most wanted to be touched.

"Cole, Cole," she breathed as he slowly, expertly caressed her, moistening his finger in the hot silky wetness flowing freely from her.

"I know, sweetheart. I know. Feels so good," he murmured, gently circling that tiny button of pulsating flesh with the tip of his finger.

An experienced lover who was more than adept at undressing women, Cole kept Marietta at a fever pitch while he managed to easily relieve her of her leather pants. When they were discarded and Marietta was gloriously naked, Cole, with his hand still between her legs, kissed Marietta. Then he drew her up into a sitting position, coming up with her. He put an arm around her. Sighing, Marietta closed her eyes and let her head sag against his shoulder.

"Baby, open your eyes," Cole coaxed. "Let's

watch together while I touch you, love you like this. You're so beautiful. So hot and wet.''

Marietta, now as naked as the day she was born, supposed that she should have been mortified, terribly embarrassed. She wasn't. She was on fire and out of her head with sexual pleasure and the sight of Cole's lean, dark hand between her legs was almost as thrilling as his masterful touch.

She knew that something wonderful and frightening was happening to her and there was nothing she could do to stop it. If a crowd of a thousand people happened upon them at this moment, she wouldn't care, wouldn't make Cole stop caressing her. The aghast crowd would just have to watch because she couldn't bear the thought of him taking his hand from her even for a second.

''Cole, Cole,'' she began to sob his name as she spread her legs wider and anxiously tilted her pelvis up closer to his loving fingers.

''Yes, baby, yes,'' he whispered. ''Let it come if you want to, but there's no hurry. I've got you. You're mine now and I'll take care of you.'' He brushed a kiss to her dewy forehead and told her, ''We've got all the time in the world, sweetheart. I enjoy loving you like this. I'd like to keep my hand on you for all eternity.''

''Co...Co...Cole...'' She began to wail loudly as her climax came, strong and undeniable.

Cole held her fast, his hand on her, his fingers

gently manipulating the wet, throbbing flesh between her spread legs. Until at last she screamed, frantically pushed his hand away, squeezed her knees together and slouched against his bare shoulder.

Twenty

Cole kissed the top of her head, then pressed her bent knees up against his chest and rocked her as if she were a fretful infant. He soothed and petted her until she was calm and sighing with lazy contentment. When that happened, Cole put a hand beneath her chin and lifted her face so he could look into her eyes.

She gazed at him and asked, "What did you do to me?"

"That's just a start, darlin'." He kissed her open lips and told her, "There's more to come."

"No, Cole. No more, please. I've had enough," she told him.

"We've only just begun," he replied. Then he lifted one of her hands, kissed the warm palm and lowered it to his straining groin.

Marietta felt the awesome power beneath her palm and shivered. And when he coaxed, "Unbutton my pants. Touch me." She found herself curious and thinking, *If he can give that kind of pleasure with just his hand, what could he do with...with this...?* Marietta fumbled with the buttons of his trousers. Cole let her struggle for a few moments, then smiled, kissed her and took over the task.

His heated mouth fused to hers, Cole, one-handed, unbuttoned the tight trousers, shoved his white underwear down his brown belly and let his fully formed erection spring free. Then he drew Marietta's hand to him.

Awed by the heat and hardness of him, Marietta tore her lips from his and blurted out, "But, Cole, you…you're so big. You're huge."

Cole grinned at her. "Don't worry, we'll fit together just fine."

"I don't know, I—"

Cole silenced her with a kiss. With his hand atop hers, he guided her slender fingers up and down his stirring erection. Feeling as if he couldn't wait one more second to be inside her, he abruptly pushed her hand away.

Marietta pulled back, gave him a look of puzzlement. She innocently asked, "Don't you like to have me touch you?"

"Sure, baby, but you keep that up and I'll come in your hand."

Marietta quickly drew her hand away and frowned. "You wouldn't dare!" she exclaimed, appalled by the prospect.

"Then help me get undressed," he said. He lifted his hips off the blanket and began wiggling out of the trousers and underwear.

Marietta didn't help. Instead, she stared with childlike curiosity as Cole made quick work of shedding the garments. In seconds he was as naked as she, and Marietta held her breath when he turned and took her in his arms.

When he felt her tremble against him, Cole said softly, "Trust me, Marietta. I won't hurt you. I'll wait until you're ready for me."

Cole lowered them down onto the blanket to lie facing each other. He pressed his warm, naked body to hers, purposely letting her feel the size and hardness of his aching erection. Marietta gasped when she felt that heavy masculine power surging against her quivering belly. She was, for just one fleeting moment, terrified. He intended to thrust and fill her with all that awesome male strength!

Cole kissed her then and the swift, enveloping hotness of his seeking mouth made her sigh and snuggle closer. She felt his hand move down her back, slide over the swell of her bare buttocks and slip into the crevice between. She tried to object, but his mouth was covering hers and the only sound she could make was a weak, strangled moan.

That murmur of protest turned into sighs of shocked pleasure when she felt those lean, talented fingers begin to tease and toy, coming at her from a different direction, but spreading the same kind of incredible heat as before.

Of its own volition, her knee began to bend and to edge up his lean body. She hooked a leg around his back and drew him closer. How exciting it was to have his heavy erection jerking rhythmically against her belly while at the same time his fingers teased at the pulsating flesh between her legs. She breathed through her mouth, leaned closer and rubbed her rigid nipples back and forth against Cole's hair-covered chest.

Marietta had, at least a thousand times, wondered just what it would be like to make love with a man. A darkly handsome lover with a lean, beautiful body who knew how to use it to please a woman. In her wildest dreams she had never imagined it could be like this. Such a total loss of inhibitions. Such undiluted joy to have this naked Adonis do wonderfully forbidden things to her.

Cole wanted Marietta fever hot.

So he spent a long, lovely interlude in pleasingly passionate foreplay. He kissed her and held her and caressed her until the blood was zinging through her veins and she was restless for all that he could give her. Knowing the exact minute when to make his move, Cole rolled Marietta onto her back, urged her long slender legs apart and moved between them.

In a haze of sexual excitement, she looked up into his humid eyes and whispered, "Cole, Cole, kiss me. Take me. Love me."

Cole kissed her and as he did, he put his hand between them, gripped himself and slid the smooth tip of his erection just inside her. He raised his head, balanced his weight on his stiffened left arm and said,

"I want to look into your eyes while I make love to you."

"And I yours," she breathed.

Neither managed to do so. While Cole meant to slide slowly into her, he couldn't make himself do it. Her hot little body was too sweet, too tight and he was far too aroused. His eyes slid closed and so did hers as he thrust forcefully into her.

He had never been hotter, never wanted a woman as much as he wanted this one. So aroused he was totally oblivious to Marietta's obvious lack of sexual experience. He made heated love to her as the setting summer sun bathed their naked entwined bodies in its blood-red afterglow.

Cole thrilled and shocked the unskilled Marietta with his intensely intimate lovemaking. She felt incredible joy engulfing her and thought she would surely faint. He kissed her and kept on kissing her throughout the fiercely passionate lovemaking.

She was divinely aware of his tongue and his tumescence probing together in sensual stimulating rhythm. She loved it. Loved the way his tongue filled her mouth while his throbbing length filled her body.

Marietta learned quickly, moving with him, bucking against him, taking him completely, squeezing him, loving him. And all the while she felt as if he was a magnificent instrument for giving pleasure, one which the gods of love had fashioned solely for her.

Cole sank all the way into her, pulled almost out, then thrust into her again. He was, Marietta mused, like mighty waves on an ocean. She found his pounding rhythm and rolled with him, surging against him, drawing him to her, holding him as if she would never let him go.

Until all at once the pleasure became so intense Marietta felt as if her female body was bursting into fire and that only the liquid that would come from his powerful male body could save her from total incineration.

"Cole, Cole, Cole!" she sobbed. "I'm burning up. I'm on fire! Save me, save me!"

"I will, sweetheart," he assured and speeded his movements.

Seconds later Marietta cried out in her wild, shuddering climax. Cole groaned and joined her in paradise, the hot, thick liquid of his release pouring into her and overflowing. Saving her, cooling her, extinguishing the raging fire.

For a long time after the last little aftershocks of the orgasm had passed, the pair continued to lie there in each other's arms, reluctant to move, to let the other go. So they lay there as the last pink gloaming of light washed over them and the gentle wind through the pines and weeping willows cooled their naked bodies.

When Cole finally rolled onto his back and drew her close against his side, Marietta raised onto an elbow, looked at his face and thought he was surely the handsomest man she had ever met.

And, oh what a fantastic lover!

Sated, breathless, Marietta smiled and sighed contentedly, supposing that Cole Heflin was now deeply in love with her. He couldn't have loved her the way he had if he was not absolutely mad about her. Which was no surprise. After all, every beau she'd ever had had fallen in love with her after only one kiss.

Surely a man who had done the things Cole did to her was in love with her. And a man in love would want to give her anything she wanted. And what she wanted was to return to Central City and her singing career.

For all her wily charms, Marietta knew little about the true nature of men. She couldn't have been more wrong about Cole. And all too soon she learned the ghastly truth.

Smiling dreamily, Marietta was drawing small circles on his chest with her forefinger when abruptly Cole caught her hand and made her stop. He sat up. She sat up beside him. He turned and looked at her, then shook his head.

"I'm sorry that happened, Marietta. I shouldn't have touched you. But you finally pushed me over the brink." She was staring at him, round-eyed, lips parted. He continued, "Still, it was my fault and I accept full responsibility. I'm sorry, truly I am."

Disbelieving, she said, "You mean you're not... you aren't in love with me?"

"Good God, no. What ever made you think that?"

Horrified, Marietta covered her bare breasts with her hands. "But you...you just made passionate love to me and I thought...I...oh, you vile bastard, how could you?''

"How could I?" he replied. "How could you? Correct me if I'm wrong, but wasn't it you who lured me out here where you were waiting bare-breasted to seduce me?''

Reaching frantically for her discarded clothes, hot tears now stinging her eyes, Marietta said, "I was not...I never...you are the one who took off my...my—" she was sobbing now "—I just...I...oh, I despise you, Cole Heflin, don't you ever touch me again!"

Unmoved by her crocodile tears, Cole shrugged wide shoulders and said sarcastically, "As you wish, Your Majesty."

Twenty-One

Lightnin' debated returning to Central City. After his failed run-in with Marietta and the Texan, he had laid up in Denver for several days, recuperating.

Lightnin's idea of convalescing was eating thick steaks and drinking whiskey and visiting the sporting ladies along Holladay Street. If he could have had his way, he would just have stayed right there and enjoyed himself for the rest of his life.

Finally, he decided that he would have to go back to Central City. The prospect was less than pleasant, but he was out of money and had nowhere else to go. Might as well get it over with. Face the music. Hope for the best. Maybe the middle-aged man was over the snooty red-haired singer by now and would forgive him for not bringing her back.

The very next day Lightnin' rode back into Central City. The word of his return quickly spread and curious townsfolk gathered, wondering if he had found Marietta. They didn't dare ask. They knew better than to question Lightnin' for he had a reputation of being disagreeable and dangerous. They would have to wait and wonder.

Lightnin', looking neither left nor right, rode up Eureka Street and directly to the Tivoli Opera House. He assumed that Maltese would be exactly where he had left him. Sleeping in Marietta's bed. Hugging her shoes. Waiting for her return.

Lightnin' dismounted in the alley outside the stage door. He ground-tethered his mount, removed his hat and raised a hand, knocking loudly. No answer. Minutes passed. He knocked again.

At last the door opened a crack and Maltese himself, looking frail and haggard and wearing a gray silk dressing robe, stood peering at him from red-rimmed eyes.

"Lightnin'!" Maltese finally exclaimed, and threw the door open wide. "Oh, thank God. Thank God. You've found her! You've found my darling—"

"No, Maltese," Lightnin' said. "I haven't." He urged the older man back inside and followed. "I searched night and day, but I found no sign of Marietta. Absolutely nothing." He wasn't about to admit that he had indeed found the Texan and Maltese's flame-haired spitfire and that she had not wanted to come back with him. Had, in fact, almost killed him, damn her to hell.

"No sign of her," Maltese repeated, shaking his silver head. "Lightnin', you...you promised me. You told me you'd bring her back. Where is she? I want her! I want my darling Marietta!"

"I tried, I did everything I could think of," Lightnin' said. "I alerted the authorities in Denver. They helped with the search. Put several of their best men on the job. But she's gone, Maltese. She's gone. It's been too long, the trail is cold. No telling where they are by now.''

"Texas!" Maltese snapped his fingers and raised his voice. "You said yourself that a Texan took her."

"I did, but—"

"Well, there you have it! They're in Texas and you will turn right around and go after—"

"Maltese, be reasonable. Texas is a huge place. I'd have no idea where to begin looking. Besides, just because her abductor is a Texan doesn't mean he took her to Texas."

Maltese thought it over and his shoulders sagged. "No, of course not. They could be anywhere," he admitted sadly. He was silent for a moment, then said, "So you didn't talk to anybody who had seen them? They left no clues along the way, no cold campfires or articles of clothing or…anything? They just vanished into thin air?" Maltese slowly raised his hands and covered his face as tears filled his eyes. He began to weep and his slight body shook with his sobs.

Lightnin' gritted his teeth in annoyance, but reached out and laid a comforting hand on Maltese's trembling shoulder. "I'm sorry I failed you, Maltese. I guess you mean to fire me for this."

Maltese lowered his hands. He looked up at Lightnin' through tear-filled eyes. He coughed, drew a white silk handkerchief from the breast pocket of his dressing gown and wiped his tear-stained cheeks.

He said pitifully, "You didn't see her? No one saw her?"

"No one," said Lightnin'. "I'll be going now and—"

"No," said Maltese, turning. "Come on up and have a drink with me. I'm all alone. When my sweet Marietta disappeared, I shut down the opera house. I paid off all the players and sent them back East. All but Marietta's voice coach, Sophia. She wouldn't go. Said she was going to stay in Central City until we heard from Marietta. You'll have to go over to Sophia's house and tell her that Marietta won't be coming back."

Maltese turned and wearily began climbing the stairs to what was once Marietta's private quarters. Behind him, Lightnin' smiled to himself. Looks as though he was going to keep his job and all the benefits that went with it. He had done the right thing in coming back.

And he had damn sure done the right thing in keeping quiet about his encounter with the Texan and the singer. Lightnin' lifted a hand, rubbed the knot on the back of his head and scowled. He was glad Marietta was gone and out of his hair. Good riddance to the haughty, no-talent bitch. She had never liked him and the feeling had been mutual.

Hell, he pitied the fool Texan who took her. Eight to five said the unsuspecting bastard was sorry he had ever laid eyes on her.

* * *

"Do you suppose I'll ever really lay eyes on her?"

"Why, sure you will."

"I don't know, Nettie," the weak, bed-fast Maxwell Lacey said to his trusted housekeeper, a stout, graying widow who had been with him for more than twenty years. "I keep hoping she'll come walking in here…" His words trailed away, but his arthritic hand remained outstretched toward the open bedroom door.

Nettie took hold of that hand in both of her own and gently placed it back on the bed. Then she made a big fuss of straightening his bedcovers and plumping up his pillows while she talked about the happy day when his only granddaughter would arrive in Galveston and come straight here to the seaside mansion and to her grandfather.

"…and we'll have a feast fit for a king. Or queen, shall I say. I'll send Nelson down into the wine cellar with instructions to bring up the most expensive bottle of…of…"

"Dom Pérignon champagne," Maxwell Lacey prompted.

"Yes, the Dom Perigon champagne," Nettie confirmed. Each night their dialogue was basically the same, but he never tired of it. Planning his granddaughter's homecoming made him happy as nothing else could, made him determined to live until she arrived.

"We'll toast Marietta with the chilled champagne," Nettie continued, "and then we'll do like they do in those European countries where they all throw their stemmed crystal glasses into the fireplace after downing the bubbly.''

Maxwell Lacey chuckled happily. This was his favorite part. "Yes, we'll break the fine crystal! She will like that! We'll have great fun."

"Great fun," said Nettie, and Maxwell's sick eyes sparkled as Nettie proceeded, discussing, as if for the first time, the dinner menu for Marietta's first meal at the mansion. "I think we'll start with fresh gulf shrimp, boiled to just the right degree of perfection and we'll have the cook's special red sauce on the side." She rubbed her chin as if pondering, then said, "After the shrimp appetizer, we'll serve thick juicy steaks for the entrée." She paused then, waiting for Maxwell to declare, as he always did, that the fine beef would come from the Lacey coastal ranch southwest of the city.

"Yes, steaks! Big, thick steaks," Maxwell said, eyes twinkling now. "And the beef will come from the ranch—we'll slaughter one of our choice Herefords. The biggest, fattest one in the herd."

"Absolutely," Nettie said, nodding. "And with the steaks we will have roasted potatoes and string beans and corn on the cob and fried okra and glazed carrots and...and—"

"Don't forget the salads, Nettie. Ladies like salads, don't they?"

"They do. We'll fix a nice large salad with big ripe tomatoes and crisp lettuce for Marietta."

"Have you thought about the dessert?" he asked.

Nettie smiled indulgently. Then recited her lines, as she did each evening. "Mmm, I don't know. How about hot fresh peach cobbler?"

"No, no, you've forgotten," Maxwell objected. "Strawberries and thick whipping cream. Her mother loved strawberries and cream and I imagine she does too."

"Strawberries and cream it is," said Nettie, shaking her head.

The two continued to talk and plan for the homecoming as the midnight hour approached and silence settled over the big house and city. Nettie was tired, but she stayed at Maxwell's bedside. She would not leave until he fell asleep. Then, and only then, would she send in the night nurse to sit with him.

For the past couple of weeks, he had had difficulty sleeping, so Nettie kept him company. She didn't want him to lie here to brood and worry and wonder if he would live to see his only granddaughter.

She didn't think he would make it. Neither did his doctor. Maxwell Lacey was a very sick man. The disease that would kill him was progressing rapidly and he grew a bit weaker with each passing day. He told Nettie that he didn't mind dying, but he had to stay alive long enough to see his granddaughter. To make things right. Then—and only then—could he rest in peace.

Nettie assured him that he would live long enough for the reunion and then some. Why, any day now

Marietta would arrive and they would all celebrate and have a wonderful time.

"Nettie," Maxwell interrupted her now as she continued to go over the plans they both knew by heart, "if I make it, if I live to see Marietta, do you think she'll…?"

"Yes, of course she will," said Nettie. "Now it's time for you to try to get some sleep, Maxwell. I'm going to turn down the lamp real low. But I won't leave. I'll sit here with you, and let's both be quiet and still."

"I'm not sleepy," he feebly protested.

"You will be," she said. Nettie went to the window and raised it higher so the slight ocean breeze could cool the room.

Maxwell Lacey closed his eyes. "Nettie?"

"Yes, Maxwell?"

"Do you suppose she's pretty? As pretty as… as…?"

The sentence was never finished. Maxwell Lacey, mercifully, had fallen asleep.

Twenty-Two

For three days, Marietta hadn't spoken to Cole.

Not since he had so callously informed her that he was not in love with her.

She still found it impossible to believe that a man could make love to a woman the way he had made love to her and not be in love with her. Not love her, at least a little. But, sadly, it was true.

Cole had not minced words, had not considered her tender feelings. He had been oblivious to the pain and shame he had caused her. Marietta had never known a man as cold and insensitive as Cole Heflin.

She despised him.

Would hate him until she drew her last breath.

She stubbornly refused to look at him or to talk to him. And she did not answer when he spoke to her. She planned never to speak to him again. Nor would she, no matter how often he asked, *ever* sing to him again. Let the hard-hearted bastard suffer the way she was suffering.

Marietta would have been even more hurt and furious had she known that Cole didn't mind her refusal to talk. He found the silence peaceful. And he sure didn't miss hearing her sing. He hadn't had a headache in days.

He did suffer a small degree of guilt for making love to her. But not because of any misunderstandings on her part. She understood all right. She didn't fool him. He had known dozens of women like her. Maybe not quite as pretty, but just as devious.

No doubt the winsome Marietta had dazzled and conquered her share of vulnerable men. The last of which was rich old Maltese, whose bed she had shared every night.

Cole knew her kind all too well. No shy, retiring violet was Marietta. No innocent maiden deserving of gentlemanly respect. More of a dangerous Delilah to be carefully avoided.

A man would be an utter fool to care about her.

Cole shifted in the saddle and looked toward the southeastern horizon. It was midmorning. They had made good time since finally leaving the towering mountains behind and heading out across the plains. They were near that narrow strip between Colorado and Texas called No Man's Land.

Tonight they would camp on the Cimmaron River, then tomorrow ride across No Man's Land and down into the high panhandle plains of Texas.

Cole squinted, rubbed his chin and did some figuring. He calculated how many miles it was from here to Tascosa, Texas. A long way, but with any luck they could be at the Longley spread in three days, maybe less.

Cole smiled at the prospect of riding up to the little clapboard house and surprising the two Longley women. He consciously touched his worn saddlebags where the all-important bank-deposit slip was safely kept. Finally, he would be able to keep the promise he had made to Keller Longley all those years ago.

Cole's smile quickly fled and a muscle clenched in his jaw. He hoped the Longleys were all right, both of them. He was worried about them. Mrs. Longley was in poor health, had been for the past couple of years. She was too sick and frail to help out much, so all the hard work fell on Leslie. Cole's eyes clouded at the thought of the pretty little girl having the weight of the world on her slender shoulders.

Leslie Longley's slender shoulders sagged with exhaustion. She was in the garden near the banks of the river a hundred yards from the house. The modest house where she lived with her mother on their little plot of land six miles north of Tascosa.

Leslie's face was shaded with a broad-brimmed sunbonnet, but her cheeks were red and shiny with perspiration. Her hands were protected with rough gloves and the sleeves of her dress were long, buttoning at the wrists. The skirts of her cotton dress dragged the ground.

Leslie protected herself as best she could from the broiling Texas sun. But she was hot. And she was tired. It was midafternoon, the hottest part of the day. She longed for the cool shade of the front porch, but she was not finished with her task.

A long-handled hoe in her gloved hands, Leslie was chopping the weeds that sprang up and grew no matter how hot or dry the weather. If she didn't keep the weeds cut, they would choke off her prized tomato vines where the plump tomatoes were starting to turn red. By next week, they would be ready for picking.

Beyond the tomato vines were row upon row of yellow squash, sticky green okra, tender shallot onions, black-eyed peas, string beans, green beans, new potatoes and cantaloupes.

Leslie paused and gazed out over the large garden she had planted in early spring. She was pleased with the fruits of her labor and planned, the first part of next week, to gather the ripe vegetables, hitch up Blaze to the old buggy and take the produce into town to sell.

She hoped, prayed, that by selling the baskets of vegetables on the town square, she would get enough money to make at least a token payment on the bank loan they owed.

Leslie frowned and sighed wearily. She was only eighteen, but she worried night and day about the outstanding debt that she and her mother owed to the Tascosa State Bank. A note secured with the deed to their property. She lived in dread that they would be unable to pay off the note and the lurking Reconstruction carpetbagger bank and its president would take possession of their home.

Her dear brother was dead at their hands. She must keep the homestead.

Leslie's eyebrows knit.

The only thing they had of value—save their property—was Blaze, her aging bay mare. It had been old Blaze who had dutifully pulled the rusty plow when she'd planted the garden. She had hated to make the gentle mare pull a plow, but there'd been no choice. The mule, Daisy, had finally dropped dead of old age last winter. So she and Blaze had plowed the garden. And she and Blaze would go into town to sell the bounty.

Leslie went back to her hoeing. She had to keep working, to keep weeding her garden. She would do whatever she had to do, work as hard as she had to work. She would not allow her dear, sick mother to be thrown out of her home.

Leslie reached the end of the row. She stopped, turned and put a hand to her aching back. She leaned an arm on the hoe handle and rested for a minute. She plucked the edge of her unbuttoned bodice out and blew down inside, attempting to cool herself. Then she took off her sunbonnet and began to fan her shiny face.

She stopped abruptly.

She heard something.

Leslie turned her head, stood totally still and listened alertly. A chill instantly skipped up her spine.

The Comanches were always a threat. Their stronghold in the Palo Duro Canyon was close, too close.

She and her mother had no one to protect them. She lived in fear that a band of renegades would ride onto their property, burn the house and steal Blaze.

Leslie exhaled with relief when she spotted a horse and buggy coming up the dirt road. She lifted a hand, shaded her eyes and studied the approaching buggy.

Then stiffened, made a face and nervously bit the inside of her bottom lip.

She recognized the rig and the driver. The president of the Tascosa State Bank. A carpetbagger straight from Cincinnati, Ohio, one of Grant's worst. The repugnant Thomas McLeish. She couldn't believe that he had driven all the way out here to collect the late payment on their bank loan.

Leslie swallowed hard. She took off her work gloves and anxiously buttoned up her undone bodice. Then she smoothed her blond hair. And she began to silently recite what she would say to the bank president, how she would ask that he give her just one more week to make a payment on the loan.

Leslie drew a deep breath, then made herself raise a hand and wave as if she was glad to see him. She bent and laid the hoe, her bonnet and gloves on the ground, intending to return to her work as soon as he left.

By the time Leslie reached the yard, the short, stocky Thomas McLeish had rolled to a stop before the little house and was climbing down out of the buggy. Leslie regarded him and felt her stomach do a turn.

Thomas McLeish, a married man with grown children, always looked at her in a way that made her uneasy. Each time he saw her he licked fleshy lips and his pale eyes gleamed demonically. She got the impression that when he looked her up and down as he often did, his thoughts were improper. She didn't like having to see him on her visits to the bank. She sure didn't want him anywhere near her home.

"Mr. McLeish," Leslie finally called a greeting to him. "What brings you all the way out here on such a hot summer day?"

The rotund president smiled, bowed and said, "Come now, I think you know why I'm here, Miss Longley."

"Well, yes, I do," she said. Then hurried to add, "Believe it or not, I was planning to ride into Tascosa early next week."

"Really?" he said, reached out and took hold of her elbow. "Then it appears I have saved you a trip."

Leslie pulled her arm free. "And I could have saved you a trip had I known you were coming. You see, I don't have the money right now, Mr. McLeish."

The corpulent bank president continued to smile, then licked his lips and looked at her in the manner that made her flesh crawl.

He said, "Why don't you invite me inside where we can talk about your little dilemma."

"There's nothing to discuss," she stated emphatically. "Monday I'm going into town to sell my vegetables. Whatever they bring, I'll give to you." She crossed her arms over her chest. "I have nothing for you today."

"Where's your mother?" he asked, lifting a pudgy hand to stroke his bushy gray mustache.

"She's inside, lying down. She's not well."

"Then let's not disturb her," said McLeish. He grinned and his eyes twinkled anew when he said, "Take a little buggy ride with me, Miss Leslie."

Leslie made a face. "No, thank you," she said. "I'm quite busy weeding my garden, Mr. McLeish, so if you'll kindly excuse me…"

"I will not excuse you," he said and again he took her arm. "I have excused you long enough, my dear. A payment on your loan was due over a week ago. But I excused the lateness because I am fond of you." Leslie didn't answer, just hugged herself defensively. He asked, "Do you want to keep this house, this land?"

"Yes, of course," she replied. "I told you, I plan on paying next week."

"Next week will be too late, I'm afraid," he said, shaking his balding gray head. "That's why I drove all the way out here today. I have been lenient with you, Miss Leslie. But now you must pay up."

"What with?" she said, her forehead creased, her arms coming unfolded, hands balling into fists at her sides. "I have no money. No assets. Nothing to pay you with."

Thomas McLeish licked his fleshy lips in that irritating way, smiled as if he had some wicked secret, leaned close and whispered, "Ah, but you do, my dear child."

Leslie, an innocent, was puzzled. "I do? What? What do I have that you could possibly want?"

"A little kiss for starters," said the smiling McLeish, his pale eyes flashing. "Take a ride with me." Before she could object, he continued, "A short ride in my buggy, that's all I ask. Nothing that would really compromise you, Miss Leslie. A few kisses. Who is to ever know?"

"Mr. McLeish!"

"You misunderstand, my dear. I'm not asking you to behave immorally. Just allow me to kiss you and perhaps touch your—"

"Get off my property!" Leslie commanded, her face afire.

"*Your* property?" he mocked. "I am not leaving here empty-handed, Miss Leslie. It's up to you. Either pay me what you owe or get into that buggy."

"I will not!" she said, horrified, and began backing away.

"No? You refuse me a few harmless kisses? Well, fine. But I'm not going back to town without taking something. You still have that old bay mare?"

"You wouldn't!" she said, her heart pounding. "Please don't take my mare. She's all I have. Without

Blaze I'd have no way to get into town. For heaven's sake, be reasonable, Mr. McLeish.''

''You're the one who's being unreasonable, Miss Leslie. I don't want your aging mare,'' he said. ''All I want is a few kisses.'' Again he reached out, took hold of her arms, tried to draw her to him. ''Please, please kiss me,'' he begged, puckering.

''Get your dirty hands off me!'' Leslie shouted and forcefully pushed him away. ''Get out of my sight, you disgusting animal! Go before I get the shotgun!''

''You, miss, are making a big mistake,'' he warned angrily. ''You're so high-and-mighty you won't allow me to touch you. Very well, I shall take the mare as your overdue payment.''

With that, he turned on his heel, circled the yard, walked out back to the barn and came out leading the loudly whinnying Blaze. Her hands to her mouth, a stricken Leslie watched as the bank president tethered her beloved mare to the back of his buggy. There was nothing she could do to stop him.

Leslie stood in the dusty road and watched helplessly as McLeish drove away with the bewildered, neighing Blaze tied to the rear of his buggy.

When they had finally gone out of sight, a beaten Leslie Longley sank slowly down onto her knees in the road, put her hands to her face and cried.

Twenty-Three

Marietta tried hard to hate the cold, uncaring Cole Heflin. She was not totally successful. While she swore to herself that she despised him, she nonetheless found it impossible to forget what it was like to be held and loved by him. She had never dreamed that such splendor was possible, had had no idea that there was a man who could make her his willing wanton.

As they silently rode knee to knee across the flat, monotonous southeastern plains of Colorado, Marietta was aware that the lovemaking had meant nothing to Cole, while it had meant everything to her. His touch, his kiss had stirred in her a fiery passion that had shocked and surprised her.

She flushed when she recalled how she had cried out in orgasmic ecstasy. And now, each time she looked at Cole, she inwardly shivered, recalling all the wonderfully forbidden things he had done to her, the way he had made her feel when she was naked in his arms.

She wondered, sadly, if she would ever in her lifetime feel that way again. She knew the answer. She would not. It was only in his arms, and his alone, that she would experience such incredible bliss.

And she would never be in his arms again.

Her heart aching, Marietta glanced covertly at Cole from beneath lowered lashes. He slouched in his saddle in an attitude of lazy indifference. Eyes squinted, hat brim pulled low, he looked straight ahead, not at her. Never at her. He didn't want to look at her when it was all she could do to keep her eyes off him.

Cole was unaware that Marietta was secretly examining him. She was on his mind, but his thoughts were quite different from hers. For him the hot love-making had been enjoyable but nothing more. The knowing, naughty Marietta had teased and tempted him until he had finally taken her. Simple as that. She was willing. She was convenient. He was aroused.

A mindless roll in the hay with a beautiful, brazen young woman who, in all likelihood, had had more than her share of rolls in the hay.

At that unpleasant thought, Cole's forehead knit and his jaw tightened. Since he'd made love to her, something had nagged at him, worried him, had stayed in the back of his mind. When he had taken her, there had been a fleeting second when—just as he had entered her—he could have sworn she was a virgin. She had been so incredibly tight and small and…oh, for Pete sake, who the hell was he trying to kid.

Marietta was no virgin. Hadn't been for years. She used her luscious body as a bargaining chip. Old metals millionaire Maltese was but the latest in a long line of lovers she had favored with her charms in return for something she wanted.

Now she wanted something from him, that's why she had seduced him. She wanted him to let her go so she could run back to Central City and her singing career.

Cole knew enough about women to suppose that Marietta, despite her protestations to the contrary, would likely come into his arms again if he wanted her, reached out to her. She had, he could tell, enjoyed the lovemaking more than she had expected.

The prospect of making love to her again was tempting, no denying it.

But he would resist.

He wished to hell he had never touched her in the first place and he vowed to himself that he wouldn't touch her again.

For two reasons.

One, he felt bad about making love to Maxwell Lacey's granddaughter.

The second, more important reason was that he was half-afraid. Afraid of her. Afraid of himself. Afraid that if she were to lie in his arms again, she might take more than his body. He was, he realized, in danger of foolishly falling in love with this beautiful, selfish woman who he was sure used men then tossed them aside when they were no longer needed.

He wouldn't let that happen.

He wouldn't let her get her claws into him.

Cole abruptly turned his head and looked at Marietta. She was staring straight ahead, not at him. Hungrily he gazed at her, recalling the faint intoxicating perfume of her hair and the pale perfection of her bare, warm body pressed against his own.

Cole felt his heart squeeze in his chest. God, how could a woman make love the way she had when it meant nothing to her.

Cole turned his attention back on the trail ahead. To hell with her. It was a world full of women with perfumed hair and pale bodies. She was no different than the others. Soon as he had delivered her to her grandfather, he would go right out and find himself one just as desirable as Marietta.

In Central City, an unhappy Maltese had given up on Marietta ever returning. If Lightnin' couldn't bring her back, nobody could. His precious darling was gone forever and his life was now meaningless. All his great wealth and power meant nothing to him.

Not without Marietta.

After losing count of the long, lonely days without her, Maltese finally forced himself to leave Marietta's silent, empty quarters. Despondent, he dressed and went out to dine alone one hot noontime.

He chose his favorite restaurant—Marietta's favorite—the Castle Top. But the fine meal served on fragile china and sparkling crystal was tasteless to him. He hardly touched his food nor tasted the fine red wine. Maltese sighed, pushed the plate away, left the restaurant and strolled aimlessly down Eureka Street.

Soon he stopped short.

He blinked and anxiously lifted a hand to shade his eyes against the blinding summer sunlight.

A few yards ahead stood a tall, well-groomed and attractive woman. Her pale-blond hair was glittering with golden highlights and her slender frame was handsomely garbed in a tight-bodiced dress of yellow organza.

She was gazing fixedly into a shop's glass window. Maltese stared for a long moment, his heartbeat beginning to quicken, his fingertips to tingle. His eyes aglitter, he lifted his hands and straightened his gray silk cravat, brushed imaginary lint from the lapels of his custom-cut frock coat then ran his fingers through the thick wings of his long-neglected silver hair.

Maltese cautiously approached the young woman. He reached her and saw that she was admiring a pair of kid-leather slippers attractively displayed in the glass shop window.

Maltese could hardly contain his rising excitement. Afraid she might bolt and run, he waited a long moment, allowing her time to become aware of his presence.

At last he said, ''The shoes are quite lovely, aren't they?''

''Yes,'' the young woman replied, never taking her eyes off the leather slippers, ''but much too expensive.''

"Allow me to purchase them for you," said Maltese, then held his breath.

The young woman turned to look at him. She was beautiful. She favored him with a dimpling smile and said, "You'd do that? You'd buy the shoes for me when you don't even know me?"

"I would," he said. "I'll buy you the shoes. I'll buy you all the shoes you want, my dear child. Would you like that?"

"I would, sir," she said in a soft, honeyed voice. "Of course I would."

Maltese took the young lady's arm. "Let's go inside, shall we?"

Twenty-Four

"You hear something?"

"No."

"You sure?" Cole asked and drew rein.

"I said no," Marietta replied sarcastically and rode on.

"Sorry I bothered you," Cole said and again put the black into motion.

"So am I."

The curt exchange was the first time Marietta and Cole had spoken in hours. Nonetheless they were intensely aware of each other. The physical attraction between them had become nothing short of palpable.

In silent mutual agreement, when nighttime came, they no longer slept side by side. Each took a blanket and spread it safely apart from the other. They usually ended up directly across the dying campfire from one another.

There were, however, those unavoidable occasions when they accidentally bumped into each other. When that happened, both profusely apologized and backed away as if they had come in contact with a hot stove.

The mere brushing of their tense bodies caused

each to shudder with unspent desire. They were of the same mind.

Neither wanted to make love to the other again.

Both were dying to make love to the other again.

They said very little to each other, but Cole had casually informed Marietta earlier that, at last, they had left Colorado behind. Had crossed the narrow strip bordering the top of Texas known as No Man's Land. They were finally riding down into the northernmost part of the Lone Star State, that three-thousand-foot-high tableland called the Texas Panhandle.

It was a desolate, windswept, lonely land of dry ravines, shallow canyons, deep arroyos and precious few trees. Scattered cedars and junipers and mesquite dotted the prairie, and the occasional stand of cottonwoods and willows wherever there was a little water.

In this lonely land the sky was a huge blue dome and the earth as flat as a floor, stretching endlessly in every direction. Marietta felt it was as if they were the only two people on earth.

But Cole knew better.

On this sweltering-hot July afternoon, as the sun was westering, the pair rode southward in strained silence. Marietta was awed by the barren grandeur surrounding them and she idly wondered how many people had crossed these vast high plains of Texas. And, she wondered, had anyone actually settled there?

She noted that Cole was more alert than usual, although slouched comfortably in the saddle.

His squinted gaze was carefully scanning the trail before them. Periodically he turned to look over his shoulder at the trail behind them. It was as if he was expecting trouble.

Cole sat up straighter in the saddle when he spotted a small cloud of dust on the southern horizon. His heartbeat accelerated, then slowed as two riders approached at a gallop.

He looked at Marietta and said calmly, "I told you I heard something. We have company, but there's no cause for alarm. Likely just a couple of buffalo hunters. You go along with anything I say or do, you understand?"

Marietta nodded. "I understand."

Marietta tensed when she noticed Cole's right hand move down to rest on the butt of his Colt .45. The riders neared and Cole saw that he had guessed correctly; they smelled of buffalo. One was leading a couple of remounts weighed down with untanned hides.

The hunters came to a stop a few feet away and the younger of the pair, a big, bearded fellow with a mouthful of broken, blackened teeth, said, "Folks, I'm Jesse Vance and this here's my pa, Nate Vance."

"Nate. Jesse," Cole acknowledged, "Cole Heflin. The lady is Marietta."

Marietta nodded.

Jesse rubbed his bearded chin and grinned, showing all his rotted teeth as he stared hungrily at Marietta.

He said, "Me and Pa was 'a fixin' to bed down for the night. It's mighty lonely out here on the prairie. What say we camp together? We got some fresh buffalo meat for supper."

Cole knew the best way to handle the hunters was to befriend them. Or pretend to. If he showed any reluctance to accept their hospitality, he would have a fight on his hands. A fight that he would lose and Marietta would be at their mercy.

Marietta was surprised and incensed when Cole smiled and said, "Sounds like a good idea to me, Jesse."

Marietta didn't like the looks of the two big, unkempt men and couldn't understand why Cole would agree to camping with them. But she held her tongue, stayed close to Cole.

Soon the men had gathered mesquite kindling and had a fire going. They began roasting buffalo steaks on a spit and telling tall tales as full darkness enveloped the high plains. When Jesse broke out a bottle of whiskey, Cole drank and laughed with the two rough-looking customers.

As soon as the meal was finished, Marietta rose, took her blanket and walked away from the crackling fire and the laughing men. She lay in silence beneath the stars, angry with Cole for allowing these two dangerous-looking characters to spend the night with them.

She listened as the men talked and laughed loudly and soon she heard the young one, Jesse, say, "Cole, you're our friend, now, ain't you?"

Cole replied levelly, "Friends to the end, Jesse."

"Well, what'd you allow if I was to tell you I'm kinda taken with that pretty, red-haired gal with you."

Cole laughed easily. Then said, "I'm pretty taken with her myself."

Jesse took another swig from the bottle, wiped his mouth on his dirty shirtsleeve and said, "Well, now, friend, looks like you have her all the time. How about if I have her jest for the night?"

Marietta's blood ran cold and she stiffened with fear. Not daring to breathe, she waited for Cole's reply.

Cole chuckled, slapped Jesse on the back and said, "Jesse, that little gal's my wife."

"Does that mean I can't have her?" asked Jesse.

Before Cole could reply, the older, quieter Nate spoke up. "Damn it all, boy, didn't your ma and me teach you no better than that? You can't jest take a man's wife with him right there. It ain't neighborly."

"Your pa's right, Jesse. If she wasn't my wife, why, I'd say go ahead."

Jesse tried another tack. "If'n I give you all them hides we got, could I have her for an hour?"

"No, Jesse." Cole kept his voice low, level. "I love my wife. She's a good, virtuous woman." He paused, then added, "I'd kill any man who tried to touch her. Is that clear?"

"It's clear, Cole," said Nate. Turning to his son, he said, "Ain't it, Jesse?"

Jesse nodded, then sighed with disappointment.

Cole yawned, rose to his feet and said, "We've got a long ride ahead of us tomorrow, so I'll be turning in now."

"'Night, Cole," said Nate.

Cole took his blanket and walked directly to where Marietta lay. His back to the two buffalo hunters, he stood just above her, put his forefinger perpendicular to his lips, warning her to keep silent.

He then sank to his knees, turned around and stretched out next to her. Marietta lifted her head to give him a questioning look. Cole cautioned her with his eyes and put a supportive arm beneath her head. He never said a word, but he wrapped his arm around her and drew her into his embrace.

Marietta didn't fight it. Afraid of the buffalo hunters, she snuggled close and draped an arm across Cole's chest. He felt her trembling and drew her closer still, his intent to comfort and reassure. His arms tightened around her when the chilling exchange between the drunken buffalo hunters carried on the still night air.

Jesse said, "Pa, I'm gonna go on over there and take that red-haired gal for myself."

"No you're not, you damn fool," said the older man. "Don't you know who that fella is?"

"I don't care who he is, I want that pretty woman." Jesse started to rise.

His pa grabbed his arm, pulled him back down. "Jesse, that there's the man who burned Hadleyville back in the war. I seen the wanted poster in Tascosa last spring, offering a reward for his capture. Hellfire, he's as mean as they make 'em."

"Damnation!" Jesse swore, but sank back down and lifted the whiskey bottle to his lips.

Cole grinned and relaxed.

Marietta put her lips close to Cole's ear and admitted, "I'm afraid, Cole."

He whispered, "Don't be, baby. I've got you, I won't let anybody hurt you."

She believed him, but still she couldn't go to sleep. She lay awake long after the rowdy buffalo hunters were snoring loudly, no longer posing a threat.

It was not fear that kept her awake. It was Cole. What he'd said to the hunters kept ringing in her ears and causing her heart to flutter, "That little gal's my wife. I love my wife." The way he had said it, the inflection in his tone—it was almost as if he had meant it.

All at once Marietta was too keenly aware of being in Cole's strong arms. Her head on his shoulder, she could feel the slow, steady beating of his heart beneath her ear. Her hand—she wasn't sure when—had moved down from his chest. It now rested on his abdomen just above the waistband of his trousers.

She was certain he was asleep. And so, of their own volition, her fingers slipped into his shirt—between the buttons—and touched his warm, smooth flesh.

She was glad he was dead to the world and unaware of her forward action. After a guilty moment wherein she allowed her fingertips to lightly stroke the crisp line of raven hair going down his flat belly, Marietta slowly, cautiously raised her head to look at Cole's sleeping face.

Her hand stilled.

Her heart raced.

He was wide awake and staring at her, his eyes flashing in the darkness. It was a moment she would never forget. His glittering gaze holding hers, he reached down and deftly unbuttoned his shirt. He pushed the open shirt apart and drew her hand up to the sculpted band of muscle covering his heavily beating heart.

They stared at each other as Marietta raked her nails through the dense hair, then trailed her fingertips down the very center of his chest and belly until she reached the waistband of his trousers.

She wasn't sure, but she thought he smiled before he drew her head back down onto his shoulder and covered her hand with his own. She held her breath when he gently urged her open hand just down inside his trousers. She shivered as her tingling fingertips came in contact with the tip of his hot, hard erection.

She desperately wanted to touch him, stroke him, release him. Instead, she anxiously withdrew her hand, abruptly coming to her senses, appalled by her own bold behavior.

And then she wanted to smack Cole's smug face

when she heard him chuckle softly and felt his lean body shake with laughter. She huffed with indignation and turned over onto her side away from him.

Then Marietta gritted her teeth when he turned with her, drew her back against him, put an arm around her and whispered, "Me too, darlin', me too."

Twenty-Five

The next day things were back to normal.

The buffalo hunters were long gone north and the barren plains ahead lay deserted. Marietta and Cole, riding south, were making good time.

Once again they were like polite strangers and their respective guards were up. The closeness of the previous night was behind them and forgotten.

Both intended to keep it that way.

The morning and early afternoon passed uneventfully. Quietly. The two exchanged few words, each engrossed in their own troubled thoughts.

It was now late afternoon, not long until sunset. Boredom and exhaustion had set in; both were half-sleepy, half-sullen.

Then all at once Cole's head snapped up, he frowned, drew rein and brought the black to a swift halt. Marietta rode on a few yards, finally pulled up and turned the piebald mare around.

"What is it?" she asked irritably. "Why are you stopping here in the middle of nowhere?"

"Quiet," Cole ordered, a hand raised to silence her.

Marietta made a face when he swung down out of the saddle and turned slowly in every direction, listening intently. She shook her head and rolled her eyes heavenward when he sank to his heels, leaned down and put an ear to the ground.

"Have you lost your mind?" she asked.

Cole gave no reply. Just kept his ear pressed to the ground for several long seconds. When he rose to his feet, Marietta could tell that he was worried.

She automatically tensed and said, "Oh, Lord, don't tell me it's more dirty buffalo hunters."

"No. It's not hunters," he said, climbing back into the saddle. "Ride!" he shouted, kicking the black into motion. "It's Comanches!"

"Comanches?" she called out. "How do you know? I don't see anybody!"

"You soon will!" he shouted, urging the black into long, ground-eating strides.

Cole heard the hoofbeats growing louder, drawing closer. He glanced back over his shoulder—a band of renegade Comanches appeared on a rise behind them. He counted quickly. At least a dozen whooping, painted half-naked young warriors were riding fast across the dusty plains.

Cole turned back, then looked anxiously ahead. Some two hundred yards away was a large, dense thicket of cedars, mesquite and scrub oak.

Cole shouted to Marietta, "Lay your heels to the piebald and head for that stand of trees up ahead on the right."

Marietta nodded. Looking back over her shoulder she saw the fierce-looking braves coming at a fast gallop, lances raised, knees controlling their snorting, blowing mustangs. Terrified, she obeyed Cole's command and they raced headlong toward the safety of the bosque.

Neck and neck they galloped.

Cole called out, "Listen to me and do exactly as I say! See that sharp bend ahead, when we go around it, we'll be out of sight. Once that happens, jump off your mount, run up into the thick trees and hide."

"What about you?" she yelled and looked anxiously at him.

"I'll keep riding," he shouted as he wrapped the reins around the saddle horn, reached down and drew his rifle from the leather scabbard. "The Indians will follow. You'll be safe."

"But what about you?" she asked again, terror-stricken.

"You hide and stay put," he ordered. "I'll find you!"

They continued to ride, full out, drawing ever nearer to the dense forest of scrub oak and cedars. In seconds they were rounding the sharp bend bordering the forest.

"Now!" Cole shouted and Marietta didn't hesitate.

She tumbled off her galloping mount, picked herself up and scurried into the trees, slapping low branches out of her way and running as fast as she could through the knee-high underbrush.

Behind her she heard the report of a rifle and the Comanches' bloodcurdling shouts as they galloped past, racing after Cole. Trembling despite the heat of the day, Marietta ran fast through the woods, tripped and fell, got up and staggered on into the darkness of the thick, impenetrable forest. She continued to run and thrash through the brush and thorny bushes until her weak legs would carry her no farther and her lungs were burning from her labored breaths.

The whooping and shouting and distant rifle fire continued. Marietta imagined the worst. She sank tiredly onto her knees and sat back on her heels. She put a hand on her racing heart and fought for breath, swallowing with difficulty. When finally her heart had stopped pounding and her breath had slowed somewhat, she sat totally still, careful not to move or make a sound.

Frightened and worried, she wondered what was happening to Cole. She licked her dry lips and told herself he could outrun the Comanches. He was smart, he would lose them, ride to safety.

Another rifle report and Marietta jumped as if it was she who had been shot. She sat flat down in the underbrush, pushed a chinaberry limb out of her hair and hugged her arms to her chest. She looked around, but could see nothing. The forest was too thick, too dark with leafy tree limbs entwining overhead and thick underbrush below. How could Cole ever find her? He *would* find her. He said that he would.

Marietta patiently waited, careful not to move or

make a sound, as time dragged slowly by. The sounds beyond the forest grew steadily fainter, came from farther away. Then they stopped altogether. She strained to listen, but could hear nothing.

The sun was almost down. Marietta could tell because it was growing even darker. She trembled and her teeth began to chatter. She had never felt so alone and frightened in her life. What would she do if Cole didn't come for her? Maybe he hadn't been able to outrun the Comanches. Maybe they had caught up with him. Had dragged him down off his horse and killed him. Had slit his throat and left him to die in the dust.

Marietta felt tears sting her eyes.

Day turned to night.

There was a moon, but it didn't penetrate the thickly foliaged forest. It was extremely dark now. Pitch black. So dark you couldn't see your hand before your face. Marietta was terrified. It had been too long. Cole wasn't coming. The Comanches had killed him. He was dead, she knew he was. If he were not, he would have long since found her. Cole was dead and she was alone and the Comanches were looking for her. Wouldn't give up until they found her.

Marietta's fear rose to choke her when she heard the distinctive sound of dead leaves softly crunching. Her head whipped around and she listened, eyes round with fright.

Dear God, the Comanches had found her. She

would be raped and scalped. She sat there, tense and motionless, waiting to meet her fate.

The sound of leaves being crushed underfoot grew steadily closer and Marietta was afraid to move or breathe. Then the leaf-crushing abruptly stopped. The Comanche brave was, she knew, standing directly above her. Marietta braced herself, expecting to feel the blade of a tomahawk slice away her hair. She stiffened and her eyes widened in horror when a hand touched her cheek, then covered her mouth so that she couldn't make a sound.

She was flooded with relief when Cole crouched down, put his lips against her ear and whispered in that distinctive southern drawl, "You're safe now, darlin', but be very quiet."

A grateful Marietta looked up, trying to see his face. She couldn't. It was too dark. He took his hand from her mouth and she felt his protective arm come around her, draw her close. Biting back a sob of relief, she automatically leaned into him. They sat there still and quiet in the darkness for several long moments, neither moving, neither making a sound.

Then, unable to see his face, Marietta sighed when Cole's hand gently captured her chin and tilted it up. She felt his breath on her face. And then his warm, smooth lips covered hers. It began as a sweet, comforting caress, a tender, silent statement to reassure her that she was now safe. But it swiftly escalated into a hot, penetrating kiss of blazing passion.

When their heated lips finally separated, they embraced, holding each other tightly, fiercely. Then they broke apart and began to undress in silent, unspoken agreement. Taking care to be as quiet as possible, they helped each other disrobe, kissing in triumph each time an article of clothing came off.

Cole carefully placed the Colt .45 next to their discarded clothing.

The only way they could be sure that the other was totally undressed was by touch. And they found it highly pleasurable to carefully examine one another with exploring fingers in search of any lingering, unwanted garments.

When they were certain the other was totally naked, they put their arms around each other again, kissed and sank onto their clothing. They couldn't talk to each other, the Comanches were still rampaging nearby.

Couldn't see.

Couldn't talk.

Could only feel. But it was enough. It was plenty. It was exciting. It was erotic.

Her arms around his neck, Marietta silently swooned when she felt Cole gently urge her legs apart. He reached down and cupped her groin with his hand in a gentle yet possessive way that silently seemed to say she belonged to him. And she wanted to shout that she was his and nobody else's.

His hand lightly closing over her, Cole kissed Marietta and she shivered with pleasure when he whispered into her mouth, "Is this mine, sweetheart?" He flexed his fingers slightly. "Can I have it? Can I have you?"

He never allowed her to reply. He kissed her deeply, his tongue seeking hers. In the middle of that invasive kiss, Cole took his hand away and agilely moved atop her. He ended the kiss by playfully biting her lower lip and sucking it into his mouth. He teased it with his tongue, then released it. His lips left hers and his mouth trailed down over her chin and to the hollow of her throat.

Marietta held her breath as he kissed her there. She released her breath as he nibbled and nuzzled his way down over the swell of her breasts. Her back arched when she felt his lips capture a peaking nipple.

She looked down, but could see nothing. So she lay there and luxuriated in the tugging of his lips, the raking of his teeth, the teasing of his tongue.

When he began to suckle the wet, sensitive nipple, Marietta's eyes closed. Then, immediately recalling that they were cocooned in covering darkness, she smiled foolishly and opened them. The thought ran through her mind that she could do anything and everything without embarrassment, since neither could see the other.

Marietta raised a hand, slid her fingers into the thick hair of Cole's moving head. Faintly she could hear the continued shouting and whooping of the frustrated Comanches beyond the thicket. But she again smiled and softly sighed, unworried. Unable to focus on anything save this naked Adonis who was kissing her breast in the darkness.

Lying between Marietta's legs, pressing kisses to her breasts and delicate ribs, Cole knew he could tease her, taste her, kiss her all over, which was what he had wanted to do since the first moment he saw her.

He could do all he desired in the darkness of this forest fortress and she couldn't make a sound.

Her body would signal her distress.

Or her passion.

Cole's hot mouth finally left Marietta's breast. With the tip of his tongue he licked a path down the center of her chest to her small waist. He teased at her belly button and felt her hips rise slightly. He turned his head and laid it gently down on her flat belly. He felt her fingers tangle in his hair, felt her stomach jerking beneath his cheek.

He smiled in the darkness.

Then he slowly raised his head, turned his face inward and pressed a tender kiss to her bare belly. Her fingers released his hair. He felt her relax. He cupped her hips in his hands and brushed kisses all over her stomach, moving steadily down. And he was pleased when she reflexively moved her legs a bit wider apart, instinctively offering herself to him.

Cole kept one hand lying on her prominent hipbone and placed the other underneath her pale left thigh. He pushed her leg up until her knee was bent, the sole of her foot resting flat on the discarded clothing.

He turned his head and kissed the inside of her thigh and at the same time urged it outward, the action clearly commanding her to let her thighs fall completely apart.

Marietta, assuming he meant to come into her now, responded as if he had spoken the words aloud. But her body quivered in surprise when Cole put his hand between her legs. She felt his lean fingers gently raking through the curls of her groin, parting them.

And then, to her shock, she felt his hot breath on the ultrasensitive flesh he had exposed and she knew that his face was close, very close. She was even more shocked when his lips, warm and soft and gentle, kissed her there. A sweet, tender caress that made her throb and left her wanting more.

Much more.

Marietta tensed and held her breath, waiting, wondering what Cole would do next. And then she had to fling her arm across her face and bite the back of her wrist to keep quiet when he kissed her again.

This time his mouth was wide open and hot upon her. When he touched her with his tongue she instantly felt as if she were on fire. That an inferno was blazing out of control between her parted legs and she could only pray that Cole's loving mouth would extinguish it before both were incinerated.

A highly excited Marietta lay there on her back in the thick darkness while the lover of her dreams passionately kissed her where she'd never been touched by anyone before. She wanted to scream her joy and cry out in her ecstasy. She wanted to shout his name in abandon, over and over again. She wanted to see his handsome face buried intimately between her open thighs.

She gasped and bit her wrist and whipped her head from side to side as Cole leisurely licked her, lashed her, loved her. Her heart beating double time, her thighs trembling and jerking, Marietta raised onto her elbows, panting helplessly now, gazing down at him, trying desperately to see.

She couldn't really see anything, could just make out the outline of his dark head and wide shoulders. She sat up fully, leaned back on stiffened arms, both knees raised now and open wide, while he continued to thrill and shock her, his marvelous mouth and talented tongue turning her into a volcano of heat that surely had to erupt if she was to live through this.

Cole could tell when he had Marietta so hot she was about to climax. He couldn't let that happen. Not here. She could cry out and alert the Comanches. So he gave that hot, wet, pulsating button of flesh one last plucking kiss and raised his head.

He scooted agilely up, took hold of her arms, kissed her mouth and lowered her onto her back, never taking his lips from hers. With his weight supported on a braced forearm, he reached between them, gripped himself and put the tip of his erection just inside her.

He withdrew his hand and slid slowly, carefully into her. His lips at last released hers and he exhaled loudly with pleasure. Marietta cupped his face in her hands and kissed him into silence as they lunged and thrust together in urgent, rapid rhythm. Wet with perspiration, their bodies slipping and sliding sensuously together, they moved in perfect unison, the pleasure spiraling quickly toward complete sexual delirium.

Cole felt himself coming, gritted his teeth and slowed his deep thrusts in an effort to hold back. But Marietta began to pant and then to viciously bite his slick shoulder, and he knew that her release was imminent. He urged her head up off his shoulder, forcefully took her chin in his hand and kissed her hard, purposely swallowing her cries of ecstasy.

They stayed locked together, kissing and bucking and shuddering until their shared orgasm ended completely and they were totally drained and sated. Even then, their relaxed bodies remained entwined, but their lips finally parted and both gasped for breath.

Weak, but gloriously gratified, the naked pair lay there in each other's arms. Their hearts beating as one, they kissed and sighed and wondered if making love could ever again be half so exciting.

The darkness, the danger, the forced silence had made the spontaneous lovemaking all the more thrilling.

Twenty-Six

Come morning the Comanches were gone and Marietta was in a buoyant mood. She was glad to be alive. Glad Cole was alive. Unusually cheerful, she laughed and talked and looked at Cole with newfound admiration. He had proven to be quite resourceful, quite heroic. She insisted on hearing every detail of how he had managed to elude the rampaging Comanches.

Cole was modest. He told her there had been nothing to it. He had learned, back in the war, how to evade and confuse superior forces. He had used those tactics to shake the Comanches. Not much to tell, really.

"But I thought the Indians always stole the horses," she said.

"Well, now, I couldn't allow that to happen, could I?" he said, turning to smile at her. He patted the butt of the scabbarded repeater rifle. "I had this little equalizer with me. I used it to hold them back until I could get an opportunity to lose them."

Marietta's mood was still lighthearted and agreeable as they approached the little village of Tascosa early that afternoon. Cole told her they would stop in

Tascosa and buy some supplies. He didn't ask her to behave and not turn him in. He knew she wouldn't.

Marietta remained pleasant and compatible as they walked down the wooden sidewalks of the village. They passed a blacksmith shop, the post office and a surveyor's office. At Tucker's General Store, they stepped inside.

Marietta browsed while Cole picked out articles of merchandise. Most were supplies needed for the remainder of the trip. But, watching from a couple of aisles away, Marietta caught him choosing a couple of items that were unquestionably gifts meant for a woman. A soft white shawl and a delicate locket.

Marietta quickly turned away, pretending she hadn't seen him select the presents. She smiled to herself. When he gave the gifts to her, she would remember to act surprised.

Back on the trail she remained happy and talkative. She wanted to hear more about how he had eluded the Comanches.

"It's just a miracle that you got away from them," she said with admiration, hoping he would elaborate.

He did not. Making light of it, Cole turned, shrugged and said, "My biggest chore was locating you in the darkness."

"I'm glad you found me," she said, recalling how they had behaved once he had found her. It had been *sooo* thrilling.

Marietta was less than thrilled when, late that afternoon, they rode up to a small shotgun house on a barren strip of land six miles south of Tascosa on the banks of the narrow Tascosa River.

"Why are we stopping here?" she asked, frowning.

"To visit two of my favorite ladies," Cole replied with a boyish grin. "I'll tell you all about it later. You'll like them, Marietta. Mrs. Longley is the salt of the earth and her daughter, little Leslie, is the sweetest child you'll ever hope to meet."

Marietta was dismounting when "little Leslie," shouting Cole's name, came flying out of the clapboard house. Marietta's jaw dropped. Little Leslie was no child. She was a beautiful, flaxen-haired, lithe-limbed young woman who leaped into Cole's outstretched arms and kissed him.

Marietta stood with her arms crossed over her chest while Cole plucked the lovely girl up off the ground and swung her around and around, both of them laughing merrily. By the time Cole lowered the blonde to her feet, Marietta had decided that she didn't much like little Leslie.

Leslie clung to Cole's hand and gazed at him with adoring eyes as he said, "Leslie, this is Marietta. Marietta, meet Leslie Longley, the prettiest little girl in all North Texas."

Leslie punched him playfully on the arm and said, "Cole Heflin, I am not a little girl! I turned eighteen last winter."

"Why, that can't be," he said, shaking his head as if in disbelief.

"I swear it's true," Leslie said. "Just look at me. I'm all grown up." She turned this way then that.

Marietta cleared her throat.

"Oh, I'm sorry," said Leslie, tearing her gaze from Cole. "Where are my manners? I'm pleased to meet you, Marietta. Any friend of Cole's is welcome in our home. Won't you come inside out of this hot sun?"

"Thank you, Leslie," Marietta replied, wishing they had not stopped to visit the Longleys.

But she had no choice, they were here and she would have to make the best of it. While Cole got a couple of packages out of his gear, the fresh-faced Leslie extended a hand, directing Marietta up the front walk. Marietta nodded and walked on toward the house. Leslie and Cole followed.

"How is your dear mother?" Cole asked, concern in his tone.

"Not well, Cole," said Leslie. "You'll see."

Marietta stepped onto the small front porch, turned and waited. Finally Leslie let go of Cole and led them inside.

"Momma, guess who's here?" she called out. "You'll never believe it!"

Leslie disappeared into a back room and returned seconds later with a thin, graying, fragile-looking woman clinging to her arm. When the older woman saw Cole, her tired eyes instantly lighted, then filled with tears.

"Cole," she said, her voice weak. "Cole, my boy, my dearest boy."

A big smile on his face, Cole handed the packages to Leslie, swiftly crossed to the infirm woman and gently put his arms around her before he kissed her wrinkled cheek.

"It's so good to see you, Mrs. Longley." He gave her a tender squeeze, then said, "Here, let me help you sit down so we can have a good talk."

Cole guided her over to the horsehide sofa, carefully lowered her to one of the worn cushions and sat down beside her. Draping a long arm around her narrow shoulders, he introduced Marietta, explaining that Marietta was an accomplished opera star who had been appearing in Central City, Colorado. He had gone up to escort her home to Galveston for a visit with her ailing grandfather.

Peggy Longley smiled, greeted Marietta warmly and said, "An opera star? My goodness, you'll have to sing for us, dear."

Marietta replied, "I would, but I really need a full orchestra behind me to—"

"She needs an orchestra," Cole jumped in.

"Well, thank you so much for bringing my boy by to see us, Marietta," said Mrs. Longley. "Please tell me that the two of you will stay with us for several days so we can have a nice visit."

Marietta deferred to Cole. He said, "I wish we could, but Marietta's grandfather is expecting us. I'm afraid one night is all we can manage."

"No," both disappointed Longley women said in unison.

No! Marietta wanted to shout. She was as disappointed as the Longleys, but for a different reason. She did *not* want to spend even one night. Wisely, she kept silent.

"I'm sorry," Cole said, "but I promise to come back up this way as soon as I can." He grinned then and announced, "We brought you each a little present. Leslie, hand me the larger of the two packages, please." Leslie complied and he told her, "The small box is for you, sweetheart."

Marietta tried very hard not to frown as "Little Leslie" lifted a delicate chain supporting a small gold heart from the box. Mrs. Longley unwrapped the white shawl and quickly gave Cole's lean jaw a kiss.

Both women thanked him, pleased with their treasures and his thoughtfulness.

Mrs. Longley studied Cole's face. With a thin hand she affectionately patted his knee and said, "I thought we'd lost you, Cole. We heard they were going to hang you."

Marietta's lips fell open and her eyes widened. She paid close attention to the conversation. She vaguely recalled an exchange she'd had with Cole on the night he had kidnapped her. She had warned him that he would hang for taking her and he had flippantly responded, "I'll be hanged if I don't."

"You heard correctly," Cole said to Mrs. Longley. "Fact is, I was on the gallows with the noose around my neck when Marietta's grandfather stepped in to save me."

"Well, my sincere gratitude to your grandfather, Marietta," said Peggy Longley.

Marietta smiled, but gave no reply, hoping their conversation would continue and she would learn why Cole was to be hanged. It didn't happen.

Mrs. Longley changed the subject, saying, "I'll bet you two are hungry. It's almost suppertime." She looked at her daughter. "Leslie, why don't you get started with the evening meal. Fix something special for our special guests."

Leslie jumped up and headed for the kitchen. In less than a half hour they were all sitting down to a hot, tasty supper of baking-powder biscuits, cured ham and sweet potatoes. Marietta thoroughly enjoyed the home-cooked meal, but she wished everything was not quite so appetizing. It seemed that Leslie could do no wrong and Cole, rolling his eyes and rubbing his belly, profusely praised the bubbly blonde for the delicious meal she had cooked all by herself.

He also complimented Leslie on the simple cotton dress she had changed into before supper.

"What a pretty dress. The color suits you," he said. "Makes you look like a beautiful princess."

"I made it myself, Cole," Leslie said, beaming.

"Well, you are one talented young lady" was his response.

Marietta quietly seethed. Was there nothing the apple-cheeked girl could not do? Besides, what was so special about a tacky little homemade dress? And being able to cook a half-decent meal? She herself could easily do those mundane domestic chores if she so chose. Which she did not.

Marietta could hardly hold her tongue when, shortly after supper, Leslie smiled at Cole and said sweetly, "Take a walk down by the river with me, Cole." She did not invite Marietta to join them.

"Why, sure, sweetheart" was Cole's quick reply.

Twenty-Seven

A fuming Marietta was left to visit with the frail, tired Mrs. Longley, while Cole and Leslie went off to walk along the riverbank.

But within minutes Marietta was glad that she had been left behind. The gentle Peggy Longley began to talk and her main subject was Cole.

"You're a lucky young woman, Marietta."

"Am I?"

Mrs. Longley nodded. "Yes, you are. Cole obviously cares for you and he is a fine young man. The best. He has always been so good and kind to Leslie and me."

"I'm glad to hear that, Mrs. Longley," said Marietta.

The older woman smiled and said, "And, of course, he and Keller were like brothers."

"Keller?" Marietta repeated, puzzled.

"Yes. Keller, my dear son. Cole hasn't mentioned him? Why, Keller and Cole were inseparable as boys," she mused aloud. "Our two families lived just a mile away from each other back in Weatherford." She smiled sadly, shook her head sorrowfully.

"Those were the happy days, the good days. The days before everything was lost." She sighed, as if weary to the bone. But, warming to her subject, she kept talking.

"Cole's father was a cowboy and he bought his first ranch at seventeen. As a youth and as an adult, Troy Heflin owned several ranches throughout Parker County. He was a member of the Masonic Lodge and served with the Parker County sheriff's posse for years." Mrs. Longley's eyes sparkled as she recalled the big, kind rancher and his ready smile. "Troy Heflin loved life, yes he did. His creed was, 'Live fast, fight hard and leave a happy memory.' Lord knows, he did leave a happy memory with everyone who knew him. He was loved and respected by all.

"Troy Heflin was so softhearted he would often bring people home from town, offer them room and board and time to get back on their feet. That's the kind of man he was. He'd send them on their way with a new set of clothes, boots and a little money."

Peggy chuckled then and said, "He had a great sense of fun. Loved to pull pranks on the unwary. Loved to rope and often practiced on the boys, Cole and Keller. He'd chase them down the road, rope swinging! The boys enjoyed the game and the attention."

Mrs. Longley smiled wistfully as she gazed back into the past. "Cole's mother, Ailene, was a handsome, refined lady—a Baton Rouge belle—who loved to cook and to garden and who treasured the well-worn library her revered grandfather left her. Young Cole pored over those old books, mainly *Blackstone on Law*. That's when his interest in the law began. When he finished his schooling, he went down to Austin to the university to read law.'' Peggy Longley paused and abruptly stopped smiling. ''Cole never liked ranching all that much. I guess it's just as well. His father was a great cowboy but a poor business-man. Generous to a fault. Went on everyone's note until finally he lost everything he had.''

Peggy exhaled heavily and continued, ''It was dur-ing Cole's last year at the university that the War of Northern Oppression began. When Cole graduated, he and Keller went away to war together. It was while they were gone that Troy and Ailene Heflin both contracted influenza and died within days of each other.''

''Oh, no.'' Marietta spoke for the first time. ''How sad.''

''Yes, it was. Cole was brokenhearted.''

''I can imagine.''

''By then Leslie and I had moved up here. My brother passed away and left us this little piece of land. Keller and Cole thought we might be safer here, they were afraid the Yankee troops garrisoned in North Texas might sweep through Parker County.'' She paused, remembering, then her eyes twinkled when she said, ''Little did they know we'd be in a lot more danger way out here than we were down in Weatherford.'' She shook her head thoughtfully.

"The Yankees never came within a hundred miles of us as far as I know, but to this day the Comanches are a threat. They have a stronghold in Palo Duro Canyon south of here. They ride and raid across these plains, then disappear back down into the canyon. They know we're here, but thank God we've been spared so far."

Marietta nodded, but remained quiet about yesterday's encounter with the Comanches. She saw no reason to tell Mrs. Longley and further frighten her.

Peggy stopped speaking, frowned and said, "Where was I? I'm getting drifty in my old age."

Marietta prompted, "You were talking about your son and Cole."

Mrs. Longley nodded, her thin shoulders slumped, and she said, "Keller died in Cole's arms in the summer of '64 on a battlefield in Tennessee."

"Oh, I'm so sorry, Mrs. Longley," Marietta said with genuine sympathy.

"Keller was the man of the house, had been for years," said Peggy Longley. "I've been a widow since the year after Leslie was born. We counted on Keller and then when he was gone, we counted on Cole. Bless Cole's heart, he has sent us money whenever he could spare it and worried about us like we were his own family."

She fell silent and Marietta took the opportunity to ask, "Mrs. Longley, why was Cole to be hanged?" She held her breath, bracing for the worst.

"My goodness, you mean you don't know? Cole hasn't told you about the raid on Hadleyville?"

"No, ma'am, he hasn't."

"In the last days of the war, Cole attacked a northern munitions-supply station at Hadleyville. Hadleyville was burned to the ground and Yankee soldiers died. We Confederates considered Cole a hero for the deed, but the secretary of war, Stanton, declared the act a crime against the Union and Cole was named a war criminal with a bounty on his head. Stanton ordered that he be hunted down and hanged for his crime. For years he eluded the authorities, then his luck finally ran out."

Peggy talked and talked about Cole. Marietta listened in awed interest, learning about a different man than the one she'd grown to know. Cole Heflin was an educated man—he had been an attorney. He had been a hero in the war. He cared deeply about the welfare of the two Longley women.

Marietta listened and nodded as Mrs. Longley talked, and when finally she paused, Marietta cleared her throat needlessly and couldn't keep from saying, "Leslie and Cole seem to be very close."

"Oh yes, Leslie loves Cole to death," confirmed Mrs. Longley, and Marietta felt her heart squeeze when she added, "And he loves her. Nothing Cole wouldn't do for Leslie. Why, I remember when—" She abruptly stopped speaking, turned her head, listened and said, "There they are now. Back from their walk."

"Yes," said Marietta, hearing the sound of their shared laughter as her green eyes turned greener.

Bedtime.

The Longley house was very small. One tiny bedroom that Mrs. Longley and Leslie shared.

Marietta was offered the living-room sofa and a clean white nightgown belonging to Leslie. She graciously accepted both. Cole assured the Longley ladies that he would be more than comfortable out in the barn.

When Leslie brought him a blanket and pillow, he thanked her, kissed her forehead and said, "Good night, sweetheart."

"'Night, Cole," she said, throwing her arms around his neck and embracing him.

While Leslie hugged Cole tightly, he glanced over her head at Marietta. He said nothing, just looked at her with those smoldering eyes that caused her heartbeat to accelerate. Leslie released him. He turned and left the house.

"You'll be okay here, Marietta?" Leslie asked when they were alone.

"Yes, I'll be just fine," Marietta replied. "I'm so tired, I'm sure I'll fall asleep the minute I lie down."

Leslie nodded. "Well, then, good night. If you need anything, you call out to me, I'll hear you." She turned to leave the room, then, "Otherwise, I'll see you at breakfast. Nobody can fix flapjacks like I can."

"I'm sure that's true," said Marietta, frowning at Leslie's retreating back.

After Leslie left her, Marietta blew out the last remaining lamp and undressed. She drew the freshly laundered white nightgown down over her head and let it fall to her ankles. She stretched out on the uncomfortable horsehide sofa. The lamp went out in the Longley bedroom.

The house grew dark and silent.

Marietta closed her eyes and wiggled around in an attempt to get comfortable. The sofa was unbelievably hard and lumpy. She flung her arms up over her head. She tried very hard to fall asleep. Her eyes came open. She tossed and turned, first onto her right side, then onto her left. Then onto her back once more.

She thought about Cole holding Leslie's hand as they had strolled away from the house earlier in the evening. She recalled how they had been laughing together when they returned. She wondered what they had done when they'd gotten away from the house.

Marietta made a face and gritted her teeth. Mrs. Longley herself had said that Leslie loved Cole and Cole loved Leslie. No getting around it, Leslie Longley was a beauty. A young, innocent-looking beauty. It wasn't too hard to imagine Cole being enchanted with the fresh-faced girl.

Marietta gave up on sleeping.

She sat up, drew her bare feet up under her and hugged her knees. She wondered: Should she? Or shouldn't she?

Marietta rose from the sofa, tiptoed to the open front door and stepped out onto the porch. Barefoot, wearing only the borrowed batiste nightgown, she stood there in the pale moonlight, listening to the crickets chirp and the night wind stirring the leaves of the chinaberry tree in the Longley front yard.

She pushed her wild red hair back over her shoulders, stepped down off the porch and cautiously circled the small house, ducking low when she passed the bedroom window. Out back she stopped at the edge of Leslie's flower bed.

Thirty yards away, through the open door of the barn, she saw the distinctive orange glow of a lighted cigar. Her heartbeat quickened as it had when Cole had looked at her over Leslie's head.

Marietta gathered her gown up around her knees and sprinted toward the barn. She stepped into the open doorway and waited, her pulse now racing. In a stall at the back of the barn, the black stallion whinnied at the intrusion.

Cole remained silent.

Leaning back against the wall, he was seated on the blanket, which he'd spread out on the hay, his knees bent and raised. He was bare-chested and barefoot, but still wore his trousers.

As she stood there hardly daring to breathe, he took a long, slow drag on the cigar. Its glowing tip partially lighted his handsome face. He then took the cigar from his mouth, came agilely to his feet and slowly approached Marietta.

She lost her breath entirely. Cole tossed the cigar out the door into the dirt. He stepped up close to Marietta, so close she could have touched him. Towering over her, he looked at her for a long, tension-filled moment, his eyes flashing in the dim light.

Wordlessly, he reached for her. He took both her hands and drew her into the barn. The stallion shook its great head up and down rapidly and neighed loudly. The piebald mare pricked her ears, then whinnied softly, turned away and ignored them.

Cole and Marietta stood facing each other in the rectangle of moonlight spilling through the open barn door.

Cole raised his hands, cupped her soft cheeks, kissed her and said, "I was afraid you might have come to your senses and not shown up."

Twenty-Eight

Marietta swayed into Cole, raked her nails gently through the black hair covering his chest and said, "You knew very well I would come."

Cole laughed softly, kissed her again, drew her deeper into the interior of the barn and turned her so that she was facing away from him.

With no further preamble, he lifted her nightgown up over her head and dropped it to the hay. Naked, Marietta stood before him, tingling, waiting impatiently to feel his strong arms come around her.

Behind her, Cole took a moment to admire her. Lord, she was sheer perfection. Heavy red-gold hair spilling over her pale, slender shoulders, waist so small his hands could scan it, flared hips and long, shapely legs he could hardly wait to have wrapped around him.

Cole swallowed hard and drew a deep breath.

Swiftly he shucked off his trousers and tossed them aside. When at last he drew Marietta back against his tall, lean frame, he was as naked as she. Marietta sighed softly when he gripped her shoulders, bent his head and kissed the curve of her neck and shoulder.

His lips moving up and down the side of her throat, he said, "There are so many ways I want to love you, baby. Say I can. Say you'll let me."

Marietta's head fell back on his shoulder and her hands covered his where they lay atop her quivering stomach.

"I'll let you, Cole," she whispered breathlessly. "You know I will. Anything you want, I want too."

"Ah, sweetheart," he murmured, turning her about in his arms to gaze at her lips for a long moment. Then he lowered his head and kissed her.

It was a searing kiss of unrestrained passion, and Marietta, trembling with growing excitement, lifted weak arms up around his neck and drew his head down, her mouth open and eager beneath his. She felt his tongue probing, felt the blazing heat of his naked body pressed insistently against hers.

She sighed into his mouth when he filled his hands with the twin cheeks of her bottom and drew her up on tiptoe, urging her pelvis more fully into his. Her breasts were flattened against his solid chest and his heavy erection pulsed rhythmically against her bare belly.

Marietta felt the muscles along the insides of her thighs begin to jump, felt her nipples tighten and sting with sensation.

No matter how tightly Cole held her, no matter how close she got to him, she felt as if she could never get quite close enough. She adored being wrapped in his long, powerful arms, loved having him hold her, kiss her, thrill her.

It was incredibly exciting to stand naked with Cole in the Longley barn while the edgy black stallion nickered behind them. She genuinely hoped that Cole would not immediately guide her to the blanket and lay her down. She wanted to stand, wanted to be free to rub her taut, yearning body against his tall, solid length and acquaint herself fully with every inch of his magnificent male physique.

Cole had become a master at reading Marietta's thoughts. He knew what she wanted without her saying a word. So for the next several minutes he continued to stand in the wedge of summer moonlight spilling in the barn door with his bare feet apart and his arms around Marietta. He happily allowed her to play and tease and tempt him with her soft, warm feminine curves.

When she drew back a little, smiled up at him and firmly pushed on his chest, he immediately loosened his hold on her. And then laughed when she stepped out of his arms and danced around behind him. He went along with it when she slipped her hands around his waist and pressed herself flush against his back.

Cole shuddered when she began brushing butterfly kisses up and down his spine. Her lips and tongue teased him and her long silky hair tickled his skin. Already painfully aroused, Cole's hands balled into fists at his sides and he clenched his teeth.

Marietta stopped kissing him, but she laid her hot

cheek against his right shoulder and let her hands slide down his tight belly to enclose his surging tumescence. Cole stiffened involuntarily and inhaled sharply. His balled fists got tighter, his short nails digging into his palms. His eyes slipped closed in sweet agony.

But he didn't stop her or join in the fun.

Cole stood there unmoving and allowed the curious Marietta to examine and caress and toy with him to her heart's content. It was the strangest of sensations. He had to hand it to her, she never failed to surprise him. He had made love in just about every possible position known to man, but he had never done this. He had never stood bare-assed and unmoving while a beautiful naked woman made him her own personal plaything, driving him half out of his mind with her searching hands and voluptuous body.

Cole exhaled heavily when finally Marietta had played enough, released him, reached out and turned him to face her. His breath labored, his heart pounding, Cole drew her into his arms and kissed her hotly, hungrily, wedging a knee between her legs.

They continued to kiss and embrace while behind them the high-strung stallion kicked at his stall and whinnied his displeasure. The naked pair hardly heard the racket; they were too engrossed in each other.

At some point—Marietta wasn't sure when—Cole, never taking his lips from hers, walked her backward to where the blanket was spread on the hay. She felt the softness of its material beneath her bare feet.

Then, in silent agreement, they sank to their knees and knelt there on the blanket, continuing to kiss. When at long last their lips separated, they fought for breath, their hearts racing.

Both felt limp and at the same time full of coursing energy. Cole sat Marietta back a little, framed her face with his hands and said, "You told me I can love you any way I want."

"And I meant it," she whispered. "Show me, Cole. Teach me how to please you."

"Oh, sweetheart, you please me," he said, taking her upper arms and raising her back up onto her knees.

Marietta's head fell back when Cole abruptly released her and rose to his feet before her. His hand in her hair, he bent and brushed one last kiss to her open lips and said, "Stay on your knees, honey, but move them apart a little."

Marietta gave him a questioning look but complied. Cole stepped around and knelt directly behind her, his knees inside hers. He drew her back against him, urged her left arm up and hooked it behind his neck. He let his fingertips glide across her exposed underarm and she automatically shivered. He kissed her cheek and laid a hand on her lower stomach. He felt her belly contract.

He moved his hand lower.

The fire inside her leaped higher, became hotter. As she knelt on the blanket with her knees apart and Cole behind her, Marietta felt wet and open and vulnerable. She whispered Cole's name and shuddered when she felt his long, lean fingers slip between her legs to touch and test her.

"Oh, Cole, Cole," she murmured as he caressed her, arousing her, readying her to take him.

When he took his wet fingers from her, she knew instinctively what he wanted her to do next. Cole placed his guiding hands on her waist and Marietta fell forward onto her hands and knees.

"Yes, that's it, baby," she heard Cole's soft-spoken praise. "This is what I want, this is how I want to love you."

He spread the cheeks of her bottom and took her then, plunging his hard, heavy flesh into her from behind. Marietta gasped with shocked pleasure as he began the rhythmic driving thrusts deep within her.

"Cole, Cole," she murmured, her eyes closing in ecstasy.

"I know, baby," he groaned, kneeling behind her, his hands guiding her hips, his pelvis pounding and slapping against her bare buttocks.

Marietta's stiffened arms grew weak. She bent her elbows and sagged slowly forward until her cheek was resting on the spread blanket. She heard the stallion whinny and realized that she and Cole were behaving like animals in heat; mating in the barn in the very same way a stallion mounts a mare.

It didn't seem odd.

She was so hot for Cole it seemed perfectly normal to have him make love to her this way. It was erotic and exciting and she didn't care if it was right or wrong. Pleasure rippled through her and she realized that she had never felt so free and uninhibited in her life.

Cole, groaning with pleasure, leaned over her and braced himself with open palms on either side of her. Marietta could feel his weight pressing on her back and she swooned when his hot, open lips brushed kisses to her shoulder.

After several seconds in that position, Cole rose back up onto his knees, bringing Marietta with him. He then sat back on his heels and drew her down against him. Her soft bare bottom now rested on his hard thighs and his throbbing length was still buried deep within her.

He slid his hands under her arms and caressed her breasts, his fingertips gently plucking and playing with the pebble-hard nipples. Marietta sighed, ground her hips aggressively against him and laid her head back on his shoulder. Her unbound hair fell into his face, brushing his cheek, drifting across his lips.

"Is this what you wanted?" she whispered breathlessly, sensuously moving against him, her back arching, her breasts swaying.

"Exactly," he managed to say, pressing kisses to her tangled hair. "This and more, my darlin'. All of you. That's what I want."

Marietta nodded and licked her dry lips. Then she began to pant when Cole again put his hand between her parted legs and touched that tiny button of wet, pulsing flesh where all her passion was located. She emitted a strangled cry of joy as Cole began to slowly, expertly caress her.

At the touch of his fingers her pleasure instantly increased, became so intense she was immediately lost in another world. A world of eroticism where making love was all that really mattered.

She loved this dreamlike world where pure lust was totally acceptable and burning passion was praised not censured. Here in this private paradise where sexual hunger was eagerly fed and an appetite for even more was rewarded, she could surrender to every human desire without fear or shame.

The marvelous mate that dwelled within her in this sultry universe was a highly sexual male animal who could and would fulfill all her wanton desires. She wished that the two of them could stay here forever.

Just as they were now.

"Cole, Cole," Marietta said his name on a sigh, glorying in the double delight of having his hand caressing her while his hard male flesh was inside her.

If she was being swept away in a lovely atmosphere of ardor, Cole was just as lost in a world of unbridled desire. To be allowed to take this beautiful, flame-haired woman in this primitive manner was satisfying beyond his wildest dreams. He inhaled deeply and smelled the perspiration of their sexual excitement mingling with the scent of the hay beneath them.

On his hard thighs, Marietta's soft buttocks had begun to move with increasing quickness, her hot, wet warmth squeezing him tightly. It felt so good he encouraged her, telling her in very graphic terms what she was doing to him, how sweetly she was loving him.

Marietta felt her release beginning and there was nothing she could do to stop it. She didn't have to tell Cole. He knew. While she sobbed his name in near hysteria, Cole continued to thrust deeply, staying with her, giving her all she could take and more.

She cried out when the shattering release swamped her, holding her suspended for several seconds in its awesome orgasmic power.

At last she whimpered and fell forward while Cole desperately clung to her hips and continued to pump into her until his own climax came, causing him to shudder violently and groan her name.

Cole collapsed tiredly atop Marietta.

She lay on her stomach, panting for breath, her face damp with perspiration. Cole's lean body covered hers, his weight partially supported on his forearms. Their hearts pounding, they lay unmoving, saying nothing. Each surprised by the new heights of ecstasy they had attained.

At last Cole raised his head, kissed Marietta's damp temple and moved off her. He stretched out on his back, folding his hands beneath his head. Marietta stayed on her stomach for another moment. Cole turned his head, looked at her and smiled. Her hair was a mess, tangled and flyaway and falling over her face. Her body was dewy with perspiration, pale shoulders and bare bottom glistening in the dim light.

Never had she looked more beautiful.

Marietta soon sat back on her heels, pushed her hair back behind her ears, looked down at Cole and said, "Texan, don't ever do that to me again." She laughed then, a delightful, musical sound, came down atop him and whispered in his ear, "At least not for an hour or so."

Twenty-Nine

At breakfast the next morning, Cole surprised all three women when, as soon as he'd finished the last plate of Leslie's fluffy flapjacks, he announced, "Ladies, if you'll kindly excuse me, I have an errand to run." He laid down his napkin and rose to his feet. He glanced at Marietta and said, "Shouldn't be long."

"But I thought you wanted us to get an early start," she said, frowning at him.

"I do. But first I have to take care of something."

While the three women watched, Cole went out the back door, walked directly to the barn and stepped inside.

Marietta exchanged questioning glances with Leslie. Leslie shrugged and shook her head. Marietta rose, hurried through the house and stepped out onto the front porch as Cole came around the house leading her saddled piebald mare. Arms crossed over her chest, she watched him climb up into the saddle and ride away. She was truly puzzled. Why was Cole riding her mare instead of the black? And where on earth was he going?

"Help me with the dishes?" Leslie said from behind.

"Oh. Yes, of course, I...I...do you have any idea where Cole is going?"

"No, I really don't," Leslie said. She smiled and said, "Maybe he'll tell us when he gets back."

Marietta made a face and reluctantly followed Leslie back inside. While the two young women did the breakfast dishes, Peggy sat at the kitchen table. She again talked about the old days, recalling when Keller and Cole were young boys, how close they had been. Marietta listened with interest, eager to learn all she could about Cole.

Once the dishes had been washed, dried and put away, the trio moved into the sitting room, and Leslie, at her mother's request, brought forth Keller's last letter. Marietta could tell, by the way Mrs. Longley looked at the letter in Leslie's hand, that it was precious to her.

"Would you like to read the letter?" Leslie asked. "It's about Cole as well as Keller."

"Yes, thank you. I would," Marietta said.

"Be careful," Leslie cautioned. "Mother and I have read it so often, the paper is beginning to come apart along the folds."

Marietta nodded. She took the letter from the yellowed, blood-stained envelope, gingerly unfolded the one page missive, and began to read.

July 17, 1864

Dearest Ma and Leslie,
I have been badly wounded. Our regimental

surgeon, overwhelmed as he is, has spent a great deal of time and attention on me. Cole is at my side, taking all this down for me.

He has promised to stay until the end. Ma, I shall not worry about you and little Leslie because Cole and I made a pact back in Weatherford: should only one of us survive, the survivor would take care of both families. God willing, Cole will look out for you. I know he will.

Pray this terrible war will soon be over.

Please do not be sad; I have had a happy life. I would not change a thing.

Your loving son and brother,
Keller Longley
Brevet Captain C.S.A.

Marietta, tears stinging her eyes, slowly lowered the letter and carefully refolded it. Handing it back to Leslie, she said simply, "Cole and Keller must have loved each other very much."

Peggy Longley nodded and said, "Keller died in Cole's arms that very afternoon."

At a fast gallop, Cole rode back north to the sleepy village of Tascosa. Once he reached Main Street, he tied the mare to a hitching post, swung down out of the saddle and went directly to the Tascosa State Bank.

Inside, he glanced at the teller's cage. A young man stood behind the barred window. No one else was in the small lobby.

Cole walked up to the teller, nodded and inquired, "The bank president?"

"That would be Mr. Thomas McLeish, sir," said the teller with a pleasant smile.

"Where is McLeish?"

"He's in his office—" the teller indicated a door to his right "—but he's with a customer and...wait, you can't go in there."

Cole had already turned and was headed for the closed door. He didn't knock. He opened the door and stepped inside.

A customer sat across the desk from the stocky bank president. At the intrusion, Thomas McLeish looked up, frowned, lifted a short arm and began to shoo Cole out.

"Sir, you will have to wait outside."

"No, this gentleman will have to wait outside," Cole said. He took the customer's arm, smiled at him and drew him to his feet. Cole reached for the man's hat, put it on his head and ushered him out of the office, closing the door behind him.

By now Thomas McLeish was on his feet and his fleshy face was flushing red. "See here, what is the meaning of this?"

"Sit down," Cole said. Incensed, the portly president continued to stand.

"I said sit down," Cole repeated in a tone that brooked no argument.

Growing nervous now, McLeish sat back down. "What do you want? Who are you?"

"I'm a good friend of Miss Leslie Longley's," Cole announced and sank into the mohair chair across the desk from McLeish. "Know her?"

"Miss Longley?" said McLeish, anxiety showing in his eyes. "Why, yes. I...ah...she is such a nice young lady. I think the world of Miss Leslie and her dear mother."

Cole's eyes narrowed. "Save your breath, you horny, hypocritical old bastard."

McLeish's red face got redder still. He shook a short finger at Cole and said, "You cannot speak to me like that, young man!"

"Yes, I can," Cole said, disgusted by this middle-aged married man who had bullied and frightened Leslie. "How much do the Longleys owe on their outstanding mortgage with this bank?"

"I...I am not exactly certain," said McLeish, his voice going a little shrill, "I would have to—"

"How much?" Cole slammed his fist down on the desk.

McLeish jumped, eyes now round, but quickly replied, "Two hundred fifty dollars."

"Two hundred fifty," Cole repeated. "Let's see, we'll deduct a hundred for the mare you stole from Leslie and—"

"A hundred dollars! Be reasonable, that mare was

old and slow. Not worth anywhere near a hundred dollars.''

"It was to Leslie," Cole said in a low, calm voice, his eyes as cold as steel. "I am deducting a hundred dollars for the mare.''

"I sold that old nag for twenty dollars!" McLeish objected.

As if he hadn't spoken, Cole said, "Take a hundred from the two hundred fifty, that leaves a hundred fifty dollars, which I am paying you this morning. You in turn will give me a signed and dated receipt marked paid in full.''

Thomas McLeish was squirming in his chair. Perspiration dotting his forehead and upper lip, he said, "I want no trouble, mister, but I cannot...I will not...''

He fell silent when Cole abruptly leaned forward, placed both palms flat atop the desk and said in a deadly tone, "You can. You will. Not only that, if you ever again get within five miles of the Longley spread, I will come after you. Do you understand me?''

"Y-yes, I...I..." McLeish was attempting to swallow, but having difficulty.

"You asked who I am? I'm Cole Heflin. Name sound familiar? I'm the man who burned Hadleyville. That's my likeness on that old Wanted poster hanging in the post office across the street. The one that offered a handsome reward for my capture." McLeish's eyes grew round with recognition and fear. Cole continued, "When Leslie Longley comes into town, you will run the other way as fast as your short legs will carry you. You so much as look at her or her speak to her and I'll know about it. There'll be no need for the telegraph, I will know. I'll know and I'll come back and tear your head off."

"I...I will never bother Miss Leslie," said a terrified McLeish.

"I know you won't," Cole said.

He smiled then and paid off the note. Thomas McLeish's hand shook as he hurriedly filled out a Paid in Full receipt, signed it and handed it to Cole. Cole put the receipt in his shirt pocket, got to his feet and left.

"Cole's back," Leslie announced more than an hour after he had ridden away.

Marietta waited anxiously as he headed straight for the barn. When he came back out, the piebald mare had been left in the barn and he was leading the saddled black stallion. He tethered the mount to the fence and came up the front walk.

When he stepped inside, Marietta noticed that he and Leslie exchanged looks. She detected the almost imperceptible nod of his head as if he was silently assuring Leslie of something.

Leslie smiled then and said, "Cole, couldn't you just stay for a couple of days?"

Cole knew he could put off their departure no longer. He was sorry they couldn't. He hated to leave the Longleys way out here by themselves. There were so many things around the place that needed tending, chores that demanded a strong back.

But there wasn't time. He had to get Marietta to Galveston. And as soon as possible.

"I wish we could," Cole said to both Longley women. "I'll come back real soon, I promise."

They all left the little house together, walked out into the front yard where the saddled black stallion was tethered to the fence.

Mrs. Longley and Leslie both got tears in their eyes when Cole told them that he was leaving Marietta's mare behind since they had no horse of their own. Marietta started to protest, but Cole silenced her with a look.

She caught herself, smiled at Mrs. Longley and said, "We can't let you two stay way out here with no horse."

"Oh, thank you so much, dear," said Mrs. Longley. "You're awfully good-hearted. Both of you."

Marietta was glad now that she had kept her mouth shut, hadn't objected to Cole giving her mare away. He was right. They couldn't leave these two helpless women alone with no way to get into town. She felt good about the gift; was glad Cole had done it. She wished that she'd thought of the idea.

Still, her lips fell open in shock when, at the edge of the yard, Cole abruptly stopped, turned and calmly told the Longleys that he had recently deposited the sum of ten thousand dollars in a Galveston, Texas, bank. He then took two small pieces of paper from his breast pocket. He presented both to Peggy Longley.

One was a Paid in Full receipt from the Tascosa bank on their outstanding loan. The other was a bank draft signing over to Peggy Longley the entire amount in the Galveston bank.

Ten thousand, less the one hundred fifty.

The stunned Peggy Longley looked at the bank draft, looked at Cole and showed it to Leslie. Her hand began to shake.

"Oh, Cole, no, we couldn't possibly take this," she said, her eyes swimming in tears.

"Yes, you can. I insist," said Cole. He looked from Mrs. Longley to Leslie and back again. "You will have enough to cultivate this land and live comfortably for the rest of your lives."

Crying now, Peggy Longley continued to thrust the bank draft back at Cole. He smiled at her, took her hand in both of his own, closed her fingers around the piece of paper and said, "You have to take it, Mrs. Longley. Keller would want you to take it." Cole turned to Leslie. Tears were streaming down her rosy cheeks. "Make me happy, sweetheart," he said to her. "Take the money."

Leslie nodded, unable to speak. On yesterday's walk, she had told Cole about the bank loan. And about the boorish bank president's unacceptable behavior. She knew Cole. He had ridden into town this morning and straightened out the repulsive banker once and for all.

Thomas McLeish would never bother her again.

Leslie and her mother began to laugh through their tears and threw their arms around Cole. He hugged both to him. Marietta stood watching, deeply touched. She had never seen anybody do something so unselfish, so admirable.

She would bet her life that the ten thousand dollars he had just handed over to the Longleys was every cent he had in the world. And that the money had been his payment in full from her grandfather for bringing her to Galveston.

It was then, at that moment, that Marietta knew she had fallen in love with Cole Heflin. It had to be love, because by his own admission he had no money, no land, no power, no prospects. There was absolutely nothing she could get from him. Nothing he could do for her.

Except, if she had her way, love her.

Thirty

Waving goodbye, they left the Longley spread with Marietta seated behind Cole on the stallion.

For several miles, they rode in silence.

Marietta quietly contemplated the change in their relationship. She was surprised at herself. She no longer had the need to behave the spoiled, pampered coquette.

It came to her that for the first time in her life she longed to humor and indulge a man, not have a man humor and indulge her. She no longer needed to pretend and playact and promise what she never intended to deliver.

Ever since she had grown up, she had plotted and planned and practiced deception, not caring who might be hurt. But only what she might gain for herself. Marietta suddenly frowned. Her grandfather was like that. He cared only about himself. He was selfish and unforgiving and coldhearted. He hadn't even loved his own daughter enough to forgive her for making a mistake. She wondered if he had ever sorrowed over his decision?

She was not going to be like him. Unloving and unloved.

At long last she had found out what was important in life.

Love.

True, unselfish love.

She wasn't sure if she was foolish or wise, but she didn't care. She loved Cole Heflin and she wanted to make him happy. And she wished more than anything in the world that she could look into his beautiful blue eyes and see love shining out of them.

Cole's feelings for Marietta had become worrisome and confusing to him. The physical pleasure they had shared had left him constantly wanting more. And that rankled him. He wrestled with himself, striving to deny any complex feelings for her. He was not used to wanting a woman again and again. Not accustomed to caring all that much about the women he bedded.

The women to whom he had made love in the past had been for the most part interchangeable. All alike. The only real difference being that some were blond, some brunette, and very rarely, there had been a redhead.

But this particular redhead had awakened in him a new emotion. Sexual hunger, yes, but his troubling fascination was more than just the physical. Despite the fact that she was selfish and manipulative, he—like some green fool—actually cared about her. And while he had only to look at her to desire her, he was plagued by the nagging thought that other men—no telling how many—had had her before him.

Cole's jaw clenched at the distasteful thought. Then he immediately berated himself. Why the hell should he care how many men had made love to her? What difference did it make? Why should he feel protective of her? Hell, she could take care of herself.

Lord, could she.

And yet...his heart hurt when she smiled so sweetly at him. Each time she smiled, he caught himself wishing he could command her to never smile like that at any other man but him.

These were the respective thoughts of the reflective pair as they rode across the prairie. On all sides they could see nothing but the bleak, far-reaching Staked Plains of Texas—what the Mexicans called the Llano Estacado. A flat, endless expanse of high tableland where a constant wind blew and a baking sun beat down from a cloudless sky.

That sun on this scorching July noontime was high and hot. Dust devils swirled across the plains. The scenery was monotonous. A worthless part of the world that the Almighty seemed to have forsaken.

Cole, guiding the black across the stark, windswept landscape, became aware of Marietta's soft breasts pressed against his back. And of the light touch of her hands clasping his waist. That's all it took.

He wanted her.

Wanted her right now.

At once he began anxiously searching the horizon around them, looking for a stand of mesquite, a shallow arroyo, an abandoned building. Anyplace that offered at least a small degree of privacy. There was nothing. Just mile after mile of nothing.

As if she had read his mind, Marietta laid her cheek against Cole's shoulder and said honestly, "I wish you were touching me, loving me."

"You mean that?" he asked over his shoulder.

"You know I do."

Cole abruptly drew rein. The responsive stallion immediately halted. Cole turned and said, "Dismount, sweetheart."

Marietta didn't question him. She hastily swung down to the ground, but said, "Not here, Cole. There's not a tree in sight, no place where we can—"

She stopped speaking and laughed merrily when Cole leaned down, plucked her from the ground as if she were as light as a feather. He drew her up across the saddle before him and gave her a quick kiss. Then Marietta squealed when, wrapping the long leather reins around the saddle horn, Cole spoke to the black and the stallion began walking along at a slow, steady pace.

"We aren't really going to…?" she began.

"We are, darlin'," Cole said. He reached down, took off her moccasins and slipped them into the saddlebags.

Then, looking into her eyes, he unbuttoned her chamois trousers. "Ever make love atop a moving horse?" he asked with a wicked grin.

"Certainly not."

"Me neither," he admitted. "Want to give it a try?"

"You're teasing me," she accused. She studied his face and added, incredulous, "You're not kidding, are you?"

"I would never kid about something so serious," he said and winked at her.

"Cole Heflin! What if someone should come by?"

"They won't," he assured her. "We are way off the main trail. Trust me."

Cole scooted back out of the saddle, giving it over to her. Then, with her help, he managed to get Marietta's trousers down and off. He anxiously stuffed them into the overflowing saddlebags. Now naked from the waist down, Marietta, with his help, agilely maneuvered about so that she was seated backward astride the saddle facing Cole.

"You're absolutely sure nobody will happen past?"

"Positive, so relax," he said. "And unbutton my pants."

Muttering that this was foolish and disgraceful and they should be ashamed of themselves, Marietta none-theless complied. Then emitted a little gasp of pleased surprise when she pushed the open trousers apart and he burst free, big and hard and ready to give pleasure.

"We're crazy, you know that," said Marietta, then laughed, threw her arms around Cole's neck and said, "Kiss me, Texan."

The black pranced proudly along as Cole and Marietta kissed. Quick, chaste kisses at first, then long, probing caresses that grew steadily hotter.

At last Marietta tore her lips from Cole's and said, "I've changed my mind. We can't do this, Cole. It's indecent."

His reply was, "Lick your fingers, baby."

Marietta smiled, sighed and nodded. She lifted her right hand, put out her tongue and licked the tips of her fingers.

"Yes, that's it," Cole said. "Lick all four fingers real good. Make 'em wet." Marietta licked her fingertips until they were gleaming.

She turned her hand around to show him. "See, they're wet."

"Good," he said. "Now make me wet."

Marietta lowered her eyes and her hand to him. She rubbed her moistened fingertips over the velvet-smooth tip of his fully formed erection until he was shiny wet. She raised her head then, looked into his smoldering blue eyes.

"Like this?" she asked, licking her fingers again and spreading the moisture down the length of his rock-hard shaft.

"Yes," he said and shuddered. "And you? Are you wet, sweetheart?"

He felt his heart hammer in his chest when she

replied honestly, "Yes, I'm wet and burning hot for you, Cole."

Cole's hands left her waist, moved around to her bare buttocks. He said, "Climb up here onto me and put it in."

Her breath coming fast, her heart beating in her ears, Marietta moved forward, slipped one slender leg up over his trousered thigh and, guiding him with her hand, put the gleaming tip of his hard flesh just inside. She released him then and, clinging to the strong column of his neck, surged up, then slowly, carefully impaled herself upon him.

"Make love to me, Cole," she whispered, leaning her forehead against his.

"No, darlin'," he said, his hands gently kneading the pale flesh of her bare bottom. "You make love to me this time."

Marietta raised her head, looked at him and said, "But I don't know how."

"Yes, you do," he said, smiling. "Go on. Practice on me till you get it right."

Marietta took the challenge. "If that's what you want."

"It is," he told her. "Make love to me as you've never made love to anyone else before. Drive me crazy with your beautiful body. Do it to me, baby. Take it from me. Bring me. Make me come. Love me, darlin', love me."

"I will," she promised breathlessly, "Oh, I will, Cole, I will."

And she set about to do just that.

Her hands now atop his broad shoulders, her legs draped over his thighs, a wildly excited Marietta surged up against him, pushed his head back and kissed him. She thrust her tongue deep into his mouth and at the same time sensuously slid up and down his hard, pulsing flesh.

She had learned from him. She would rise until their joined bodies would almost come apart, then gyrate her hips and slide back down until he was deeply buried in her.

The stallion, as if attempting to match their rhythm, had picked up the pace. His strides grew longer, quicker and the motion of the moving horse beneath the entwined pair only added to the thrill of their love-making.

Mounted atop the stallion while mounted atop Cole, Marietta rode both big males with total abandon and was so carried away with this unorthodox coupling, it wouldn't have mattered to her if a wagon train of curious settlers had come upon them. She couldn't have stopped what she was doing.

Neither could Cole.

The delectable Marietta had him at a fever pitch and he wanted her to never, ever stop what she was doing to him at this minute. He wanted to ride like this forever across these barren plains under a hot broiling sun while this half-naked temptress rode him. He wanted to keep his bold, beautiful lover astride him like this for all eternity, to have her hot, wet flesh clasping him, squeezing him, driving him out of his mind.

Cole knew they were not in danger of actually being seen. He was confident that there was no one within miles and miles of them. But even if there had been riders on the horizon, he would have kept Marietta right where she was, doing exactly what she was doing. In fact, he might just keep her here like this the rest of the way to Galveston.

Cole soon gritted his teeth in an attempt to stave off his coming climax while the wild, wanton redhead gave him the loving of his life. He held out for as long as was humanly possible.

And then there was no holding back when the very naughty Marietta put her lips to his ear and whispered on a fiery breath, "You can let yourself go now, darling. I'm ready for you. I'm almost there. Come with me to paradise, Cole."

Her words triggered the most wrenching release he'd ever experienced in his life. He hoped she really was ready, because he couldn't stop himself.

Feeling the hot, thick liquid of love inside her immediately brought on Marietta's incredible orgasm. Together they climaxed. Fiercely. Loudly.

She screamed his name. He groaned hers. The excited black whinnied.

When it was over, when at last their hearts had begun to slow and they had regained their lost breaths, the pair stayed as they were for a while longer. Resting. Coming back down to earth. Murmuring endearments. Soothing each other.

Finally Marietta raised her head, looked at Cole and they started laughing.

"We should be ashamed of ourselves," she declared happily, shaking her head.

"I don't see why. Nobody saw us," he said. "Besides, tell me you didn't enjoy it."

Marietta gave him a sly look and admitted, "That was the most pleasurable ride of my life."

Thirty-One

It was not yet dawn in Galveston, but the gravely ill Maxwell Lacey was wide awake and impatient for daybreak. From his bed, he looked across the room, saw that the night nurse was sleeping soundly in her chair. He could wake her and ask for pain medication. But he didn't want to take anything today. He wanted his mind to be totally clear.

Maxwell Lacey had the strong premonition that today would be the day his granddaughter arrived in Galveston. That possibility so excited him, he could hardly wait for the sun to rise so that he and Nettie could make the necessary arrangements.

Maxwell smiled when finally, as the first pale rays of the rising sun streamed into his bedroom windows, Nettie breezed into the room. The loyal housekeeper looked at the sleeping nurse, made a sour face then glanced at Maxwell. His eyes following her, Nettie tiptoed over to the snoring nurse. She leaned down close to the woman's ear and shouted, "Boo!"

The nurse awakened with a start and Maxwell laughed out loud. The nurse was not amused. Nettie didn't care. "I've warned you, Mrs. McCain, for the last time," she said. "You were hired to watch Mr. Lacey throughout the nighttime hours. Not to sleep in your chair. Get your things together and leave at once."

"But...but...I just dozed off," said the nurse. "I stayed awake all night and...and...it won't happen again."

"No, it won't happen again," Nettie said, "because you're fired."

"Well, now, just a minute, I—"

"Out," said Nettie, pointing to the door.

Maxwell was still chuckling as the dismissed nurse flounced out of the room in a huff.

Nettie came to the bed, patted Maxwell's thin shoulder and said, "I never liked her anyhow, did you?"

"She was mighty poor company," admitted Maxwell.

Straightening his bedcovers, Nettie said, "What do you say we do a run-through today?"

"A run-through?" Maxwell repeated, puzzled. "You mean you practice being my night nurse?"

"My goodness no. We'll hire a new nurse. Dr. LeDette will have someone here before nightfall. I don't mean that." She paused and her eyes sparkled. "I mean, what if today we rehearse Marietta's homecoming right down to getting all gussied up in our finest clothes and serving a scrumptious evening meal?"

Maxwell's pale eyes lighted with pleasure and he

confided, "Nettie, I don't believe it will be just a run-through. I have the strongest feeling that today will be the day she gets home."

"Really?" said the faithful housekeeper, as if surprised.

She wasn't actually surprised. She knew Maxwell Lacey better than anyone. Knew when he was in horrific pain even if he swore he wasn't. Knew he had spent long, lonely years regretting the foolish actions of his past. Knew that he was determined to cheat imminent death long enough to get one fleeting glimpse of his only granddaughter. Knew exactly what he was thinking. So she played along with him.

"...and when I awakened around three-thirty this morning," Maxwell was saying, "it came to me that today might well be *the* day. You think it's possible?"

"Why, it certainly is," Nettie replied, then hastily added, "but even if it's not, if we have to wait a few more days, today we can have what we'll call a dress rehearsal. How does that sound?"

Nodding eagerly, Maxwell was already attempting to rise up off the pillows, eager to get out of bed.

"Whoa, hold on, Maxwell," Nettie gently scolded, urging him back down onto the bed. "I'll get Nelson right away. Send him in to get you up and dressed."

"Tell him to hurry!" said Maxwell, as excited as a boy, his pain-dulled eyes agleam.

"I will," Nettie promised and left the room smiling.

Outside his door, her smile quickly fled. Her shoulders slumped. Bless his old heart, he thought Marietta would get home today. She knew better. Central City, Colorado, was a long way off. The journey could take at least another week, perhaps more.

But Nettie knew there was no use upsetting a dying old man. Better to go along with his optimism and pretend that the big celebration would take place any day now.

Today she would keep Maxwell occupied and entertained by having him help her and the rest of the staff get ready for their anticipated visitors.

Nettie and Maxwell spent most of the morning in his paneled library going over—one more time—the menu for the all-important homecoming meal. When finally they exited the library, they went directly to the kitchen where the head cook, Sanders, and his two helpers awaited instructions.

After a half hour, Nettie and Maxwell left the kitchen. The cooks were already firing up the ovens and taking down the necessary pans. Like a general with her eager aide-de-camp, Nettie, followed by Maxwell in his wheelchair, moved about the mansion, issuing orders in staccato fashion to the corps of cleaning girls.

When she was confident they would make the furniture gleam and see to it that the entire mansion was spotless, she motioned Maxwell out onto the broad front veranda.

"It's time we settle on which flowers to choose. I think roses would best fit the occasion, don't you, Maxwell?" she asked.

"Yellow roses!" he declared. "Lots of big white porcelain vases filled with dozens of yellow roses. And I want several bouquets in her room."

"Absolutely. Yellow roses it is," said Nettie, running down the front steps calling the head gardener's name.

Within the hour, dozens of fragrant yellow hothouse roses had been brought into the house. Nettie and Maxwell sat before a long worktable in the mansion's sunroom, carefully arranging the yellow blooms into white porcelain vases.

Setting the table was saved for the very last. When one of the serving girls offered to help, she was shooed away. As the afternoon shadows grew steadily longer, the industrious Nettie and Maxwell were in the dining room where the long table was covered with a snowy-white damask cloth.

"How many places shall we set?" Nettie asked, taking a stack of gold-rimmed plates from the china closet.

Maxwell, a clean cloth in hand, was busily polishing crystal wineglasses. "Well, I feel like we ought to invite Cole Heflin to stay to dinner, don't you?"

"By all means," Nettie said, placing the stack of plates on the table. "I would imagine that the two young people will have become good friends on the long journey. Marietta would want us to invite Mr. Heflin.''

''That's my thinking,'' said Maxwell and, suddenly struck by a stab of excruciating pain, dropped the glass he was polishing. It crashed to the floor and broke.

''I'm sorry, Nettie,'' he managed to say, and tried to lean down from his chair.

''Let it go, Maxwell,'' Nettie said, continuing with her chore as if nothing had happened. Waving a dismissive hand, she told him, ''The cleaning girl will take care of it.'' She smiled then and added, ''Besides, weren't you just practicing for the moment when we all break our glasses in the fireplace?''

The pain now eased, Maxwell nodded and grinned. Nettie could tell he was enjoying himself, so she kept up the charade for the remainder of the day. She helped him choose the clothes he would wear and supervised the brushing of his thinning gray hair. She saw to it that he got a good close shave and checked to make sure the shoes he wanted to wear had been properly shined.

But try as she might to stretch out their tasks, the summer sun had begun to set and still no one had arrived at the seaside mansion. It was then that a disappointed Maxwell asked Nelson to wheel him out onto the broad veranda.

Nettie spoke up. ''Yes. A good idea, Maxwell. I'll go out with you and we can—''

''No, Nettie.'' Maxwell shook his head and raised

a hand to stop her. "You stay inside and oversee the preparation of this evening's meal."

"As you wish," she replied.

Nettie stood in the marble-floored foyer and watched, sadly, as the man who had, throughout the day, worked tirelessly and laughed often, once again became dejected and somber.

Outside, Maxwell sat alone in his hospital chair. He looked out over the calm Gulf of Mexico, the gentle waves now pinkened by the dying sun. His bony shoulders slumped tiredly. He clenched his fists against another wave of pain. His eyelids drooped.

He was a fool. An old, pitiful fool. Marietta wasn't coming home today. More than likely, she was never coming home. It was senseless to wait and hope any longer. He could give up the struggle. Stop fighting. Surrender to the inevitable and let death take him.

"No. I can't do that," he finally murmured, tears filling his eyes. "She'll come. I know she will. And, when she does, I will be here to greet her."

Thirty-Two

The granddaughter that Maxwell Lacey hoped to see before he departed this earth laughed merrily as she rode behind Cole across the forbidding Llano Estacado of North Texas.

Marietta was happy as she had never been before. She was having the time of her life, enjoying one heart-stopping adventure after another.

Cole was a great companion. He was smart and witty and he knew everything there was to know about this vast tableland of Texas.

There were, he told her, no ranches or homesteads ahead for at least a hundred miles. They would have to make do with only the black stallion; would have to ride tandem until they reached Lubbock.

Marietta was secretly glad. While she pitied the dutiful black having to carry such a heavy load, she loved riding behind Cole. Loved clinging to his trim waist and laying her cheek on his shoulder. Loved feeling his broad chest move with his breaths or his laughter.

And she was glad they were a good three-day ride or more from Lubbock. Gladder still that they were a long way from Galveston and the end of their journey. She realized that these golden days would end all too soon. A woman in love, she wanted to be with Cole forever.

If she couldn't make him fall in love with her before they reached Galveston, it would never happen. He would deliver her to her grandfather as promised and leave her.

Marietta was determined to enjoy and savor every lovely minute of the time she had left with Cole. She would not dwell on the dreadful hour when he would walk right out of her life and she would never see him again.

''Hear that?'' Cole asked over his shoulder.

Marietta lifted her cheek from his shoulder and listened. Immediately she heard a commotion and spotted great clouds of dust on the southern horizon.

''What in the world is it?'' she asked. ''A sandstorm?''

''Buffalo,'' Cole said as the stampeding herd's first big bulls appeared, snorting and blowing, racing due north. Directly toward them.

''Dear Lord,'' Marietta said, alarmed. ''We'll be trampled to death.''

''No, we won't,'' Cole said, unworried. ''We'll just get out of their way. Hang on, sweetheart.''

Marietta nodded and wrapped her arms tightly around his middle while Cole wheeled the black about, pointed him eastward and put him into a gallop. Once they were well out of harm's way, he drew rein and the black immediately halted. Cole quickly dismounted.

He turned and offered Marietta a hand. She hesitated. "Those big beasts won't change course, turn and head this way, will they?"

Cole laughed easily. "Not a chance," he assured her.

Cole knew from experience that buffalo could be mean and savage. They charged anything or anyone who intruded. But he wasn't concerned. They were out of the path of this stampeding herd.

"Come on, get down and let's give the stallion a rest while we wait for the buffalo to pass."

Marietta dismounted. She stood next to Cole as the herd went thundering by in front of them, not fifty yards from where they stood. The black neighed and danced around, his natural instinct to gallop after the buffalo. But Cole held firmly to the reins, pulling the stallion's head down.

Marietta shaded her eyes against the blinding sun and watched in wonder as the huge creatures thundered past. She had never seen a herd of buffalo before and she was amazed by their size and speed. They were a sight to behold with their hairy bodies, puffing nostrils and pointed horns.

They ran so close together they became blurred into one dark moving mass and the noise they made was deafening. The very earth shook from so many sharp hooves striking the ground at once.

No longer afraid and now delighted with the spectacle, Marietta turned and smiled at Cole. He laughed, drew her over to stand directly in front of him and slipped an arm around her waist. She leaned back against him, clapped her hands and laughed with joy.

And then, as swiftly as the stampede had begun, it was over. Marietta foolishly waved goodbye as the herd grew smaller and smaller and finally disappeared, leaving a great cloud of dust hanging in the still air. Cole loosened his hold on her waist and she quickly turned to face him.

"Have you ever seen anything like that in your life!" she declared, looking after the departing herd. "Why, there must have been three or four hundred of those big woolly animals."

"That's about my estimate," said Cole, then shook his head. "Not long ago there would have been three thousand. Hope you got a good look, sweetheart. The buffalo are swiftly disappearing from these plains."

"The Indians killing them off?"

"No. The Indians only kill what they need for food and clothing. They use every part of a slaughtered buffalo." He made a face of disgust. "It's the hunters. Like the pair we ran into on our back trail. They kill the buffalo, take the hides and leave the carcasses to rot in the sun."

"I knew I didn't like those two big, ugly men," said Marietta.

"There are dozens, hundreds just like them," Cole replied. "Five, ten years from now there will be no more buffalo roaming the land."

"That's sad," she said.

"It is," he agreed. "So much for civilization."

"Well, if they are a dying breed, I'm glad I got to see them today."

Finally Cole looked down at her and grinned. "I knew you would be. That's why I had them come running past us."

"Ah, so you staged the impressive performance?"

"Just for you." He smiled and asked, "Anything else you'd like, miss?"

"Yes," she was quick to reply. "A bath. A nice long, cooling bath."

"Is that all?" he said.

"That's all."

Cole squinted up at the sun, then looked back at her. "In less than an hour, you, my dear, will be dipping your delicate toes into a swiftly flowing river."

Without turning to look around, Marietta knew there was nothing to see in any direction but the flat, dusty, waterless plains. There couldn't possibly be a river anywhere near where they now stood.

"I don't believe you for a minute," she said.

"No? Wanna bet?"

"Sure. I know I'm right, so what will I win?"

"If you win, I have a little something in my saddlebags just for you."

"Good. May I have it now?"

Ignoring the question, he said, "And if I win, I get a nice long back-scrubbing from you."

Marietta laughed and threw her arms around his neck. "I hope you win."

"I will," he said and kissed her.

Back on the trail, a highly skeptical Marietta needled Cole about the river she was certain did not exist. The brutal Texas landscape had not changed one whit. Nothing stretched before them but the same barren grandeur of the flat, pitiless plain they had been riding across all day.

"I can hardly wait. Only a few more minutes," she said into Cole's ear, "and I'll be dipping my feet into the river's cool, refreshing water."

"That's right," he replied, sounding totally confident. "And I'll be getting my back scrubbed."

"Strange, isn't it?" she commented conversationally. "I see no stand of cottonwoods or willows along the river's edge. No sunlight reflecting off the water. No wildlife rushing down to have a drink." She jammed her finger into his back and told him, "Texan, you better start looking in your saddlebags for the prize I am going to win." She then laughed gaily.

"Keep it up," Cole said, unfazed. "I will get the last laugh."

Marietta was still smiling broadly when Cole abruptly drew rein, bringing the black to a swift and total halt. Without explaining, he wrapped the reins around the saddle horn, threw his leg over and dropped to the ground.

Certain that she had won her bet, Marietta clapped her hands with glee, assuming that he had stopped to rummage through his saddlebags for some little trinket to give her.

"Close your eyes, Marietta," Cole ordered.

"Aha! So you admit I've won the bet."

He shook his head, reached up, put his hands to her waist and hauled her down off the horse.

"Now, close your eyes," he repeated. "And keep them closed until I tell you to open them."

Marietta smirked, but closed her eyes. Cole drew her forward a couple of steps, keeping a hand wrapped firmly around her upper arm. When he stopped her, he sternly cautioned, "Do not move! You hear me?"

"I hear you," she said, but giggled.

"Dammit, Marietta, I mean it. Not an inch."

Marietta promised to behave. She stood there perfectly still, waiting. But she frowned, puzzled, when she felt Cole's free hand grip the waistband of her trousers in back so tightly the fabric pulled across her stomach.

"What the...?"

"Open your eyes now, sweetheart, but keep very still," came Cole's low, drawling voice just above her left ear.

Marietta opened her eyes.

And immediately lost her breath.

They stood on the rim of a deep, gigantic canyon, the floor of which lay far, far below. Standing stock-still on the brink of the great abyss, Marietta stared, dumbstruck, at the yawning void hundreds of feet below, stretching beneath them with no termination in sight.

A vast and stunning panorama, the deep, gaping canyon floor was cut in half by a wide, winding river.

Thirty-Three

"P_{alo} Duro Canyon," Cole proudly announced, continuing to cling tightly to her waistband. He knew she was overwhelmed because she said nothing. Didn't make a sound. "The canyon was named Palo Duro by the Spanish when Coronado and his boys came through here in the spring of 1541." Cole chuckled then, and added, "I imagine old Coronado took himself a good long bath in that fork of the Red River you see down there slashing through the canyon."

Marietta remained speechless with awe and disbelief. Not daring to move, she peered over the rim into the depths of the seemingly bottomless gorge and saw a landscape as different from the flat Texas plains it cut through as night was to day.

"Cole," she finally spoke. "I had no idea. It's magnificent."

"Isn't it," he said and drew her a few steps back from the rim. He finally released his hold on her waistband.

She turned to face him. Her eyes now flashing, she

said, "You big devil! You tricked me. That's not fair."

"Sore loser," he teased. "I win. Be a good sport and admit it."

"Okay, you win, but the canyon appears to be awfully large, so we can't possibly—"

"Six miles wide in some places. Directly below is the narrowest part," he said, interrupting. "And Palo Duro stretches southeastward for a good sixty or seventy miles."

"My point exactly," she said. "We'll have to go all the way around it."

"No. We're going down inside," he said and winked at her.

Marietta frowned. "Now, Cole, I don't know about that. Even if we could find a way down, which I'm not sure we can, Mrs. Longley said that the Comanches live in the canyon."

"As I said, it's a huge canyon. The Indians will never know we're there."

"Promise?"

He nodded. "Their stronghold is in the northernmost reaches of the canyon. We're well to the south of them." He told her, "You and I are going down into the canyon and make camp by the river. You lose the bet, baby, and I mean to collect."

Relishing the thought of a bath, Marietta said, "What are we waiting for, Texan?"

Back in the saddle, Cole carefully guided the black along the edge of the canyon's rim until he found a place to start a safe, gradual descent. While a nervous Marietta clung tenaciously to his waist, he neck-reined the responsive stallion down a serpentine trail where the towering cliffs were layered with bright bands of orange, red, brown, yellow, purple and maroon. Patches of juniper, mesquite, sunflower and prickly pear grew along the colorful slopes.

Adding to the canyon's rugged grandeur were numerous pinnacles, buttes and mesas rising majestically from the level floor. When at last they reached the flat, grass-covered floor, Cole began scouting for just the right place to spend the night.

Thick groves of cottonwood along the river offered ample shade and total privacy. Firewood was plentiful. Grass covered the smooth riverbanks, making it ideal for spreading the blankets. But it was the distinctive sound of unseen water splashing that piqued his interest.

Cole pulled up on the black, turned his head and listened. "Hear that water falling into the river?" he asked.

"I do," Marietta said, delighted.

Sunset in Palo Duro Canyon.

Marietta, unashamedly naked, stood thigh deep in the river, singing as she shampooed her long, heavy hair. Cole, fully clothed, lounged lazily on the blanket, smiling with pleasure as he watched her.

The bloodred rays of the sun fell on the red-walled canyon and on the winding Red River below. On the

far side of the expanse, directly across from where
they'd made camp, the mist of spray spilling over the
rocky eight-foot waterfalls was tinged a luminous red-
gold from the fading sunlight. The calm waters of the
river were painted that identical soothing hue.

And the pale flesh of the woman standing naked in
the river was tinted the same warm reddish-gold.

Smiling, Cole watched her.

Then all at once, like a bolt out of the blue, it
dawned on him.

Marietta was singing.

She was singing and she wasn't all that bad to hear.
Not nearly as punishing as he remembered. Miracu-
lously, the sound of her singing no longer grated or
gave him a headache. It was, incredibly, almost pleasurable to listen to her.

Cole's forehead knit. What the hell was happening
here? Had she suddenly improved? Had he been too
hard on her before?

Baffled, Cole rolled up into a sitting position and
stared at Marietta. Arms raised, flaming hair now
richly lathered, mouth open wide in song, she was a
vision in all her naked glory. She looked so young
and beautiful and happy, he felt his eyes smart. He
wished he could keep her just as she was now for all
eternity.

Cole swallowed hard.

He knew that the sight of her standing naked in the
dying sunlight of this yawning canyon would be
etched in his memory forever. His chest suddenly felt

tight. He stopped smiling. His eyes clouded. He realized, as he watched her sink into the water to rinse the soap from her hair, that even after he had left her, he would never escape her.

She would still be there in his heart.

"I'm ready to scrub your back!" Marietta called out to him, sweeping her clean hair back off her face and holding up the piece of soap.

Cole's smile immediately returned. For the moment she was his. He wouldn't think past the here and now.

"I'm coming," he shouted and swiftly stripped down to the skin.

"Bring a cloth," she instructed.

Cole snapped up his silk bandanna and draped it around his neck. Marietta squealed when he came splashing into the warm water and grabbed her. He drew her up against his long, lean body, clasped his hands behind her, lowered his head and brushed a kiss to her smiling lips. She swooned and curled up against his chest contentedly. But he didn't let her stay there. He laughed, released her and sank into the water.

Cole sat down flat on the sandy river bottom, looked up at Marietta and said, "Payoff time, sweetheart." He gestured over his shoulder to his bare back.

Marietta nodded and started to move around behind him. He stopped her. He wrapped his arms around her thighs, drew her to him and pressed his face against her glistening belly.

"If you do a good job of washing my back," he told her, "I might be persuaded to return the favor."

Marietta shoved him away, freed herself from his grasp, reached down and slipped the bandanna from around his neck. She stepped behind him, went down on her knees and dipped the neckerchief in the river. She dribbled water across his bronzed shoulders. His taut muscles gleamed wetly in the fading sunlight and she thought him the most beautiful creature God had ever created.

"What are you waiting for?" he said over his shoulder. "Get to work, woman."

"Who says you're the boss around here, Texan?" she asked with a laugh, reached up and yanked hard on a dark lock of his hair. When he grumbled and threatened to retaliate, she smiled and began slowly rubbing the bar of soap in tiny, tantalizing circles over his brown back.

"Ahhh," Cole moaned his approval. "That feels good."

"How's this?" she asked and dragged the soaking bandanna over the spots she had lathered.

"Heaven," he said, then sighed contentedly when she dipped the neck piece back into the river and thoroughly rinsed his back.

If he was enjoying it, so was she. Marietta found scrubbing Cole's back to be a highly sensual experience. His was such an exquisite back, darkly tanned and deeply clefted and skin as smooth as silk. It was all she could do to keep her mind on her task.

When she finished giving his back a leisurely, thorough scrubbing and had rinsed away the last traces of suds, she couldn't resist slipping her hands under his arms and around his chest. Cole groaned his approval. As she had done with his back, Marietta began making soapy circles in the hair covering his chest.

But when she allowed an inquisitive hand to start sliding down his slippery belly, Cole gripped her wrist and stopped her.

"No you don't," he said and pulled her around in front of him. "Your turn, baby. Give me the soap."

"I'd rather you didn't," she said with a laugh and scooted back away from him.

"Fine. But you don't know what you're missing," he told her, rising to his feet.

She squealed, supposing that he intended to come after her.

To her surprise, Cole waded right past her, moving swiftly out into the deeper water. When the river rose up past his waist, he fell over onto his belly and began swimming.

Marietta stopped laughing. She tossed the soap and soggy bandanna onto the bank, turned and anxiously waded after Cole, calling out to him, "Wait for me!"

He didn't.

He continued to slice through the water, his powerful arms pulling him farther and farther away. Marietta frowned, irritated, but sank into the water and began to swim after him.

He was much the swifter of the two, his legs and

arms longer. The distance between them quickly widened. Marietta was annoyed with him. Twilight was not a half hour away and she was ready to get out of the water. She did not want to be all the way across the wide river when night fell.

"Cole," she called, spitting water as she attempted to stroke more rapidly, "you're getting too far ahead. Come back here. I can hardly see you."

No answer.

Cole continued to swim across the river. Marietta, already growing tired and short of breath, doggedly swam after him. And suffered no small degree of panic when all at once she could no longer see him. He had disappeared. Her lungs burning, her body growing chilled, Marietta swam on, not sure she could make it to the far side. Equally worried that she might not be able to swim back to where she had started.

Short of breath and frightened, Marietta finally reached the loud splashing falls on the river's far side. But there was no sign of Cole. She dog-paddled and turned in the water, squinting, searching nervously for him. She opened her mouth to call to him and closed it without making a sound. She hadn't thought about it before, but suddenly she was worried that there could be Comanches nearby and they would hear her.

Her eyes widened with fear and she could hear the beating of her heart in her ears. What if Cole had gotten the bends, slipped beneath the surface and drowned? What would she do if something had happened to him?

Marietta flipped around and stared at the rushing falls spilling down over the rocks. She hoped she would spot Cole treading water beneath the loud, splashing water. She saw nothing but great torrents of water plummeting into the river.

"Damn you, Cole Heflin!" she shouted, the danger of lurking Comanches quickly forgotten. He hadn't drowned. He was an excellent swimmer. He was playing games and she was not amused. "Where are you? Answer me this minute, Texan!"

Treading water, she turned to look back out over the river. And screamed when a muscular bronzed arm snaked out through the rushing falls and grabbed her.

Thirty-Four

"What kept you?" Cole shouted to be heard as he drew the startled Marietta back through the roaring water and into a totally dry cavern behind the falls.

Quickly turning to face him, an angry Marietta swept her hair back off her face then began pummeling his chest with her fists.

"Damn you, Heflin," she shouted. "I will never speak to you again!"

"Now, there's an attractive idea," he teased, easily deflecting her blows with raised hands. "A totally speechless woman. I didn't know there was such a thing." He laughed and slipped his arms around her.

"Very funny!" she said, squirming to free herself. "Let go of me, I'm not staying here with you."

"Ah, sweetheart, I'm sorry," Cole said, refusing to release her. "Don't be angry."

Continuing to push futilely against his chest, she said, "Why shouldn't I be angry? You swim off and leave me, then hide from me while I..."

"It was the only way to get you over here," he explained. "Had I suggested you swim across the river, would you have done it?"

"Certainly not. It's too far. And for your information, my arms got very tired and I almost drowned. I'm not sure I can make it back."

"You won't have to," he promised. "I'll take you back. You know I will."

"Fine. Let's go right now before it starts turning dark."

"Not just yet," he said. "Look around you, Marietta. I wanted to show you this cavern. It's my secret place. Now it's our secret place."

Beginning to soften a little, Marietta grudgingly glanced around. She was immediately enchanted. They were standing in a small, dry crater carved from the rock. A cozy room that was softly illuminated in an ambient red-gold light from the rays of the setting sun filtered through the splashing water. A hidden private place where the only entrance was directly through the rushing falls.

"You knew this grotto was here?" she asked at last.

Nodding, Cole said, "I did. I found it one summer when Keller Longley and I camped in the canyon." He released her, stepped back and said, "There's something I want to show you."

Ducking to keep from bumping his head on the cave's low ceiling, he moved to the back wall and sank to his knees. Marietta followed, stopping to stand beside him. Cole smiled when he located the initials he had carved in the stone one hot afternoon that long-ago summer.

"Look, Marietta, here are my initials in the rock," he said, tracing the crudely etched C.H. with his forefinger. "It's been more than a dozen years since I put them there."

Intrigued, Marietta slowly sank to her knees beside him and studied the initials. "Just think, Cole, those initials will be there long after you and I are gone. They'll stay just as they are forever." Then, childlike, she said, "I wish you had a knife with you."

"I didn't use a knife," he said, then looked around for a loose rock. When he found one that was suitable, a piece of rock with a sharp edge, he told her, "I used an Indian flint arrow. Shall I add your initials to mine?"

"Yes," she said, smiling, liking the idea very much. "Put them right next to yours, please."

Cole immediately went to work. While he scraped at the canyon's rock wall, he looked at her and asked, "Your name really is Marietta, isn't it?" When she hesitated, then nodded, he said, "And Stone? Is that actually your last name, or is it your stage name?"

Again he detected the slightest hesitation before she replied, "One initial is enough. Just carve the M for Marietta."

Puzzled, Cole said, "If you're sure that's the way you want it."

"It is."

In moments, the letter M was artfully carved directly beside the C. H. "There," Cole said, admiring his handiwork. "Does that suit you?"

Marietta smiled at him, reached out, traced her initial and said honestly, "You'll never know how much. Thank you, Cole."

"You're very welcome, sweetheart." He touched her cheek and said, "Sure you don't want me to add the S for Stone?" She shook her head. He asked, "Ready to go back now?"

"No," she said and laid a hand on his chest.

"No? I thought you wanted to get back across the river before nightfall."

"I've changed my mind," she said and began to smile. She looked into his eyes and admitted, "I don't think I can wait that long."

"Wait that long for what?"

"To be in your arms. Could we make love here in our secret place?"

"Ah, darlin'," he said, turned, rose onto his knees and drew her up into his arms. "Sure we can. Kiss me, Marietta. Kiss me."

Cole brought his mouth down on hers and fire instantly surged through their wet pressing bodies. When at last his lips left hers, he kissed her cheek, her ear, her throat and the curve of her neck and shoulder, leaving a trail of fire with each soft caress.

Her arms around his neck, hands clasping the thick damp hair at the back of his head, Marietta clung to him as if she would never let him go.

His lips took hers again, urgent but gentle, teasing, tasting. Then abruptly he deepened the kiss and she sighed her approval. The enveloping hotness of his seeking mouth closed firmly over hers and sucked the very breath from her body. Her pulse pounding, Marietta trembled against his chest. Weak with desire, she tore her lips from his and pressed her face against his throat.

Cole set her away and hurriedly stretched out on his back. He immediately reached for her, lifted her atop him. Settling herself astride his hips, Marietta leaned down and kissed him. She kept kissing him for several minutes, her breasts flattening on his chest, her knees hugging his ribs.

Cole responded to her sweet, probing kisses and did not rush her to do more. Marietta loved kissing. Couldn't get enough. Wanted to kiss and be kissed over and over again. He humored her. If it took dozens of kisses to satisfy her to the point where she was ready for total lovemaking, he would do all he could to hold his raging passion in check.

It was far from easy.

She was so incredibly desirable. So warm and soft and beautiful. It was sweet torture to have her draped naked atop him like this, kissing him, pressing her breasts into his chest, sensuously rotating her hips against his thighs. With each kiss, he grew hotter. So hot he felt as if he couldn't wait one more second.

But he had to, for her sake.

Cole became conscious of the hard pounding of blood through his veins, the involuntary surging and seeking of his aching erection. The sound of the water rushing over the falls somehow added to the sensation. The hammering water was allowed to spill unfettered into the receptive river. He badly needed to spill into the receptive flesh of this tempting woman.

Cole heaved a sigh of relief when finally Marietta's lips left his and she sat up. Fighting the powerful impulse to turn her onto her back, take her and hammer forcefully into her, he bit the inside of his jaw when she scooted down his body.

He drew a sharp intake of air when she impulsively lowered her face and brushed a butterfly kiss to the smooth head of his masculinity. It jerked against her lips and she lifted her head.

"I could," she told him, "lick my fingers and make you wet the way we did atop the stallion. Or, I could simply lick you wet with my tongue. Which will it be?"

His breath dangerously short, Cole tried to speak, to tell her it wasn't necessary, that he was still wet from the river. But he didn't say a word. More than anything in the world he wanted to feel her lips and tongue upon him. At the same time he was afraid he would climax if he allowed it.

Finally he said, "No, baby, I—"

But Marietta didn't listen.

Delicately, taking great care not to hurt him, she bent to him, put out her tongue and licked lightly upward, all the way from the base to the tip. A great paroxysm of air rushed out of Cole's tight lungs and he anxiously grabbed her arms and pulled her up.

"I thought you would like that," she said, her green eyes afire.

"I do like it," he said. "Too much."

Marietta smiled, catlike, and laid a gentle hand on the hard flesh she had just licked. "Shall I do the honors?" she asked.

"Yes, please," he croaked and placed nervous hands on her thighs.

"Watch, to make sure I do it correctly," she said.

"I will," he ground out.

Choking with sexual excitement, Cole watched unblinking as she raised onto her knees, wrapped a gentle hand around his rigid male flesh and carefully placed the tip just inside her. She took her hand away and slowly, sensuously, lowered herself onto him.

"Ahhh," Cole groaned as he easily slid up into her wet warmth.

"Ohhh, Cole, Cole," she echoed his ecstasy.

Matching Cole's lust with her own, Marietta gripped his ribs and began the erotic, rolling motion of her hips. Thrusting, she held him prisoner with her strong gripping thighs, pounded him with her rocking pelvis, punished him with her gyrating hips.

Loving it, loving her, Cole reveled in this wild, uninhibited display of fierce sexual hunger. A deep, powerful hunger that matched his own and lifted him to new heights of carnal pleasure.

Flexing the muscles of his buttocks, driving rhythmically into her to meet each of her frenzied thrusts, Cole watched her and was as excited by the sight as the feel of her. Her heavy hair, still damp from the river, whipped around her face and shoulders, one wet lock clinging to her cheek. Her breasts, with their tightened wet nipples, danced and swayed with her sensual movements. And between her gripping thighs, the dampened fiery curls were meshed with the raven coils of his groin.

Such a powerful aphrodisiac.

"Cole, Cole," Marietta began to call his name as she panted anxiously.

"Yes, baby," he groaned, grateful her release was at hand, knowing that he couldn't last much longer.

"Oh, oh, oh!" she gasped as he gripped her thighs and speeded his movements, driving into her, triggering her deep and lingering orgasm.

For several long seconds Marietta was lost in the throes of a shattering release, out of control, begging Cole for an end to a joy so intense she could stand it no longer.

The fervent squeezing of her burning body took Cole with her into paradise. His deep groans matched her whimpering cries as together they attained the ultimate in ecstasy.

When it subsided, Marietta sagged down onto Cole's chest and they fought to regain their lost breaths. When finally their intermingled heartbeats slowed and they could breathe freely again, a happy Cole grinned and teased, "I almost came that time. How about you, darlin'?"

Thirty-Five

The sun's last rays had faded when the pair left their grotto and plunged back out through the falls. As promised, Cole, with one arm wrapped loosely around her chest, effortlessly ferried Marietta back across the river to their campsite.

Once they reached the shallow water, Cole rose with Marietta in his arms and carried her to the spread blanket. She squealed her protest when he sank to his knees and dumped her. He fell over onto his stomach, gasping for breath, pretending he was exhausted. He didn't fool Marietta.

Laughing, she gave his bare bottom a playful, open-handed slap and said, "Don't tell me you're actually tired after that short swim supporting my feather-light body?" She made a mock face of disgust and asked, "Do I have a weakling on my hands here?"

Chuckling, Cole turned over, guided her hand to his groin, and said, "No, you have a weakling *in* your hands."

"You're terrible," she smilingly accused, released

him and laid her hand on his chest. "It's getting dark. We better get dressed."

"You first," he said, too content and lazy to move.

"Help me dry my hair?" she asked.

"Sure, sweetheart," he said and rolled up into a sitting position.

Marietta snatched up a towel. She rose to her feet and stood before him, leisurely drying herself while he watched, bewitched. The flames from the dying campfire danced and flickered, momentarily lighting her tall, slender frame, then casting it in shadow. Cole caught himself straining to see better.

Too soon she was finished. She tossed him the towel, turned and sat down between his legs. Cole enjoyed the task of blotting the moisture from her luxurious hair.

As he worked, they talked and laughed and Cole told her, "I have a fantasy about this beautiful hair of yours, Marietta."

"Tell me," she coaxed.

"We are alone in a room where there is a nice soft bed with clean white sheets. I am lying naked on that bed and I am not allowed to move, no matter how much I am tempted to do so. You are sitting on the edge of the bed beside me. You do not touch me with anything but your hair.

"You bend your head and let your hair spill over onto my chest. Then you slowly move down my body, letting the loose locks tickle and torture me until I can stand it no longer." He paused, then laughed and asked, "Think I'm crazy?"

"No. I think you're very innovative. Thank heavens. And, if we ever get back to civilization where there are still such things as beds, we might give your fantasy a try."

Cole grinned. "I can hardly wait."

When a full white moon rose over the darkened canyon, Marietta and Cole, fully clothed now, lay on their backs atop the blanket, yawning, holding hands, counting the stars in the heavens. Twigs snapped and crackled in the dying campfire and somewhere in the distance a lonely whippoorwill called to his mate.

It was a warm, beautiful summer night and Marietta, listening to Cole's deep, drawling voice as he pointed out a constellation of brilliant, clustering stars high above, was engrossed. And content. Happy beyond belief. She loved lying beside Cole in this ruggedly beautiful canyon. And she loved the fact that this ruggedly beautiful Texan was, surprisingly, a tender, caring man whom she had seen unselfishly hand over every cent he probably had in the world to the destitute Longleys.

When Cole fell silent, Marietta said softly, "Know something, Texan? I have found you out."

"Have you?"

"Yes." She raised onto an elbow and smiled at him. "You're a kind, gentle man. And I learned from Mrs. Longley that you are an attorney."

"*Was* an attorney, Marietta. And only for about five minutes." He turned his head and looked at her. "I'm a convicted felon. Felons cannot practice law."

Marietta smiled. "Mmm. You're a felon because of Hadleyville?"

"That's right."

"Tell me about Hadleyville. Mrs. Longley said you were a hero for what you did there and that—"

"I'm no hero, Marietta. Never was. Far from it."

"I don't believe you."

"It's true. All I did was follow orders," Cole said, setting her straight.

"Oh, Cole," she murmured.

"A price was put on my head," he continued. "I spent seven years eluding the authorities, moving from town to town, job to job, hiding out, lying low."

"And finally they caught you?"

He nodded. "I attempted to rob a bank and they nabbed me."

Marietta frowned and said, "Why would you take such a chance when…when…" She paused, thought it over, then said, "I know why! You did it for the Longleys. You knew how badly they needed money. That's why you robbed that bank. You meant to give the money to them. Didn't you? You risked your life for Mrs. Longley and Leslie."

Cole shrugged and gave no reply.

Marietta urged, "Oh, Cole, please tell me the rest. They caught you and meant to hang you?"

"I was standing on the gallows with the noose

around my neck,'' Cole said, ''when your grandfather's attorney arrived with the documents necessary to stop the execution.''

''Thank the Almighty,'' she said.

''No, thank Maxwell Lacey, your grandfather. He is a very powerful man, Marietta. He pulled the necessary strings to spare me. God knows what markers he called in. I owe him my life and I'm grateful to him.''

Marietta wrinkled her nose and steered the conversation away from her grandfather and back to Cole and his life before the war. Coaxing him sweetly, drawing him out, she listened, intrigued, as he talked of the happy times when he was a boy back in Weatherford.

He spoke fondly of his tall rancher father and his pretty, genteel mother. Said they had loved him and spoiled him and made his childhood carefree and happy. He reminisced over the good times he and Keller Longley had shared, telling her about their many escapades and laughing about the numerous pranks they had pulled together. Even though he had hated to leave Keller behind, the fun and adventure had continued when he went away to university to read law.

As she listened, Marietta couldn't help being envious; it was evident that Cole had crammed enough adventure into his life to provide ample excitement for a dozen men.

Cole laughingly confided that back in the days of

his golden youth he had never encountered a problem that couldn't be solved. Said he'd had more than his share of fistfights, but had always come out the victor. And what hard muscle alone could not fix, his intellect could. Life had been joyful and exciting.

Then the war had come. Overnight things had changed forever.

Cole stopped talking.

Marietta, plucking gently at the buttons of his shirt, said she knew he had lost both his parents. Peggy Longley had told her.

"I'm sorry," she said. Cole nodded, gave no reply. Then she couldn't keep from asking, "Were you married, Cole? Was there…is there a wife waiting somewhere in Texas?"

"No. I've never been married."

"I'm glad," she said, unable to hide her relief. But she couldn't let the subject alone. "Was there a special girl?"

Cole laughed. "I thought there was. I was wrong."

"Oh?"

"I was engaged to a young lady I had known most of my life," he said without emotion. "She promised to wait until I got back from the war."

"And she didn't?"

"I hadn't been away six months before she ran off with a New Orleans cotton broker."

"She married someone else?" Marietta made a face of disbelief. "Why, she must be a fool. You're better off without her."

Cole grinned. "Enough about me. Tell me about you. About your life, your family, your—"

"Some other time," she said and yawned dramatically. She lay back down, snuggled close and said, "I'm *sooo* sleepy. Aren't you?"

"A little," he said.

Her lips against his throat, she said on a sigh, "Cole, can we please stay in this beautiful canyon for at least part of the day tomorrow?"

"We'll ride all day in the canyon," he told her. "Then day after tomorrow, we'll make our way back up top. Once we're out of the canyon, we'll begin to drop due south along the Caprock escarpment toward the village of Lubbock." No response. "Marietta? Sweetheart?"

Marietta had fallen asleep.

Cole exhaled and gently pulled her closer, drawing her slender arm across his chest. He pondered her reluctance to talk about herself and her childhood. He knew nothing about her, other than the fact that she was an opera singer and that she had a rich grandfather down in Galveston whom she did not wish to visit. What about her mother, her father? Where were they? When had she left Texas?

Cole yawned and closed his eyes. But sleep did not come. He opened his eyes and again gazed up at the bright stars he had pointed out to Marietta earlier. And he counted the days he had left with her. Days that would pass too quickly.

He slowly turned his head and gazed at her sleep-

ing face. She looked so innocent, so vulnerable. It
struck him that hers was the face he longed to wake
up to every morning for the rest of his life. He had
known many women, but had fallen in love only this
once.

No. No. No. He didn't love her. How could he? He
knew what she was. Hell, he wasn't that foolish. Cole
turned his head away. He assured himself that there
was no woman on earth—not even this one—with
whom he wanted to spend the rest of his nights.

All the next day, the pair rode southeastward
through and around the soaring cliffs and majestic
spires in Palo Duro. They stopped often to water the
stallion and to cool themselves off. They napped in
the shade after their noonday meal. Well rested then,
they walked for a couple of miles, allowing the black
to follow at a slow, easy pace.

Come nightfall they again made camp along the
banks of the river and bathed in the cool, clean water.
They didn't get dressed after their swim. In silent
agreement, they stretched out on the blanket and allowed the heat of the campfire to dry their bodies.

Lazy, relaxed, they considered putting on their
clothes but never did. When the canyon winds rose
and the night air chilled, Cole drew the blanket up
over them.

"You sleepy?" he asked.

"Not that sleepy" was her whispered reply.

Thirty-Six

At sunrise they slowly, carefully, climbed out of the cool, cliff-shaded canyon and up onto the sunbaked Caprock of Texas. The terrain was once again brutal. Trees were few and far between. Water holes were scarce. The mercury quickly climbed past the century mark.

If all that were not enough, at midafternoon Cole spotted dust devils swirling on the near southern horizon. A sandstorm was coming. A savage duststorm that was quickly gathering steam, sweeping toward them in the constantly blowing winds.

Cole swore as he pulled up on the black. Marietta, dozing, her cheek resting on his shoulder, was jolted awake. "What is it?"

Hurriedly dismounting, Cole said, "A duststorm."

"Oh, no. What can we do?"

"Ride it out," he told her and reached for the canteen. "Get down."

"Why?"

"You heard me."

Nervously eyeing the gathering tempest sweeping toward them, Marietta dismounted. She watched as

Cole slipped the bandanna from around his throat and wet it down.

"Hold this," he said, shoving the canteen at her.

He tied the soaked neckerchief loosely around the stallion's muzzle. The black neighed and blew, shaking his head up and down. While Marietta frowned, Cole yanked the long tails of his shirt free of his trousers. He unbuttoned the shirt and whipped it off.

Sure he had lost his mind, Marietta stood holding the canteen, staring at him. Swiftly, he ripped one of the long sleeves from the shirt, then the other. He tossed both torn sleeves over Marietta's shoulder while he put his shirt back on.

He grabbed the sleeves, held both out and said, "Pour water over them. Wet them down thoroughly." She nodded and poured. "That's it," he said, and handing her one of the soaked sleeves, said, "Tie it over your mouth and nose."

"For heaven's sake, Cole, I don't—"

"Do it," he commanded and she did.

Cole tied the other sleeve around his lower face, climbed back into the saddle and reached for her. When she was seated behind him, he said over his shoulder, "Bury your face against my back, close your eyes and don't open them until I tell you."

Marietta didn't argue. Already the winds were swirling the loose dirt around them and just ahead a solid sheet of golden dust looked to be impenetrable. She closed her eyes, wrapped her arms tightly around Cole and felt the stallion go into motion.

In seconds the storm had completely enveloped them. Blowing sand stung their faces like the jabbing of hundreds of tiny needles. The fine sand filtered into their hair and down inside their clothes and the wind deafened them with its relentless howling. The black labored on through the roar and whine of the wind-driven sands, whickering his distress.

"It's okay, boy." Cole patted his neck and tried to calm the poor creature. "You're doing fine. Keep going. You'll make it."

Marietta, curious by nature, foolishly opened her eyes and was immediately sorry. Grains of sand stung like fire. Tears immediately filled her eyes and spilled down her dusty cheeks. She pressed her face against Cole's back and wondered how long they could survive such a terrible storm.

The howling winds and whirling sand continued to assault them for more than an hour, growing steadily worse until finally it reached a loud crescendo of wailing and roaring that was frightening in its intensity.

Then it stopped.

The wind tapered off.

The sand stopped eddying.

Cole drew rein. He yanked the wet shirtsleeve down off his face and turned in the saddle to ask, "You okay? You hurt?"

Marietta tugged the dirt-crusted sleeve down from her mouth and nose. Sand crunching between her teeth, she told him, "I'm all right, but there is not one inch of flesh on my body that is not covered with

sand." When he laughed, she said, "You think that'
funny? How about you in a shirt with no sleeves
You look silly, Texan."

"Perhaps, but it's cooler this way" was his reply
"You should try it."

After two miserable days when they endured sev
eral brief but fierce sandstorms and tolerated the op
pressive heat and constantly blowing winds, a ho
unhappy Marietta shouted with joy when they ap
proached the outskirts of a small settlement.

"We've finally reached Lubbock," Cole said
"How would you like to make the rest of the journe
by train?"

"Can we get a sleeper?" she asked.

"Sure thing," he replied and kicked the black int
a canter.

The dusty little settlement rising from the blea
South Texas Plains was not much of a city. It boaste
only one saloon, one hotel, one general store, on
livery stable and a tiny train depot.

But Lubbock, Texas, looked awfully good to Mai
ietta. It was the first settlement they had come acros
since leaving tiny Tascosa, a hundred miles back u
north in the Panhandle.

"Cole," she said, ignoring the stares they drew a
they rode down the street, "is Lubbock the prettie
place on earth or is it just me?"

Cole grinned and said over his shoulder, "It'

beautiful, but nonetheless let's hope we won't have to stay overnight.''

He guided the black directly to the train depot. He dismounted, tied the lathered, alkali-crusted horse to the hitch rail and went inside. Marietta eagerly followed. She stood at his elbow while Cole asked the ticket agent when the next southbound train would be leaving Lubbock.

''In exactly one and a half hours,'' said the man. ''You going to Abilene?''

''Galveston,'' Cole told him. ''Book us a sleeping compartment if one is available.''

''Certainly, sir,'' said the agent.

Cole paid for the tickets, stuffed them in his breast pocket, took Marietta's arm and ushered her from the depot.

Out on the sidewalk, Cole said, ''The first thing we must do is tend the tired, winded stallion.''

She nodded and followed as Cole led the weary black toward the livery stable down the street. While Marietta waited outside, he took the animal inside and found the stable boy.

''Unsaddle him and give him a nice long drink of water. When he's had his fill, wash him down real good to cool him off, then feed him a bucket of oats.''

''I'll take good care of him, mister,'' said the stable boy.

Cole grabbed the saddlebags, draped them over his shoulder and said, ''I'll be back for him in an hour.

The torture's over, old friend,'' Cole said to the stal
lion. ''You're going to get a long rest.''

The stallion raised his drooping head, nickered an
affectionately nudged Cole's shoulder. Laughing
Cole turned and stepped outside.

''What are we waiting for?'' he said to Marietta
''Let's go get ready for our train ride.''

Badly needing some new clothes, the pair walke
directly to the general store. The choices were limited
The railroad had come to Lubbock, but the latest fash
ion had not yet arrived. But neither cared. Cole picke
out a plain white shirt, a pair of tan trousers and blac
cowboy boots. Marietta found a simple dress of blue
and-white checked gingham, white cotton underwea
and petticoats and white kid slippers.

With their newly purchased treasures, the pai
rushed to the town's only hotel. They checked into
second-story room and waited while a porter filled th
claw-footed tub with hot water. Then once he wa
gone, they laughed and scuffled as they hurriedl
stripped, each attempting to beat the other into th
steamy water.

It was a draw.

Marietta stepped into the filled tub, then squeale
when Cole joined her. They stayed in the tub for
good half hour, washing the sand from each other'
hair and soaping their slippery bodies.

''I never knew that the simple act of taking a batl
could be so pleasurable,'' Marietta said with
happy sigh.

"Think how enjoyable it will be to sleep in a bed tonight," he said and kissed her.

She wrinkled her nose. "You need a shave, Texan."

"Coming right up," he said, shooting to his feet, splashing water all over her and the floor.

The train whistle blew.

A half-dozen travelers had gathered on the platform, ready to board the southbound train.

Near the end of the train, Cole led the shiny clean stallion up the plank gangway into a hay-filled stock car. He gave the big black a slap on the rump, turned and jumped down to the ground.

He looked up the tracks and saw Marietta. She stood on the platform in her gingham dress, her red-gold hair aflame in the afternoon sunlight. Anxiously she waved for him to hurry. Cole sprinted along the tracks, reaching her in seconds.

"You look like a schoolgirl," he said. Then he plucked her off the platform and handed her up the steps and onto the train.

No sooner were they on board than the wheels of the train began to slowly turn on the tracks. The whistle blew loudly as they made their way down the cars' narrow aisles in search of their private compartment.

"Here we are," Cole finally announced, stopping before a closed door.

Inside, the window shade was raised, revealing a cozy chamber equipped with a long, upholstered sofa

with a high plush back. Both sighed and moaned a
they sank onto the comfortable couch.

The train began to pick up speed. The depot an
the false-front buildings of Lubbock were left behind
For a while neither Marietta nor Cole spoke. Instead
both leaned back and relaxed, gazing out the window
at the parched land rushing by.

His head resting on the sofa's high back, his lon,
legs stretched out before him, Cole reached for Mar
ietta's hand. She turned and looked at him. H
yawned and stretched, rippling his muscles like a bi
jungle cat, the fabric straining against his biceps. H
reached up and loosened the collar of his newly pur
chased white shirt.

He squeezed her hand.

Marietta felt a thrill run through her and knew tha
she couldn't wait one more day, one more hour to te
him that she loved him.

She freed her hand from his, turned more fully t
face him and said softly, "Cole, there is something
want to say to you. Something I have to tell you."

Smiling, he laid a hand on her knee and said, "A
right, but must you look so serious? Is it somethin
bad?"

"I love you, Cole," she said simply. "I am in lov
with you."

Thirty-Seven

Cole's heart skipped a beat.

For a long moment he didn't speak. Finally, keeping his tone low and level, he said, "Marietta, please don't talk like that. Such foolishness. You don't love me."

"I do, Cole, and I—"

"Sweetheart, listen to me," he cut in. "You think you love me, but you don't. Not really. It's simply that we've had some grand adventures and you've been swept away." Cole smiled and added, "Why, we managed to elude Lightnin' and his entire gang. And then when Lightnin' finally caught up with us, you knocked him senseless."

Marietta nodded and smiled.

Cole continued, "After that we encountered that pair of dirty buffalo hunters, one of whom definitely had his eye on you. And then we managed to evade a band of whooping bloodthirsty Comanches. We've seen a thundering buffalo herd and then rode down into the awesome Palo Duro Canyon and...and...don't you see, Marietta, you've been swept away by the circumstances. Once you get back to civilization, you will—"

"Still love you," she firmly stated. "I love you, Cole, and whether you love me or not I will always love you."

Cole smiled as one might smile at a precocious child. He said, "That's terribly sweet and I am very flattered. But you don't love me. I know you don't. How could you? I have nothing to offer." He paused, then said bluntly, "Marietta, there isn't anything you can get out of me. Not a thing I can do for you."

Stung by his hurtful words, she stiffened and said, "I don't want you to do anything for me except love me." Cole made no reply. He glanced away, stared out the window. She said, "Look at me, Cole. Please, just look at me." Cole slowly turned to face her. She said, "Didn't you hear me? I said I love you and I only want you to love me."

Cole exhaled slowly and shook his head. "Nice try, but it won't work, Marietta. I'm on to you, sweetheart. I can see why you'd suppose that all you need do is profess your love and I'd give you anything you asked me for."

"That is not true."

"It is true and we both know it," he said, determined he would not be as easily conquered as her other past admirers. "No offense, sweetheart, but it's obvious that you have been pampered and spoiled all of your life." He paused for a heartbeat, then added,

"And that you are an expert at using men to get what you want."

Angered now, Marietta's face flushed and she said hotly, "You don't know what you're talking about, Cole Heflin! You think you're so clever, think you know everything about me. But you don't. You know nothing. Nothing at all. You don't know who I am or what I am or anything about me! You believe me to be a child of privilege? Coddled and indulged every moment from the cradle forward? You suppose I've led a life of ease and indulgence with never a care in the world? Nothing could be further from the truth. Did my dear old granddad tell you why I wouldn't want to come to Galveston with you? Did he? Tell me!"

Cole straightened. "No. No he didn't, but—"

"Then I will tell you," she said, her delicate jaw tightening and her eyes flashing fire. "When my mother became pregnant with me at the young age of seventeen, she was not married. As soon as he learned of her pregnancy, my spineless father deserted her. Left her to face my grandfather alone."

"Marietta, you don't have to tell me—"

"Yes, I do, so don't interrupt," she warned. "My grandmother was dead and my mother's brother was just a child. My coldhearted grandfather, shamed by my mother's condition, banished her from his sight without a dime to her name. Can you imagine? That old bastard tossing out his only daughter?"

"No, I can't."

"Well, he did. He told her that she had shamed the Lacey name and he never wanted to see her again. There she was, pregnant and on her own, with no skills and nowhere to turn, no place to go. She walked away from her home and accepted a ride out of town with a traveling drummer.

"Months later she wound up in Wichita, Kansas. She had me all by herself. We were dirt poor. We never had any luxuries, hardly had the necessities. We were fortunate to have a roof over our heads. My mother was so beautiful and sad and I watched her grow old before her time. She cooked and cleaned at a boardinghouse for our keep, and by the time I was twelve years old I had decided that my mother's life was not going to be mine. No matter what anyone thought about me, no matter what they said about me, I was going to do whatever it took to have a better life."

Marietta paused to get a breath and Cole felt a sudden ache in his throat. Seeing the bright tears shining in her eyes, he reached out to lay a comforting hand on her arm.

She irritably brushed his hand away and declared, "You're a man, you can take care of yourself, can't you?"

He did not even trust his voice to answer. He simply nodded.

"Of course you can. You can come and go as you please. Do anything you set your mind to." She glared at him and said, "You have no idea what it's like to be a woman all alone in a man's world! While my worthless father blithely turned his back on me, my mother could hardly do the same, now, could she? She couldn't just walk away from me like he did.''

"No, she couldn't, sweetheart," Cole said softly.

"When I was seventeen, my mother died from overwork and a broken heart." Tears sprang to Marietta's eyes and spilled over when she said, "She was only thirty-five, but she was no longer young, no longer pretty. She was an old woman." Marietta shook her head sadly and continued, "After I buried her, I could have stayed and been a serving girl at the boardinghouse where my mother had worked. But I didn't. I left that very day."

Continuing to talk, revealing things she had never shared with anyone other than the motherly Sophia, Marietta told Cole about her fears, her loneliness, her struggles, her constant striving to be somebody, to make something of herself.

Cole listened as she told of the terrible hardships she had endured and of how she had—all of her life— yearned for a family that loved and cared about her. Deeply touched, loving her more than ever, he wanted to draw her to him, to comfort and reassure her. But he knew that she was too upset to allow it.

"I am far from perfect," she admitted, "but I am not the terrible person you believe me to be. I have done what I had to do to take care of myself. And yes, I've used men to get what I wanted, but weren't they using me as well?''

Cole started to reply, but she threw up her hand and stopped him. "I wanted the things my mother never had. I wanted pretty clothes and a nice place to live and an exciting life. I wanted to be an opera singer more than anything in the world! Can't you understand that?" She exhaled and continued, "It is true that Maltese gave me the opportunity to sing at the Tivoli Opera House. But did he get nothing in return? Did he look unhappy to you? Is it acceptable for a man to use a woman, but not the other way around? If so, who made those rules? A man? Who else!" She was openly crying now.

"God, Marietta, honey, please, don't. I'm sorry for all the cruel things I said."

As if he hadn't spoken, she sobbed, "I am not proud of the things I've done, but I'm not ashamed either. I am not the scarlet woman you believe me to be. I'll admit to playing the flirt with a number of well-heeled gentlemen, but it never went any farther than that." She stopped, sucked in an anxious breath, brushed a wayward lock of hair back off her face and stated emphatically, "I have never known a man before you. Never." She paused and looked at him with sad, tear-filled eyes.

For a moment Cole was stunned, couldn't speak. Then softly he asked, "What are you saying, Marietta?"

"Cole, you were my first and only lover. I never gave anyone else anything more than a chaste peck on the check, so help me God. I am telling you the truth and I don't care if you believe me or not.''

Cole was deeply affected by her admission. He loved her and he couldn't help be relieved and happy to learn that he was her first and only lover. That confession made her all the more precious to him. Made him feel even more protective of her.

And he was incensed that her heartless grandfather had been so cruel to her mother. He swallowed hard, straightened his legs, reached out and put his hands to her narrow waist.

He hauled her over and sat her on his lap. He dried her tears and said, ''Darling girl, I'm so sorry for all that you've been through. I apologize for the mean things I've said and for the way I've treated you. Can you ever find it in your heart to forgive me?''

Her arms slipping around his neck, she sobbed, ''Cole, don't take me to Galveston. I've never met that mean old man who is my grandfather. I don't want to meet him. I hate him.''

Cole comforted her, sympathized with her, but said, ''Sweetheart, your grandfather saved me from the gallows and I vowed to him that in return I would bring you safely home. I must keep my word.''

''No,'' she cried. ''If you don't love me, at least let me go. Tell him I got away and—''

''Listen to me, Marietta,'' Cole said. ''I can't do that, you know I can't. But don't worry, I'll be there with you when you meet him and I'll take you away from his house anytime you say the word.''

"You promise?"

Cole hugged her closer. "I promise." He kissed her then and said, "Darling, I love you. I've never said that to a woman in my life. I love you, Marietta, and I want you to be my wife. When we get to Abilene, let's get off the train and get married."

"You mean it?"

"I do. Marry me, Marietta, the sooner the better. Marry me."

"Oh, Cole, the answer is yes, yes, yes. The one thing in this world I want even more than I wanted to be an opera singer is you, my love. I love you so much, Cole, but there's something else I must confess to first."

"All right, sweetheart," Cole said, then tensed and waited.

Sniffing, she told him, "I've called myself Marietta Stone for years, but that isn't my name. I'm really just plain old Mary." Fresh tears spilled down her cheeks when she added, "I don't even have a last name."

Into Cole's mind flashed the moment back in the grotto at Palo Duro Canyon when she'd said, as he started to carve her initials in the rock, "Just carve an M." Now he knew why. Bless her heart.

Cole hugged her tight and said, "Darlin', soon your name will be Mrs. Cole Heflin."

Thirty-Eight

"**B**y the powers vested in me, I now pronounce you man and wife," said Sam Willingham, Abilene's bearded, slightly inebriated justice of the peace.

The minute the justice spoke those words, Mr. and Mrs. Cole Heflin, laughing happily, hurried out of his office. Holding hands, they ran swiftly down the wooden sidewalk toward the train depot. The locomotive's wheels were already beginning to turn on the tracks when Cole swept Marietta off her feet and handed her up the steps.

"Cole!" Marietta shouted anxiously as he jogged along beside the tracks and the locomotive began to pick up speed. "Cole," she sighed with relief when he grabbed a handhold and swung up onto the moving train. She impulsively wrapped her arms around his waist and said, "For a second there I was afraid you weren't going to make it."

Cole grinned and hugged her. "And miss my own honeymoon? Not on your life. What are we waiting for, Mrs. Heflin?"

Marietta laughed, took his hand and pulled him along behind as they made their way through three cars of day coaches to their private sleeper. Once inside, Marietta was pleased to see that during the half-hour stop in Abilene, the porter had prepared the compartment for the night. The couch was pulled out and made into a bed, complete with clean white sheets and fluffy lace-trim cased pillows.

Suddenly feeling shy, Marietta turned to Cole and said, "But, darling, it's only three in the afternoon."

"We'll pretend it's nighttime." He touched her cheek with his fingertips. She felt it all the way down to her toes. She trembled. Cole kissed her, raised his head and looked into her shining eyes.

"Do that again," she said with a smile and he did.

Once their lips separated, Cole told her, "I have a little wedding present for you, Mrs. Heflin."

She made a face of puzzlement. "How could that be? I was with you every moment we were off the train. We hardly had the time to get married."

"I always plan ahead," Cole told her with a mischievous grin.

He kissed her forehead, then set her back and reached for his saddlebags. He withdrew a white paper bag and handed it to Marietta. She took it and on seeing that Lilly's Ladies Apparel was written on the bag, her eyebrows knit. She looked at Cole suspiciously.

"Go ahead. Open it," he coaxed.

Marietta gingerly opened the bag and peeked inside. Her lips parting, she took out a folded article of clothing that was soft and blue and shiny. She dropped the bag, shook out the beautiful ice-blue lace and satin nightgown and held it up. For a minute she was speechless. She stood staring at the beautiful nightgown, shaking her head.

Finally she drew it to her, pressed it to her breasts and said, "You bought this back in Central City, Cole Heflin!"

"Guilty as charged," he said, crossing his arms over his chest. "The day we met."

Marietta smiled and said, "And you bought it for me?"

"Who else, darlin'?"

She playfully swatted him with the nightgown and said, "Aren't you the presumptuous one, Texan."

Cole stopped smiling, uncrossed his arms and said earnestly, "The truth is, sweetheart, that never in my wildest dreams did I dare to hope I'd one day see you in the gown."

She liked his answer. She smiled and touched his tanned jaw. "You will see me in it this very afternoon, my love. Give me a few minutes?"

"As long as you want, sweetheart," he said. "I'll be out on the observation platform smoking a cigar."

"Fifteen minutes is plenty of time," she said and raising up on tiptoe, brushed a kiss to his lips.

"I'll count the seconds," he said, turned and went out the door.

Alone in the compartment, Marietta carefully placed the beautiful blue nightgown on the bed, then hastily lowered the window shade against the blazing

Texas sun. She kicked off her kid slippers and began unbuttoning the bodice of her gingham dress.

In minutes she was naked.

She turned and stepped in front of the closed door, on the back of which hung a full-length mirror. She frowned. She didn't like the way she looked. She unpinned her hair, which she had haphazardly wound into a knot atop her head before they'd gotten off the train in Abilene. She shook her head about, picked up the hairbrush and began to vigorously stroke through the long, tangled locks. She laid the brush aside, pinched her cheeks and bit her lips to give her face some color.

She turned and picked up the nightgown. She lifted it over her head, stretching her arms up, one at a time. When the lace straps lay softly atop her shoulders, she released the gown. It slithered down her bare body to the floor.

Again she turned to the full-length mirror. She blushed. The gown's low-cut bodice was lace all the way to the waist. The pale rose-hued nipples of her full breasts showed through as if the lace were transparent.

The gown's slinky satin skirt was cut on the bias, accentuating the feminine curve of her hips and delineation of her flat belly. The fit of the garment was so snug, the small indentation of her navel was well defined, as was the triangle of springy curls between her thighs.

Marietta shuddered.

She felt hot and cold at the same time, and oddly embarrassed, although she didn't see how she could be. It wasn't as though Cole hadn't seen her naked. He had. Yet somehow this was different. Now she was his wife. Now they were newlyweds and she desperately wanted to please him. To have him find her pretty. Desirable. Irresistible.

A soft knock on the door caused her to jump. She stepped back away from the mirrored door. Her heart began to pound. Her breasts rose and fell, pressing against the diaphanous lace. She had the foolish urge to throw her arms across her chest and hide herself. She didn't immediately answer Cole's knock.

"Marietta?" came his distinctive drawl, soft, but clearly audible. "Sweetheart, may I come in?"

Marietta took a quick breath and managed only a hesitant, "Y-yes."

The door opened only enough for Cole to slip inside. He closed it quickly behind him and threw the lock. He turned and looked at his bride in the revealing nightgown and lost his breath. For a long moment, he leaned back against the mirrored door and gazed at the flame-haired vision in blue satin and lace.

"You are," he said when he trusted his voice to speak, "the most beautiful woman I have ever seen. I can't believe that you are mine. That you are my wife. Surely you aren't real. You're so incredibly divine, you must be an angel."

Marietta smiled seductively and said, "Nothing could be further from the truth, as you well know."

Certain now of how much she pleased him, Marietta relaxed completely and was once again her sassy self. Swaying provocatively to him, she slid her arms up around his neck. Thrusting her satin-clad pelvis against his, she said, "I'm no angel, Texan, and I plan on spending the afternoon showing you just that."

"Ah, baby, that's what I wanted to hear," he said and kissed her.

Her eyes closing, Marietta's lips parted beneath his and she felt his sleek tongue slide between them. They kissed hotly and when at last their lips separated, Marietta said, looking directly into his eyes, "I've heard it said that all men want to be a woman's first lover, while all women wish to be a man's last. You were my first, Cole. Let me be your last."

"You will, sweetheart," he promised. "I'll be forever faithful to you."

"And I to you," she said, eagerly wrapping her arms around his trim waist.

They kissed again and kept on kissing for several minutes, each kiss growing hotter, probing deeper, lasting longer. When finally Marietta tore her lips from his, Cole gently turned her in his arms so that she was facing away from him.

Marietta sighed and leaned back against him, her head falling onto his left shoulder. Cole pressed his smooth cheek against hers and slid his arms around her.

"We have a bed now, Cole," she softly reminded him.

"I know, but let's stay like this for just a moment," he said as he lifted a hand to her lace-covered breasts.

"You'll get no arguments from me on our wedding day," she said as her eyes slipped half-closed.

"I would like," he told her, his voice low, his drawl pronounced, "you to leave the nightgown on. Just for a while." Through the covering lace, the tip of his index finger was making tantalizing circles around her rigid left nipple.

"Whatever you want," she said on a sigh. "I told you you'll get no arguments from me today." She laughed softly, and added, "Or tonight."

Cole brushed a kiss to her cheek, gently plucked at her nipple through the gauzy lace and felt her squirm against him. He moved to the other nipple, but never slipped his hand inside the gown's bodice. Her covered nipples stood out in twin points of sensation, the lace mildly abrasive, Cole's fingers gentle.

She could already feel the sexual heat languidly spreading throughout her body. That heat quickly flared into blazing passion when one of Cole's hands swept down over her satin-covered belly to her groin. Gently, he cupped her and she shivered.

Against her temple Cole whispered, "Sweetheart, move your legs apart just a little."

Marietta didn't question him. She moved her bare feet slightly apart, then exhaled anxiously when she felt his hand go between. Once again using only his long index finger, Cole purposely pressed the gown's slick satin into the delicate cleft of her soft female body. Carefully, he slid his finger up and down repeatedly, gently parting the springy red-gold curls pressing against the satin. He continued until the slick satin was molded against her, the feather-soft fabric sticking to her.

Through the sensuously slippery barrier, he began to caress that tiny button of highly sensitive feminine flesh. Marietta drew in a shallow breath and began to murmur her approval. Her eyes closing, she turned her face inward, her body tingling, her breath coming in short, anxious gasps.

It was, she thought, incredibly thrilling to be standing on a moving train in the middle of the day in a slinky lace and satin nightgown while the handsome man of her dreams, the man who was now her husband, showed her a new method of making love.

"Cole, I'm on fire," she whispered as an incredible heat radiated upward from that burning spot where he was caressing her. "I'm hot all over."

"I know, baby," he said, continuing to gently circle and caress her until the shiny satin barrier between his fingers and her flesh was wet with her body's physical response to unchecked sexual desire.

Marietta found it wildly exciting. The wet satin, the tantalizing fingers, the taboo aspect of it added to the awesome pleasure. She loved the feel of Cole's fingers touching her through the damp satin, loved the idea of climaxing like this. Thrusting her pelvis forward, her arm bent and raised up around Cole's neck, she heard the train's whistle blow loudly. That, too, added to her rising ecstasy. The mighty locomotive letting off steam matched her body's growing need for a blaring release of its own.

"Ooooh, Cole," she said, her eyes growing wide, her heated body beginning to spasm against Cole's loving hand as her climax began.

Knowing just how to handle her, Cole held her firmly with one strong arm wrapped around her waist as his dexterous fingers stayed between her legs and continued to carefully coax the climax from her.

When it came, Marietta screamed loudly in her ecstasy, but the sound was drowned out by the shrill blowing of the train whistle. The lengthy scream and the blasting whistle peaked simultaneously. The train raced swiftly on while Marietta sagged weakly back against her smiling husband.

When she regained her lost breath, a sighing, sated Marietta turned in Cole's arms and said, "I've ruined my beautiful nightgown."

"Who cares?" Cole said with an impish laugh. "Tell the truth, darlin'. Wasn't it worth it?"

"It was, you wicked devil," she said with a happy smile.

With his help, she peeled the gown up and over her head. Cole tossed it aside, drew her into his arms and said, "Besides, I like you naked even better."

"Mmm," she replied, and began unbuttoning his shirt. "It's high time you get naked with me."

"Sounds good to me," Cole said and they laughed as together they stripped him of his clothes.

When he was as bare as she, Marietta swept a han
over his broad chest and said, "Remember your fan
tasy, Cole?" She moved her head, swirled her lon
loose hair around her shoulders. "Get ready to liv
it." She began to push him toward the bed.

"Sweetheart, you don't have to…"

'I want to," she said. "Now lie down, darling."

Cole stretched out on his stomach, placing a folde
arm beneath his cheek. His head turned to the side
he watched expectantly as Marietta sat down on th
edge of the bed. He tensed as she lifted her hands an
combed her fingers through the heavy tresses.

He watched as she scooted up higher on the be
and abruptly flipped all that wild red hair over he
head. She then bent to him, her hair making a silk
curtain of reddish-gold across his face. He inhale
deeply of its clean scent and kissed a silky strand a
it fell against his nose and mouth.

Too soon the mass of glorious hair was taken awa
Cole groaned when he felt it fall onto his bare shou
ders, tickling him, exciting him. For the next te
minutes his playful bride teased and tormented hi
with her abundant red tresses. The feel of all tha
glorious hair falling onto his bare flesh was intensel
pleasurable and arousing to Cole.

Enjoying every second of his fantasy, he stood
as long as he could while Marietta languidly move
down his long, lean body, her hair brushing light
over his back, his waist, his flexed buttocks, his lon
legs. When she reached his feet, then started back u

Cole swiftly turned over. Lifting his head off the pillow, he watched with growing excitement as Marietta, head still bent, hair still spilling down, worked her way back up his tense body.

When she reached his groin, she purposely paused, knowing what would happen.

It did.

Cole's aching erection surged up against, and then through, the cloud of hair lying over his pelvis.

"That's enough," he choked. Marietta smiled and finally raised her head. "Come here to me, you beautiful witch," he said and pulled her into his arms.

He kissed her, turned her over onto her back and took her with no further preamble. She was, to his delight, as ready as he. While the train clickity-clacked steadily down the tracks, the naked newly-weds made love in a clean white bed for the very first time.

It was, they decided, most enjoyable.

The afternoon loving was only the beginning of a long, lovely honeymoon. As the summer sun set outside the closed window shades, the lovers were once again surrendering to their blazing passion. Vowing they would stay naked all the way to Galveston, they finally, around 9:00 p.m., got so weak from hunger they had put on clothes.

But as soon as they'd finished their meal, they left the empty dining car, rushed back to their compartment and raced each other to see who could get naked first.

Cole won.

But not by much.

When Marietta stretched out beside him, she kissed his chest and said, "While I have learned that a woman can make love anytime at all, I was wondering...can a man?"

"Sweetheart, the only man you'll ever need to worry about is me," Cole told her, "and the answer to that is, it's entirely up to you."

Marietta raised up, looked at him. "Me?"

"Yes you. It depends on whether you are woman enough to arouse me. You want it up, you have to get it up."

"Is that all?" she said flippantly. "Tell you what, Texan, if I can't get it up in five minutes flat, feel free to divorce me."

Both laughed as Marietta happily went to work on him.

Thirty-Nine

"Maxwell, won't you please let Nelson help you get out of bed?" urged Nettie.

Maxwell Lacey didn't bother turning his head on the pillow. The weak man had not left his bed for the past five days. He was sicker than ever. And he had all but lost hope that he would ever see his granddaughter. He had faced the sad fact that she was not coming.

"Who knows," Nettie continued, making her voice sound cheerful, "today might well be the day that Marietta arrives."

No answer. No movement on the bed. Nettie glanced at the nurse. The nurse shook her head. The message was clear. Maxwell Lacey's days left on this earth were few in number. The sick old man would not live out the week.

"All right, lazybones," said Nettie, her tone remaining bright, "why don't you take a nice restful nap and then this afternoon you can sit out on the veranda for a while. How does that sound?"

Finally, a muffled response from the bed. Nettie

hurried forward. "What? I didn't quite hear you, Maxwell. What did you say?"

At last the gray head slowly turned on the pillow and a pitiful Maxwell looked up at Nettie. Tears were swimming in his eyes and his sunken cheeks were ghostly pale.

"It's no use, Nettie," he said, barely above a whisper. "She isn't coming. She will never come home."

"Such nonsense," Nettie scolded, shaking her head. "Why, this isn't like you, Maxwell Lacey. You've never been a quitter. Don't give up now."

"I'm awfully tired," he said in apology.

"I know you are," Nettie said softly and, stepping closer, reached out and smoothed back a lock of thinning hair from his damp forehead. "You rest now and perhaps later today you'll feel better." She smiled at him, took one of his frail hands in both of her own and asked, "Shall I sit here with you a while?"

"Cole, I'm nervous."

"Don't be," he said, his tone low, level. "I'm here with you, I'll never leave you."

"I know, still…do we have to…to…?"

"We do, darlin'. But we don't have to stay," he soothed. "We'll put in an appearance, that's all. Just stay long enough so your grandfather knows I kept my word."

The pair had finally arrived in Galveston. It was midafternoon as they rode in a hired carriage toward the home of Maxwell Lacey. When they neared the

Gulf shores, the coach turned into a long, pebbled driveway. Lips parted, Marietta stared at the gleaming two-story mansion rising to meet the sun at the end of the palm-bordered avenue.

Her jaw tightening, she said, "Why, he's filthy rich, isn't he?"

"He is," Cole confirmed. "He certainly is."

Marietta made a sour face. "Well, perhaps he can take it with him. I'm sure he'll try."

The carriage rolled to a stop. Cole opened the door and stepped out. He reached for Marietta. She reluctantly allowed him to help her down.

As soon as her feet touched the ground, she turned and said to the carriage driver, "Don't leave. Wait right here for us. We'll only be inside a few minutes."

As Cole took her arm, Marietta drew in a slow, deep breath. Together they went up the front walk and climbed the mansion steps.

On the wide veranda, Cole turned her to face him and said, "I love you, Marietta. I'm on your side and I understand how you feel. Remember that." She nodded, but gave no reply. "Ready?" he asked.

"Yes," she said. "Let's get this over with."

The heavy wooden front door was open. A screen door was closed. Cole raised the brass door knocker beside it and gave it a forceful thump. A uniformed butler immediately appeared in the portal.

Through the screen, Cole said, "I'm Cole Heflin and this is—"

"Who is it, Nelson?" Nettie stepped up beside him. The minute she saw the handsome couple standing on the veranda, she stepped past Nelson, threw the screen open wide and exclaimed, "You must be Marietta!"

"Yes, ma'am," Marietta replied. "And this is—"

"Cole Heflin," Nettie interrupted. "I've heard so much about both of you. Come in, come in."

Cole handed Marietta inside and followed. In the cool, high-ceilinged foyer, a beaming Nettie said to Marietta, "Thank heavens you've come. And just in time! Your grandfather has been steadfastly clinging to life in the hope that he would get to see you."

Marietta was not swayed. "Yes, well, he'll see me, but only briefly," she said in clipped tones. "I've no intention of spending any time with him."

Nettie nodded. "A mere glimpse of you will mean the world to Maxwell."

"Fine," Marietta replied, vowing she would remain as hard-hearted as her grandfather had been. "Where is he?"

"Follow me," said Nettie and led the way. Marietta and Cole followed her down a long, wide corridor. When she stopped before a closed door at the rear of the house, she said, "This is Maxwell's room. He's bedfast, hasn't been up in days. When you go inside, just nod to the nurse and she will leave."

"No need for her to leave," said Marietta. "I told you, we're not staying."

When she reached out to open the door, Cole said, "I'll be right here, sweetheart, just outside the door."

Her eyebrows knit. "You aren't coming in with me?"

"No. It is you he wishes to see."

Marietta didn't argue. She straightened her back and, her heart in her throat, entered the sickroom. She did not nod to the nurse. She didn't have to. On seeing her, the woman rose, opened the heavy drapes to let in some afternoon sunshine, then silently left the room, closing the door behind her.

For a long, tense moment, Marietta continued to stand just inside the door, saying nothing. After what seemed an eternity, the pale, pain-stricken Maxwell Lacey sensed a presence, turned his head and saw her. At once his sick old eyes lit up.

"Oh, child, child," he rasped, raising his head from the pillow. "Please, come closer."

Years of bitterness having made her immune to his pain, Marietta approached the bed, glared down at the grandfather she had never met and said coldly, "What do you want, old man?"

"Just to see you," he said honestly.

She smirked. "It's a little late to be claiming your bastard granddaughter."

He lifted a weak hand from the bed and reached out to her. She ignored the gesture. "You have your mother's eyes," he said, his own swimming in tears. "Can you ever forgive me, Marietta?"

"No, never!" she declared hotly and pivoted.

"Oh, please, child," he begged, "don't go. Stay for just a moment." Jaw clamped tight, Marietta slowly turned back to face him, crossing her arms over her chest. "There's so much I want to tell you," he said.

"Yes, well you have five minutes and not one second longer."

Scowling, she stood by the bed and listened quietly as her repentant grandfather begged for her forgiveness. He said he knew he had made a terrible mistake and that he had paid for it every day of his life. He told her she could rest assured that his had been a lonely, meaningless existence filled with unhappiness and regrets.

Marietta stared at him. Her arms came unfolded.

He looked so frail and pitiful lying there with bright tears shining in his eyes. There was little doubt that he truly had suffered for his sins. Since she was now so fulfilled and happy herself, so secure in the knowledge of Cole's love, it made her more understanding, more forgiving.

Knowing that her grandfather was dying, Marietta finally took his withered hand in hers, but gently accused, "You turned my mother out because she was in love and made a mistake. How could you have been so cruel to a young, helpless girl? Your own daughter?"

"I don't know, child," he admitted, "I was a pig-headed fool and I should have been horsewhipped for it."

They talked and talked and Marietta, by nature a kind, loving person, finally decided to ease her suffering grandfather's conscience by telling him that he was forgiven. She saw the relief flood his pain-clouded eyes and was touched. In that minute she decided that she would do what she could to cheer him in the final days of his life.

She kept to herself all the struggles and loneliness she'd suffered through the years. Instead, she told him how she had been a popular opera singer in Central City. And she told him that she and Cole Heflin, the man he had sent·to Colorado after her, had fallen in love on the journey to Galveston and had gotten married in Abilene. She could tell by the look on his face that he fully approved.

Just outside the door, Cole and Nettie waited anxiously, wondering what was going on inside. Both were surprised that Marietta had stayed with Lacey as long as she had. Several long minutes had gone by. What, they wondered, was happening? Was she continuing to torture the dying old man by telling him how much she hated him?

Cole's jaw dropped open and Nettie blinked in surprise when all at once they heard the distinct sound of laughter erupt from inside the sickroom. Maxwell Lacey was chuckling loudly with delight. Marietta was laughing as well, the sound musical, genuine. Cole and Nettie exchanged pleased looks.

"...and then after Cole got me down out of the mountains it was one unbelievable escapade after an-

other," Marietta was saying, squeezing her grandfa
ther's hand, entertaining him with the many thrilling
adventures she had experienced on the trail.

Maxwell listened with glee, living vicariously
through her. She said, "Can you believe this one? We
had to outrun a band of Comanches! I tell you it was
touch-and-go, but Cole outsmarted them and thus
saved our scalps!"

"Thank God," said her beaming grandfather, "you
have such beautiful hair. Your mother had glorious
red-gold hair just like yours."

"Yes, she did. That's where I got it. Now, where
was I?" Marietta said. "Oh, yes, and before that we
met up with two wild-and-woolly buffalo hunters
They camped with us." She wrinkled her nose
"They smelled bad."

Her grandfather laughed.

"And then there was the day we almost got run
down by a thundering herd of buffalo. It was the first
time I'd ever seen hundreds of those shaggy creatures
They raced across the dusty plains like Satan himself
was after them."

Marietta continued to enthrall her grandfather with
tales of the days and nights she and Cole had spent
on the trail. She asked if he had ever been to Palo
Duro Canyon in far North Texas. When he shook his
head that he had not, she painted vivid pictures with
words.

She artfully described the canyon's rugged beauty
and made his old heart beat with joy when she added

"You get to feeling better, we'll all go back up there and camp out under the stars. Wouldn't that be fun?"

The thought so excited him, Maxwell Lacey attempted to raise up off the bed. His granddaughter shook her head, gently urged him back down and said, "I've stayed too long, tired you out."

"No, don't go," he said, his disappointment evident.

"Now, now, it's all right. I'm going to let you get some rest."

"You'll come back? You won't leave?" he asked hopefully.

"I'll be back," she said, nodding. "I promise."

"Thank you so much for coming, Marietta," he said. He squeezed her hand and added, "You've made a dying old man very happy."

"I'm glad," she said and meant it.

"I don't suppose that you...you..."

"What? Tell me."

"Would you consider calling me...grandfather? Just once?"

Marietta flashed a dazzling smile and said, "I'm glad that you and I have finally met, Grandfather."

Maxwell Lacey died the next day.

Peacefully.

His granddaughter and her husband were at his bedside when he drew his last breath. Marietta was holding his hand. When they came out of the room, Nettie was waiting.

Marietta said softly, "He's gone, Nettie."

Tears shining in her eyes, Nettie said, "You're a kind young woman. I appreciate you for making his last hours happy." She blinked back her tears and announced, "Mark Weathers, Maxwell's attorney, is waiting for you in Maxwell's library." She extended her hand, pointing the way up the long corridor. Then she turned and went into the sickroom to say her last farewell to the man who had been a dear friend as well as her employer.

Her hand enclosed in Cole's, Marietta walked up the hall to the darkly paneled library. As soon as she stepped inside, her attention was drawn to the fading poster advertising an opera in which she had been the star.

That, for some unexplained reason, brought hot tears to her eyes. For the first time since arriving in Galveston, she cried. Cole hugged her, kissed her forehead, then guided her to the massive mahogany desk where he had first laid eyes on Maxwell Lacey. The attorney, Mark Weathers, was now seated behind the desk.

He rose to his feet as they approached. They reached the desk and he said, "Mark Weathers, Marietta. My condolences."

"Thank you," she replied and lifted a lace handkerchief to dab her damp eyes. "You've met my husband, Cole Heflin?"

"Yes, I have," said the attorney, reaching across the desk to shake hands.

Mark Weathers said, "Won't you please have a seat. Both of you."

When they were seated, the attorney sat back down. He picked up a legal document and explained, "Maxwell's last will and testament. Shall I read it to you, Marietta?"

She nodded.

Weathers read the will aloud. Marietta learned—to her pleasant surprise—that, with the exception of a substantial inheritance left to Nettie, she was the sole heir to a vast fortune. For a long moment she was speechless. Finally the attorney cleared his throat needlessly, handed the will across the desk and got to his feet.

"Now, if you'll excuse me, I'll get back to my office and leave you two alone."

Once he had gone, Marietta turned to Cole and said, "You're an attorney, aren't you, Cole?" She got up out of her chair.

Cole rose to face her. "*Was* an attorney. I can't practice law, Marietta. I'm a disbarred felon, remember?"

"Good!" she said. "I don't want you to practice law. I want you to take over the task of overseeing and maintaining this expansive estate."

"Are you sure? There are experts who, for a fee, would be more than willing to manage your estate."

"*Our* estate, Cole. Yours and mine." She put her arms around his neck and said, "And *you* are the expert I want handling it. Say you will, darling."

Cole grinned. "I will."

"One more thing, I want my voice coach to move down here from Central City. Sophia has no family and she's such a dear, she's been like a mother to me. I'm sure we have opera here in Galveston, don' we?"

He nodded. "But of course. Even we Texans appreciate the higher arts."

Marietta smiled. "Sophia could give voice lessons."

"That's a wonderful idea," Cole said. Then "So...you're still as interested in the opera as ever?"

"Well, certainly. I'll want to attend every production."

He noted that she said "attend" not "appear in." But after a pause, he said, "Marietta, if you could sing in any opera house in the world, where would i' be?"

She laughed gaily, took one of his lean hands placed it lightly on her flat stomach and said, "I'll be singing only lullabies in the nursery soon."

Cole blinked in surprise. "You mean, you...?"

"No, I mean *we*. We are going to have a baby." Speechless, Cole stared at her. "Please, darling," she said, "tell me you want the baby. Tell me you wan' me."

His arms going around her, Cole said, "Ah, sweetheart, I want you both. I love you both and always will."

Bestselling Author

TAYLOR SMITH

On a cold winter night, someone comes looking for Grace Meade
and the key she holds to a thirty-five-year-old mystery. She is
tortured and killed, and her house is set ablaze. Incredibly,
the prime suspect is her own daughter, Jillian Meade, a woman
wanted in connection with two other murders of women Grace
knew during the war. And FBI Special Agent Alex Cruz has to find
Jillian before her past destroys her for good.

DEADLY GRACE

A "first-rate political thriller."
—*Booklist*

On sale April 2003
wherever paperbacks are sold!

MTS945

*Introducing an incredible new voice
in romantic suspense*

LAURIE BRETON

FINAL
EXIT

Ten years ago tragedy tore them apart….

But when FBI Special Agent Carolyn Monahan walks back into
the life of Homicide Lieutenant Conor Rafferty, the sizzle
is undeniable. They are back together, albeit reluctantly,
to find the serial killer who is terrorizing Boston.

As the pressure builds to solve the murders, so does the attraction
between Caro and Rafferty. But the question remains:
Who will get to Caro first—the killer or the cop?

Available the first week of April 2003 wherever paperbacks are sold

MIRA®

If you enjoyed what you just read,
then we've got an offer you can't resist!

Take 2
bestselling novels FREE!
Plus get a FREE surprise gift!

Clip this page and mail it to The Best of the Best™

IN U.S.A.	IN CANADA
3010 Walden Ave.	P.O. Box 609
P.O. Box 1867	Fort Erie, Ontario
Buffalo, N.Y. 14240-1867	L2A 5X3

YES! Please send me 2 free Best of the Best™ novels and my free surprise gift. After receiving them, if I don't wish to receive anymore, I can return the shipping statement marked cancel. If I don't cancel, I will receive 4 brand-new novels every month, before they're available in stores! In the U.S.A., bill me at the bargain price of $4.74 plus 25¢ shipping and handling per book and applicable sales tax, if any*. In Canada, bill me at the bargain price of $5.24 plus 25¢ shipping and handling per book and applicable taxes**. That's the complete price and a savings of over 20% off the cover prices—what a great deal! I understand that accepting the 2 free books and gift places me under no obligation ever to buy any books. I can always return a shipment and cancel at any time. Even if I never buy another The Best of the Best™ book, the 2 free books and gift are mine to keep forever.

185 MDN DNW
385 MDN DNW

Name	(PLEASE PRINT)	
Address	Apt.#	
City	State/Prov.	Zip/Postal Code

* Terms and prices subject to change without notice. Sales tax applicable in N.Y.
** Canadian residents will be charged applicable provincial taxes and GST.
  All orders subject to approval. Offer limited to one per household and not valid to current The Best of the Best™ subscribers.
  ® are registered trademarks of Harlequin Enterprises Limited.

BOB02-R   ©1998 Harlequin Enterprises Limited

NAN RYAN

66893	THE SCANDALOUS MISS HOWARD	___ $6.50 U.S.	___ $7.99 CAN
66814	THE SEDUCTION OF ELLEN	___ $6.50 U.S.	___ $7.99 CAN
66591	THE COUNTESS MISBEHAVES	___ $6.50 U.S.	___ $7.99 CAN
66521	WANTING YOU	___ $5.99 U.S.	___ $6.99 CAN

(limited quantities available)

TOTAL AMOUNT	$_____
POSTAGE & HANDLING	$_____
($1.00 for one book; 50¢ for each additional)	
APPLICABLE TAXES*	$_____
<u>TOTAL PAYABLE</u>	$_____

(check or money order—please do not send cash)

To order, complete this form and send it, along with a check
or money order for the total above, payable to MIRA Books,
to: **In the U.S.:** 3010 Walden Avenue, P.O. Box 9077, Buffalo,
NY 14269-9077; **In Canada:** P.O. Box 636, Fort Erie, Ontario,
L2A 5X3.

Name:_____
Address:_____ City:_____
State/Prov.:_____ Zip/Postal Code:_____
Account Number (if applicable):_____
075 CSAS

*New York residents remit applicable sales taxes.
Canadian residents remit applicable
GST and provincial taxes.

Visit us at www.mirabooks.com

MNR0403BL